CANDLELIGHT
Ecstasy Supreme

"I TOLD YOU I DON'T WANT TO GET INVOLVED," MANDY PROTESTED.

"I think it's too late," Clay whispered. "We're already involved."

"Then, we'll just have to get uninvolved."

"We can't. Didn't you enjoy the last few minutes as much as I did?"

"Well, yes, but . . ."

"Mandy, we're both adults."

"But one of us is not consenting."

"You sure?" he asked her provocatively, playing with her hair. "It's a slow, lazy day, and we're all alone in a secluded cabin in the woods. You have to admit it's a romantic place to . . ."

"No!"

With an indulgent smile he threw up his hands. "Well, you can't blame a man for trying."

"And you can't blame a woman for being cautious."

"There's such a thing as being too cautious, though. I'll have to see what I can do about freeing you of some of your inhibitions."

CANDLELIGHT ECSTASY SUPREMES

53 AUTUMN RAPTURE, *Emily Elliott*
54 TAMED SPIRIT, *Alison Tyler*
55 MOONSTRUCK, *Prudence Martin*
56 FOR ALL TIME, *Jackie Black*
57 HIDDEN MANEUVERS, *Eleanor Woods*
58 LOVE HAS MANY VOICES, *Linda Randall Wisdom*
59 ALL THE RIGHT MOVES, *JoAnna Brandon*
60 FINDERS KEEPERS, *Lois Walker*
61 FROM THIS DAY FORWARD, *Jackie Black*
62 BOSS LADY, *Blair Cameron*
63 CAUGHT IN THE MIDDLE, *Lily Dayton*
64 BEHIND THE SCENES, *Josephine Charlton Hauber*
65 TENDER REFUGE, *Lee Magner*
66 LOVESTRUCK, *Paula Hamilton*
67 QUEEN OF HEARTS, *Heather Graham*
68 A QUESTION OF HONOR, *Alison Tyler*
69 FLIRTING WITH DANGER, *Joanne Bremer*
70 ALL THE DAYS TO COME, *Jo Calloway*
71 BEST-KEPT SECRETS, *Donna Kimel Vitek*
72 SEASON OF ENCHANTMENT, *Emily Elliott*
73 REACH FOR THE SKY, *Barbara Andrews*
74 LOTUS BLOSSOM, *Hayton Monteith*
75 PRIZED POSSESSION, *Linda Vail*
76 HIGH VOLTAGE, *Lori Copeland*
77 A WILD AND RECKLESS LOVE, *Tate McKenna*
78 BRIGHT FLAME, DISTANT STAR, *Blair Cameron*
79 HOW MANY TOMORROWS?, *Alison Tyler*
80 STOLEN IDYLL, *Alice Morgan*

PLAYERS IN THE SHADOWS

Donna Kimel Vitek

A CANDLELIGHT ECSTASY SUPREME

Published by
Dell Publishing Co., Inc.
1 Dag Hammarskjold Plaza
New York, New York 10017

Dell ® TM 681510, Dell Publishing Co., Inc.

Candlelight Ecstasy Supreme is a trademark
of Dell Publishing Co., Inc.

Candlelight Ecstasy Romance®, 1,203,540, is a registered
trademark of Dell Publishing Co., Inc.

ISBN: 0-440-16925-9

Printed in the United States of America

First printing—July 1985

To Our Readers:

Candlelight Ecstasy is delighted to announce the start of a brand-new series—Ecstasy Supremes! Now you can enjoy a romance series unlike all the others—longer and more exciting, filled with more passion, adventure, and intrigue—the stories you've been waiting for.

In months to come we look forward to presenting books by many of your favorite authors and the very finest work from new authors of romantic fiction as well. As always, we are striving to present the unique, absorbing love stories that you enjoy most—the very best love has to offer.

Breathtaking and unforgettable, Ecstasy Supremes will follow in the great romantic tradition you've come to expect *only* from Candlelight Ecstasy.

Your suggestions and comments are always welcome. Please let us hear from you.

Sincerely,

The Editors
Candlelight Romances
1 Dag Hammarskjold Plaza
New York, New York 10017

CHAPTER ONE

Someone was following Amanda Mills. Someone was watching. She was sure of it. The uncomfortable feeling of being secretly observed had first come over her during lunch, and even after returning to the store she had sensed somebody was waiting outside for her to show herself again. As she locked the shop for the day, the feeling lingered. Prickles rose up her spine, her breathing quickened. Pushing a strand of strawberry blond hair back from her temple, she turned away from the store and glanced as casually as possible up and down the street. There were several people on the sidewalks but none of them seemed to be looking at her. She nibbled her lower lip. Maybe no one was watching her after all. Maybe she had simply imagined it. But she didn't think so, because the feeling of being observed was growing stronger now, beginning to crawl slowly over her skin.

Amanda slipped the strap of her purse over her shoulder and strolled to the store next door, where she stopped and pretended to window-shop. The glass reflected the street behind her, and there she saw the man, on the other side of the street. He had stopped when she did. Who the devil was he? She'd never seen him before in her life. But he was keeping a close eye on her without being outrageously obvious about it. When she moved on to the jewelry store and pretended to admire its window display, he remained where he was, merely

9

following her with his gaze. Why was he staring, and why had he been hanging around waiting for her all afternoon? Amanda was accustomed to admiring glances from men but this was something different. This guy seemed to be stalking her—well, perhaps that was a slight exaggeration. Tall, broad-shouldered, clad in gray slacks, white shirt, and a black jacket, he looked too relaxed to be called a stalker. He glanced at his wristwatch, then sat down on the bench at the bus stop, stretching his long legs out in front of him leisurely. Yet she still felt his gaze was boring through her back. On impulse, she spun around and stared directly at him. For several long uneasy moments he looked right back at her.

Enough was enough. After waiting for a break in traffic, Amanda walked quickly across the street into White's Bakery. Rosalyn White smiled at her from behind the counter.

"What can I tempt you with today?" she asked. "Croissants? Pecan tarts?"

"Just the croissants," murmured Amanda, looking back over her shoulder toward the bus stop. "Half a dozen, please."

"You seem a little uptight," Rosalyn remarked, placing the freshly baked rolls into a bag. She leaned over the counter. "What's the matter? Bad day at the store? Did some of your little customers give you a hard time?"

"No. Today, most of the kids who came in seemed fairly tame and agreeable. Actually it was a pretty peaceful day." Amanda was the manager of a children's clothing store, which her family owned.

"What's wrong, then?"

"I'm not sure." Amanda thoughtfully tapped a fingertip against her chin, then inclined her head toward the plate glass window. "See that man out there? The brown-haired one sitting at the far end of the bench."

10

Untying her white apron, Rosalyn came around the counter and peered out. "I see him. What about him?"

"He's watching me."

"Hmm, he's not bad-looking. If I weren't married, I wouldn't mind if he wanted to watch me." Rosalyn grinned. "He just likes your looks. What's the problem?"

"I don't think that's all that's on his mind. I doubt he'd stay around all afternoon and wait for me to close the store simply because he likes the way I look."

A frown replaced Rosalyn's grin. "You mean he's been watching you for hours?"

"Well, I didn't actually spot him until a few minutes ago, but since lunch I've had the feeling somebody was watching me. I can't imagine what he's doing."

"Maybe you don't want to find out. There are some odd people running around loose in this world, some of them dangerous. I don't mean to scare you but . . ."

"I know, I know. I'm not scared though—not yet. Just uneasy. I wish he'd go away." Paying for the croissants, Amanda shrugged. "Ah well, I can't hide in here forever. The best thing to do is go home and forget about him."

"Aren't you worried he'll follow you there?"

Amanda's heart skipped a beat. "Now that you mention it . . ."

"I have an idea. I'll get my purse—It's closing time anyhow. You leave first, if I see he's going to follow you, I'll stop him long enough for you to lose him."

"How are you going to stop him?"

"I'll think of something. I can ask him for directions, or the time—anything. I'll keep him busy while you get away."

Amanda had to smile. "This really is crazy. Maybe my imagination's just running wild."

"But what if it isn't? You don't want to have to worry all

11

night about whether he followed you home, do you? Of course not," Rosalyn asked, and answered her own question. "My little plan will work if you'll give it a try, wait and see. All right?"

Amanda finally agreed, and the ploy was successful. She left the bakery and had gone only a few steps when she heard Rosalyn say behind her, "Excuse me, sir, do you have change for a twenty? Oh, I hope you do, because the drivers insist on the correct bus fare and I usually have it but today I simply forgot to get change and my bus will be along in less than a minute, so if you would help me I'd be very grateful. My husband's waiting for me and if I have to wait for the bus after this one, he'll . . ."

As Rosalyn chattered on nonstop, Amanda smiled faintly, hazarding a backward glance. Good old Rosalyn. She held the man's arm in an anxious grip. He could have jerked free of her hand, but that might have caused a scene. He was trapped. Humming merrily, Amanda rounded the corner and walked across the parking lot to her sky blue Mustang.

Amanda lived on a quiet tree-lined street in a suburb of Richmond. Shaded by two ancient oaks, the green-shuttered white house was small. A modest little bungalow with great potential, the realty agent had said. Agreeing, Amanda had bought it during a time when interest rates were relatively reasonable, and she'd never regretted her decision. The neighborhood was nice, the people friendly, and best of all the front lawn was perfect for flowers and the backyard large enough for a vegetable garden. Amanda had decorated the house to suit her, and enjoyed being a home owner.

Tuesday evening after dinner she watered the plants in the living room, chuckling softly when she remembered how Rosalyn had waylaid the stalker on the sidewalk. Momentarily, she wondered once again what he had been up to. But that was a mystery she couldn't possibly solve, so she dismissed the entire incident from her mind. On the cold hearth, Bossy, her golden retriever, lifted her head off her paws, gave a loud squeaky yawn and got up to stretch. She ambled slowly to her mistress's side.

"You droopy old thing. You're sure getting lazy," Amanda said, patting the dog's sleek head. "And you're only three years old. What are you going to be like when you're ten?"

Bossy yawned again in response, but she also wagged her tail a couple of times rather sheepishly. With her soft black velvet nose, she nudged Amanda's leg.

"I certainly made the right choice when I named you. You're very demanding. But okay, I'll put more food in your bowl in just a minute."

Heaving a greatly exaggerated sigh, Bossy sprawled out on the floor, watching as Amanda sprayed the last philodendron with a fine mist.

"You're always underfoot, you old poop," Amanda remarked fondly, forced to step over the animal to get to the front windows. In the deepening dusk the streetlights had come on, and as she started to draw the drapes shut, she noticed the car parked at the curb. Then she saw the man inside. He turned his head. When the light of the streetlight caught his face Amanda gulped, her heart leaping up into her throat. It was *him!* The man who had watched her all afternoon. He hadn't been able to follow her home, yet he'd known where she lived! This was serious. Remembering Rosalyn's warning, Amanda was very much afraid the man in the car might be someone dangerous. These thoughts flashed through her brain in a second, and she hastily jerked the drapes closed. Then she checked the front door to be sure it was locked securely. Bossy must have sensed her sudden tension because her entire body was rigid, her silky ears pricked up alertly.

"It's all right, girl. At least it will be in a few minutes. Now he's gone too far," Amanda murmured, heading for the phone. Reaching the police, she told the dispatcher as calmly as possible, "There's a man parked outside my house. I just noticed him watching me this afternoon but obviously he's been around longer than I thought if he knows where I live. Please send someone out to investigate right away."

The dispatcher assured her an officer would be there in a matter of minutes, but Amanda still didn't feel entirely safe as she hung up the receiver.

Outside in the car, Clay Kendall kept one eye on the house while easing sheer boredom by working a crossword puzzle with the aid of a flashlight. He glanced across Amanda Mills's yard again. He planned to stay until midnight. If nothing happened, he would talk to her tomorrow. She wasn't apt to be cooperative, which was why he hadn't already approached her. But this surveillance was proving a waste of time. More direct action was needed. He turned back to his puzzle.

When the police cruiser pulled up in front of him several moments later, Clay lifted one eyebrow. He rolled down his window, letting in more of the balmy late summer air, as the policeman got out and started toward him.

"Evening, officer," he said politely. "Anything wrong? Surely you're not going to give me a ticket for speeding."

"No, I'm not," the man in uniform answered, ignoring the humor. "Get out of your car please, place your hands palms down on the hood, and spread your legs."

Without bothering to argue, Clay opened the door, stepped out onto the asphalt, and assumed the position. He said nothing as he was being frisked. This development wasn't all that surprising. He'd suspected Miss Mills was wise to him, and

14

naturally, she'd called for help. He couldn't really blame her, although he found it somewhat humiliating to be treated like a criminal.

Amanda witnessed the procedure through a crack between the drapes, and groaned inwardly when the officer directed the strange man up her front walk. She didn't want to see this weirdo up close, she simply wanted him to be warned to stay away from her. Obviously, it wasn't going to be that simple. She answered the first knock with Bossy at her heels, opening the door only a few inches and looking out.

"May we step inside, ma'am, where the light's better?" the burly policeman requested. "I want you to have a good look at him."

"Well, I . . . Okay." Reluctantly she stood aside, allowing them to enter.

"Is this the man you reported?"

Amanda found herself looking into the darkest pair of eyes she had ever seen. They appeared almost coal black. The mysterious stalker returned her gaze evenly. She nodded. "Yes, this is the man."

"I had planned to talk to you tomorrow anyway." Clay spoke up, his voice deep and steady. "Might as well make it tonight instead."

"Just hold on there, buddy," the policeman interceded. "You have a few questions to answer and I—"

"I can show you identification, Officer— Sorry, I didn't get your name."

"I didn't give it. It's Ingram."

A tiny frown etched Amanda's brow as she watched the black-eyed man remove his wallet, open it, and show the policeman something. From where she stood she couldn't see what it was.

"We can straighten this out in no time, Officer Ingram,"

Clay continued, replacing his wallet. "Call Captain Mears at headquarters and he'll explain."

"Explain what? I don't understand what—" Amanda began.

"May I use your phone, ma'am?" Ingram asked, walking over to pick up the receiver before she answered.

Thoroughly baffled now, she needed to vent her frustration and so she glared at the mystery man, balling her hands into tight fists at her sides. "Who are you? What do you want with me?"

"I'm not a psychopath, I promise you. I know this must seem odd but—"

"That's putting it mildly! Why are you following me around? How long have you been doing it? Who *are* you?"

"Clay Kendall," he introduced himself. He stepped toward her.

She stepped back.

He stopped short, thrusting his hands into his trouser pockets. "I can explain."

"I doubt that. You—"

"Well, that clears things up," Officer Ingram inadvertently interrupted, ending his call to headquarters with a smile. He gave Clay a nod. "Sorry if I inconvenienced you, Mr. Kendall, but I had to check out the complaint. And everything's fine now. The captain vouched for you, so I can be on my way."

"Just a damn minute!" Amanda spluttered, shaking her head. "You can't leave me with this man, Officer. For God's sake, he's been following me, watching my house! I won't let you go and leave me alone with him!"

Passing her, Ingram lightly patted her shoulder. "Nothing to worry about, ma'am. Captain says it's okay, it's official business. "G'night."

"But wait," Amanda called as the policeman walked out the door. She started after him. "You can't—"

Clay Kendall blocked her way. "I told you I could explain."

"Are you saying you're a policeman?"

"No. I'm not saying that. Look, let's sit down, okay?" He moved suddenly to reach for her arm. Bossy bared her teeth and growled. Clay dropped his hand instantaneously, eyeing the dog warily before raising his gaze once again to her mistress. "Could we talk without this one around?"

"No. I'd rather have her close by," Amanda flatly insisted. She called Bossy to her as she settled on the edge of a chair, indicating with a gesture he should sit across from her on the blue damask sofa. "All right, explain. What's going on, Mr. . . . er, Kendall?"

As the retriever settled down on her haunches, Clay settled back against the cushions, his eyes never leaving Amanda Mills's face. "I'm not a policeman, but you could say I'm a private investigator. Actually, I specialize in recovering stolen property, very valuable property, such as art work, rare antiques, priceless jewels."

More bewildered than ever, Amanda threw up her hands. "Then what do you want with me? I know next to nothing about things like that."

"Maybe not, but it doesn't matter. I'm here to talk about your sister."

"Becky?" Hope lit up Amanda's face. "Do you know where she is?"

"I've been watching you, hoping she'd show up. Don't you know where she is?"

"Lord, I wish I did. Mom and Dad are worried sick about . . ." Her voice trailed off and she tilted her head to one side inquiringly. "But how did *you* know she'd left town without a word?"

"Did she?"

"What does that mean?"

"Didn't she tell you where she was going?"

"What do you think I just said?"

"You're answering my questions with questions," Clay said, leaning forward to rest his elbows on his knees, his steepled fingers supporting his chin. "Maybe you're trying to hide something."

Amanda glowered at him. "Are you calling me a liar, Mr. Kendall?"

"I'm just wondering if you'd stretch the truth to protect your sister, Miss Mills."

"Protect her from what? She ran away with a man Dad and Mom didn't approve of. What's so unusual about that? It happens all the time."

"Yes, I'm sure, but there's a difference in this case. Your sister was assistant curator at the museum before she disappeared."

"Yes, but—"

"Why didn't she go into the family business with you? You have two stores in town. She could have managed one of them."

"She didn't want to. It's that simple."

"Isn't it true Becky was always interested in works of art? And she vanished at the same time the Shalimar rubies were stolen from the museum."

Amanda bristled. "Are you insinuating she . . . Oh, what nonsense. Becky ran away three days before the rubies were stolen."

"Correction. She disappeared three days before it was discovered the rubies at the museum were excellent fakes," Clay

18

said. "No one knows exactly when the real collection was stolen and the forgeries put in its place. I think it might well have happened the night your sister skipped town."

Amanda had to laugh aloud. "You must be joking. You don't know Becky at all. She's quite naive and innocent."

"You talk about her as if she's eighteen, but I happen to know she's twenty-four, only a year younger than you."

"She acts younger. Maybe it's because she was sick a lot when she was a baby and we all tend to pamper her. Always have. But you're crazy if you think she stole the Shalimar rubies," declared Amanda emphatically, laughing once more. "Becky couldn't possibly do anything like that. She's hopelessly unmechanical, and I read that the display case holding the jewels was practically theft-proof. Never in a million years would she have been able to deactivate the alarm system. The police questioned us about the robbery, but after investigating Becky's background, they obviously realized they were on the wrong track. We haven't heard anything more from them. And you're barking up the wrong tree, Mr. Kendall, if you even suspect she had anything to do with what happened at the museum."

Clay wasn't convinced. Linking his fingers, he rested his jaw on his knuckles. "Tell me about this man she ran away with. Why didn't your parents approve of him?"

"Brad? Oh, I don't know exactly. Dad seemed to think he was too charming, too smooth. And Mom thought he was just too old for Becky."

"And what did you think of him?"

"I never had much chance to form an opinion. I only saw him twice. I guess he is more sophisticated than Becky, but if she wants him . . ."

"What's his last name?"

"Charles. Brad Charles."

"And is he mechanically minded? Maybe he was Becky's accomplice."

"You're out of your mind. Becky is as honest as the day is long. She'd never steal anything!"

"But she loves Brad Charles," Clay quietly reminded her. "Some people would do anything for love."

Amanda swallowed hard, filled with a growing dread and a sharp resentment toward this man who had waltzed into her life and disrupted it. She held her head high. "You're not a policeman, so what does any of this have to do with you anyhow?"

"The museum hired me to recover the collection. The police have too many cases to solve to spend more man-hours on this one." Clay's finely carved features grew taut. "This is serious. Even the CIA is eager to recover the Shalimar collection, since it was on loan to us from a foreign government. The theft created something of an international incident. I'm trying to make you understand how important the recovery of the collection is. And I hope you'll call me if you hear anything at all from Becky."

"No, I don't think I will. Seems to me you're trying to set her up, and I won't have anything to do with that," she replied as she rose to her feet, her tone flat. "I want you to go now."

"If you insist, Amanda."

As he stood, she bent down to stroke Bossy's back. "I'd rather you call me Miss Mills, Mr. Kendall."

Without acknowledging that request, he walked to the door, his expression somber. "I'll be in touch."

"Don't bother. I don't think I'll want to tell you anything about Becky if I hear from her."

He looked back at her. "If you won't cooperate, I guess I'd better talk to your parents."

Biting her lower lip, she shook her head. "Don't do that. They're upset enough about Becky already. Don't make it worse for them."

His darkening gaze held hers. "I don't want to hurt any of you, Amanda," he said softly, meaning it. "But I'll do what I have to do to recover the rubies."

She took a deep tremulous breath. She believed him. His obsidian black eyes seemed to penetrate the depths of her own. Then he turned and walked out of the house. She shut the door behind him and leaned against it, closing her eyes, shaken. He was out to get her sister and he seemed to be a very determined man.

Heading for his ivory BMW parked at the curb, Clay uttered a curse beneath his breath and kicked a small stone out of his path. There were moments when he wasn't all that proud of his profession. This was one of them. Amanda seemed to be a fine, decent woman. He admired her for rushing to the defense of her younger sister. And she had the most beautiful blue eyes, honest and open. Shaking his head, trying to forget such thoughts, he got into his car and switched on the engine. Okay, so she was attractive and appealing—he couldn't let those considerations get in the way. He was a professional. And he had meant what he told her. He would do whatever was necessary to recover the Shalimar rubies.

CHAPTER TWO

"Mom, try to calm down," Amanda said comfortingly over the phone. "I warned you about Clay Kendall and what he was going to say to you and Dad. I wish you hadn't let him upset you so much."

"How can I help but be upset?" Shirley Mills exclaimed softly, her voice breaking. "A perfect stranger just told us he thinks Becky is a thief!"

"But you know he's wrong, Mom."

"Of course he is, but that doesn't change the fact that he suspects her and wants to track her down. Even the CIA wants to talk to her. Oh, God, it's awful."

"It's a ridiculous misunderstanding. Becky just picked the worst possible time to leave town—it's as simple as that. It'll all get straightened out sooner or later," Amanda said soothingly. "What's Dad saying about this whole mess?"

"He's worried sick. What else? Becky's his little girl."

Amanda bit back a sigh. "She's twenty-four, Mom, hardly a little girl anymore."

"Oh, you know what I mean. She's the baby of the family. Ted would do anything in the world to find her and get her away from Brad Charles. That's who he blames for this whole situation."

"Brad didn't kidnap her. She went with him willingly."

"But he must have some hold on her. She's been gone over

three weeks and hasn't gotten in touch with us once, even though she has to know we're worried to death. He's a bad influence. I think he's convinced her not to call or write us."

"Maybe. Maybe not. But even if he has, I don't think she'll stay convinced. We'll hear from her soon, I'm sure of it."

"Oh, I hope so. That detective Ted hired to look for her acted like he couldn't even find his own way home, so we fired him. Now nobody's looking for her."

"Clay Kendall is. Maybe it would be a good thing if he found her. At least we'd know where she is."

"But if he's going to arrest her—"

"Mom, he can't do that. If he found her and talked to her, I'm sure he'd realize she had nothing to do with stealing the rubies," Amanda said. "Last night when I talked to him, I just wanted him to leave her alone. Now I'm not so sure. If he finds her it might be the best thing that could happen. Then he'll find out he never should've suspected her in the first place."

"I—I guess so. But it does look sort of bad, doesn't it?" Shirley Mills's words were choked. "I mean, she was assistant curator at the museum and the rubies were stolen about the same time she disappeared."

"An unfortunate coincidence. It does look suspicious but—"

"Oh, I wish she'd call. Or better yet, come home where she belongs. I've never seen Ted in such a state. He can't sit still. He's a nervous wreck, and I'm close to becoming one."

"I know, Mom. It isn't easy. But just try to remember Becky's not a child. She's an adult, and she can take care of herself if she has to. I'm sure she's perfectly all right. Listen, I have to go now. There's somebody I have to see this evening if possible. Why don't you and Dad have dinner with me tomorrow night. That'll help us all feel better."

23

"I suppose so. Of course, dear, we'd love to come," Shirley said, making a concerted effort to sound cheerier. "Can I bring something?"

"Um, dessert would be nice. How about one of your delicious strawberry pies. You know how much I love them," replied Amanda, relieved to hear her mother's tone finally lighten a bit as they exchanged good-nights.

Breaking the connection, she cradled the receiver with her left shoulder, pulled out the phone directory, and flipped through the yellow pages, searching for the heading Private Investigators. Two numbers were listed by the name Clay Kendall but she decided not to bother with those. It was the address she needed, and she pressed her lips firmly together as she read it.

"Twenty-nine Melrose Street," she murmured to herself, committing it to memory. She got up to examine her reflection in the oval mirror above the telephone table. Reaching for her purse, she took out her comb and ran it lightly through her hair. It bounced healthily around her shoulders. She found her car keys and started for the front door, but stopped when Bossy trotted expectantly after her.

"Sorry, girl, you'll have to stay home. I can't take you for a ride," she told the dog, stroking her golden coat. "Although I am tempted to take you along. Maybe you'd sink your teeth into Mr. Kendall's ankle for me. He deserves it. But I'd better handle him by myself."

Bossy's ears drooped a little when Amanda patted her once more before she left.

Melrose Street was located in the outskirts of Richmond, a gently winding woods-bordered road. When Amanda located number twenty-nine she was surprised by what she found. She had expected an office building but instead she faced a long rambling stone house set back on an expanse of lush lawn and approached by a circle drive. Glossy greenery cascaded down from vast stone urns, flanking the wide solid mahogany door in garlands of tumbling shiny leaves. Sweeping maples were scattered across front and back yards and early-evening sunlight filtered down between the leaves to lie in dappled pools upon the grass. The house itself wasn't grand by any standard. It was rustic and perfectly in tune with the surroundings. A flash of green caught Amanda's eye as she drove past the garage, and she spotted a vintage car parked there. She stopped by the flagstone walkway which led to the house. Unnecessarily adjusting the collar of her blouse, she got out of her Mustang and went to the door to ring the bell.

Clay Kendall answered a few seconds later. Barefoot, dressed in faded jeans and a white sweatshirt, he cocked one darkly slashed eyebrow. "Amanda, this is a surprise."

"Yes," she responded, forgetting to remind him to call her Miss Mills. "I expect it is."

"Well, don't just stand there," he insisted, ushering her into the foyer, and on into a study on the right. Bookshelves rose from floor to ceiling on two sides, paperbacks and hardbound volumes mixed. Some of the furnishings were obviously antiques. A huge old teakwood desk dominated. But overall the decor was light and airy. Modern art objects and vibrant paintings added distinctive and attractive points of interest. The mixture of styles in the room shouldn't have worked, but somehow it did. It was a nice study, cozy, lived-in. Clay motioned her toward the black leather sofa. "Have a seat."

She perched herself on the edge of the cushion, clasping her clutch purse in her lap. "I guess that's your car I saw in the garage?"

"Yes. A 1937 Jaguar roadster. Like it?"

"Very much."

"Good" was Clay's dry answer as he took the chair across

from her. "But you didn't come here to discuss cars, did you?"

"No, but now I'm wondering why you weren't driving that car when you were following me. I suppose you thought a 1937 Jaguar roadster would be too noticeable on a spy mission."

"I prefer to call it surveillance. But you're exactly right—the Jag is too noticeable. Would you like a drink?"

"No thanks. I won't be here that long," answered Amanda, her words stilted. "I only have one thing to say: I hope you're happy with yourself. You upset my parents royally today."

"I wish that hadn't been necessary, but it was."

"It was not."

"Yes, Amanda, it was. I have to talk to anybody who can give me a lead on your sister. You said you weren't going to cooperate so I had to talk to your parents."

"Only to find out they're not going to cooperate with you either."

"Your father practically threw me out on my ear. But his reaction came as no big surprise. It's painful for parents to hear what I had to tell them."

"That you suspect Becky is a thief. You really shouldn't have done that, Mr. Kendall. You—"

"Clay."

"Mr. Kendall. You don't know Becky. We do, and we know she couldn't possibly have had anything to do with the robbery."

"Sometimes we don't know people we're close to as well as we think."

"Well, we know her! We're her family. You must not have any brothers or sisters."

"Yes I do. One sister, one brother."

"Don't you trust them?"

"I trust them but I also know they're human. And people can have secrets, and may make mistakes—sometimes big ones. There are a lot of ways to get into trouble."

"You're jaded."

"I'm realistic," Clay corrected, a hint of impatience darkening his lean face. "Look, Amanda, this is a senseless argument. You want to believe in your sister's innocence, and I understand that. But there are some hard facts you have to face. She's the prime suspect in the museum heist. We know it was probably an inside job, that someone inside had to be at least an accomplice. There was no forced entry. The thieves knew exactly how to shut off the security systems, which are very complex. They had to know the precise routine of the night guards so they'd have enough time to steal the real rubies and replace them with the fakes."

"Then maybe one of the guards was in on it. Or anybody else who works at the museum. Why are you picking on Becky? It could have been someone else who . . ." Amanda's words trailed off as Clay shook his head. "But why not?"

"It's highly unlikely. All the museum employees have been checked out thoroughly and they all look clean," Clay explained, his voice lowering, his tone becoming somewhat apologetic. "Besides, Becky is the only one of them who vanished about the same time the rubies did. I'm not the only one who thinks that's significant. So do the police and the CIA."

Amanda winced. "Are you working for them? The CIA?"

"No, but I'm keeping them informed about my progress."

"Oh damn!" she softly exclaimed, shaking her head. "This is insane. The CIA is looking for my sister."

"They haven't designated this a priority case. They have their hands pretty full with international espionage. But they do want to question Becky, since the rubies were loaned to the U.S. by a foreign government. They're a national treasure,

Amanda. It doesn't look good for us that the rubies were stolen while they were in our possession."

"I know that. But for Becky, of all people, to be involved in something like this—it's so crazy!" murmured Amanda, the expression mantling her features both anxious and earnest, her glimmering blue eyes darkening with appeal. "She may seem like the logical suspect but she couldn't have done it. Believe me, Clay."

He sat back in his chair, linking long fingers together across his flat abdomen as he regarded her solemnly. "Tell me about Becky's boyfriend, Brad Charles. Anything you know about him."

"Like I said, I only saw him twice. He seemed to want to keep Becky to himself, so we didn't see as much of her after she met him. I liked him okay, I guess. He was something of a smooth operator, which is why Dad disapproved of him. And Mom worried about his age."

"How old is he?"

"Um, thirty-one, thirty-two, somewhere along there. A little too old for Becky, I guess."

"I'm thirty-two and you're only a year older than your sister. Am I too old for you?"

The question came out of the blue, and for an instant Amanda was taken aback. Then her steady gaze met his. "I'm not Becky and you're not Brad Charles. He's been around and she—well, she's been sheltered."

"And you haven't been?"

"Not as much as Becky. Independence always meant more to me than to her."

"Would you say your parents are overly protective?"

"What is this? A psychological analysis of our family life?"

A tight humorless smile scarcely moved Clay's finely shaped lips. "No. I'm just trying to understand her a little

28

better. Now, what else do you know about Brad Charles? Where did he come from? How did Becky meet him?"

"They met in the restaurant across from the museum. Becky always has—*had* lunch there. According to her, he swept her off her feet, insisted she have dinner with him that evening. She did, and it snowballed from there."

"When was this?"

"About six months ago. In March or early April. He'd just moved to Richmond."

"From where?"

"Madison, Wisconsin."

"His hometown?"

"Yes. But he went to school in Milwaukee. The university."

"Where did he work here in town?"

"Um, let me think. It was a public relations firm. Oh yes, Shiver and Burnett, that's the one." Amanda mustered a faint smile. "I guess that's the perfect profession for a man with all his charming ways. But why are you so interested in him?"

"Why not? He's the man Becky left town with," Clay said simply. "He's a suspect too."

Amanda stiffened, blue eyes flashing defiance. "I thought a person was innocent until proven guilty in this country. You're assuming Becky's a thief without giving her a chance to defend herself. That's not fair!"

"If she'll come out of hiding, she'll have every chance to defend herself. Until then, I have to go by the evidence I've found."

"I have to leave now," Amanda tersely announced, rising to her feet and squaring her shoulders with dignity. "I wouldn't have bothered you at home, but I thought the address in the phone book was for your office."

"It is. My office is here. And you haven't bothered me," Clay softly said, rising effortlessly from his chair to stand in

29

front of her, his clear black eyes searching hers. "What happens now?"

She looked up at him, shrugged. "I really don't know. Obviously, I can't convince you Becky isn't a jewel thief. If we could just find her . . . Mom and Dad had a detective trying to find her but he got nowhere. They probably want to hire another one, but they're not rich. They can't afford the daily expenses for very long." She sighed. "I guess all you private investigators are expensive."

"Some work on a set fee plus expenses. Some of us work for a percentage of the value of the property we recover. I'm one of those. Fifteen percent."

Her eyes widened. "And how much are the Shalimar rubies worth?"

"Approximately fifteen million."

"Then if you find them, you'll make . . ."

"Only *if* I recover them. If I don't, I get nothing. I'll even have to pay for my own expenses and take them as a loss. Risky business."

"Then you must be very good at what you do to be able to take that risk."

"I try hard."

She was sure he did. Depressing, considering he was out to get her own sister. She nodded, sinking the edge of her teeth into her lower lip, and then said, "One favor, please. If you have any more questions about Becky, ask me instead of Mom and Dad. I don't know if they can take much more of this."

"I'll be in touch with you, then," he promised, walking her through the foyer to the front door. The bright flare of the setting sun beamed through the small mullioned windows, catching the highlights in her reddish blond hair, setting strands aglow. He caught hold of her elbow as she turned the doorknob. And when she turned to look back at him, he gave a slow smile. "Had dinner yet?"

"No."

"I'd planned to throw a sandwich together, but we could go out somewhere and continue our discussion."

"I . . . don't think so. Thanks just the same."

"We could take the roadster, Mandy."

Her breath caught silently deep in her throat at the softly spoken abbreviation of her name. He made it sound so . . . so *intimate* somehow. Valiantly, she managed to still the silly fluttering of her heart. "Nobody calls me Mandy. Mom never cared for it."

"No? Pity. I like it very much. *Mandy.*" Clay repeated, his deep voice melodious. "There's a song by that name."

"Yes, I know. Good night," she said, rushing out the door.

Clay returned Amanda's visit Friday night. When she answered his knock wearing khaki shorts and a yellow cotton top, he allowed his gaze to linger on her long shapely legs until her dog wriggled in front of her and growled at him through the screen.

"Quiet, Bossy," she commanded while looking warily at Clay. "Have you found Becky?"

"No. May I come in? Or will Bossy attack me?"

"Not unless I tell her to."

"That doesn't sound very reassuring but I'll take my chances," he said with a wry smile. As she swung open the storm door, he stepped across the threshold, keeping some distance between himself and the watchful dog. "She's a pretty animal."

"Yes, and if you'll scratch her rump for her, you'll make a friend for life."

"Ah, so that's the secret." Taking the advice, Clay stroked

Bossy's back, then scratched the base of her tail for several seconds. Losing their alert glint, her brown eyes softened and she flicked her tongue in sheer delight.

Amanda chuckled. "Some guard dog, huh? Now, she'll probably want to go home with you."

"I'm sure she's more loyal to you than that," he commented, standing up straight, his expression sober. "I haven't found Becky yet. It's not going to be easy. But I've spent the last few days checking out Brad Charles, and I thought you might be interested in what I found."

"I certainly am," she murmured as they sat down together on the blue damask sofa. "What about Brad?"

Turning toward her, Clay draped one arm over the top of the back cushion. "I couldn't find a trace of evidence that Brad Charles ever existed before he came to Richmond."

"But that's crazy. Of course he existed."

"Of course, but obviously he wasn't using the same name. I flew to Madison and there's no record of his birth anywhere in the state. And at the university in Milwaukee, I discovered he'd never attended classes there."

"I don't understand. This must be a mistake, Clay."

"It's no mistake, Mandy."

"But how did he get a job with Shiver and Burnett?" she persisted, not yet willing to accept this news as fact. "He must have had college transcripts and references from former employers or they wouldn't have hired him."

"He had them. The personnel director at Shiver and Burnett let me see them. They're all fakes—very good ones, but fakes nonetheless. Brad Charles, or whatever his name really is, seems to be a very clever man. The addresses he gave for his references were post office box numbers. He either answered the inquiries about him himself or had someone do it for him. Anyway, the references seemed to check out, so personnel didn't bother to verify the college transcripts. Besides, they were quite impressed by his outgoing personality—thought he was perfect for public relations work."

"This is incredible," Amanda muttered, rubbing her temples to ease the dull ache that was growing there. "Then he lied to Becky. He didn't even tell her his real name. Why?"

"Maybe he had something to hide. Generally that's the reason a person uses an alias."

"Good lord, what kind of man did she run off with?"

"I hope to find out. Do you know anything at all about his family."

"He didn't have one. He told Becky he was raised in an orphanage."

"Very convenient," drawled Clay. "If he has a family, their last name isn't Charles. He couldn't let Becky meet them so he simply told her he had no relatives."

"I wonder how many other lies he told her." Amanda's worried eyes searched Clay's. "Wh-what do you think this means?"

"I can't be sure, but I have my suspicions. Maybe you're right and Becky didn't actually steal the rubies herself. Maybe Brad did."

"Well that makes a little more sense, but . . ."

"But he still had to have someone on the inside helping him —which brings us right back to Becky."

"Damn it, will you stop insisting she's a criminal! I know she's not," Amanda loyally declared, resentment faintly coloring her cheeks as she glared at him. "Becky didn't take the rubies. And she wouldn't have been Brad's accomplice. She didn't have anything to do with it."

"Mandy," Clay said softly, gently, "I know how much you want to believe that, but you've heard the facts. By now you must be having some doubts."

"I . . . no. No, I'm not. I trust my sister."

Deciding not to press the issue, Clay took an envelope out of his inside jacket pocket. "Did you ever go see the Shalimar collection, Mandy?"

"No. I planned to, but never seemed to get a chance." She accepted the color photographs he handed her, taking a swift breath as she looked at the first one. The entire Shalimar collection was pictured: the large but exquisitely delicate gold filigree crown, the heavy necklace and bracelet to match, the two rings. Huge bloodred stones sparkled in beds of diamonds set in platinum and gold. "They're beautiful," she murmured, going through all the photos. "I didn't realize the rubies were so big . . . and clear. There must not be any flaws in them."

"Very few. Imagine how much money the thief will be able to get for them."

"But who can buy them? I mean, I'm sure there are plenty of people in the world who can afford to, but do they dare?" she asked logically. "It's such a famous collection. Everyone knows it was stolen."

"There are private collectors who'd jump at the chance to buy them, and then hide them away someplace. Brad just has to make the right connections to find a buyer."

Amanda scowled. "Brad? You're making a very big assumption, aren't you?"

"More an educated guess. A hunch, but my hunches are fairly reliable."

Not knowing how to answer that, she got up quickly. "Would you like coffee? Or iced tea, since it's been so hot today?"

"Tea would be nice, thanks," he said, watching her walk down the short hall to the kitchen. When she returned a couple of minutes later carrying two tall frosty glasses, his black eyes followed the graceful motion of her body as she gave one glass to him and rejoined him on the sofa. He took a long, hearty swallow. "Delicious. Just what I needed. Today was a scorcher." She simply nodded and he put his glass down. "I know my hunch is hard for you to accept. I'm sorry. I don't enjoy being the bearer of bad tidings, believe me."

Her chin lifted a fraction of an inch. "You're just doing what you have to. Right?"

"It's how I make a living."

She sighed. "I'm just thinking, if Brad did use Becky—*if* he did—to get into the museum, then why didn't he take off with the rubies and leave her behind?"

Clay shrugged. "Maybe he really cares about her. Thieves can fall in love too."

"Would he lie about his own name if he loved—" Amanda's words cut off abruptly and her face paled alarmingly. "Oh God, what if . . . if he didn't take her with him? What if he didn't want to leave any witnesses and he got r-rid of her before he left. What if—"

"Whoa, I think you've watched too many crime dramas on television."

"But she could be . . . He could have left her lying somewhere and—"

"Don't do this to yourself," Clay softly commanded, enclosing her slender fingers in his, giving them a comforting squeeze. "She did go with him. Your father told me she left a note for them, saying she was leaving. Did you see it? Was it typed or handwritten?"

"Handwritten."

"Was it her handwriting?"

Amanda nodded, the knot of fear that had suddenly clutched at her stomach beginning to ease its grip.

"There you are, then. She went with him. He didn't get rid of her."

35

"I forgot about the note for a few seconds," Amanda acknowledged, smiling wanly. "Sorry. I didn't mean to get so rattled."

"You're entitled. She's your sister."

"And I'm worried about her, but there are moments when I could give her a swift kick and enjoy doing it. If she is all right, she could at least let Mom and Dad know that. She was upset with them because they didn't like Brad, but that's no excuse for what she's doing to them now. I'd like to give her a good shaking."

"You're entitled to feel that way too," said Clay, his gaze darkening as he surveyed her face. "In a way, you wish I would find her, don't you?"

"I wish she'd be found."

"And soon. She's in enough trouble already. With Brad Charles, she could get into more."

"Dandy. Just what she needs. What Mom and Dad need too. I don't want you to tell them what you found out about Brad. It would upset them even more than they already have been."

"I won't tell them."

"Thank you," she half whispered. "You can be a very nice man."

"You're just realizing that?" he retorted teasingly. "Of course I'm a nice man."

As he moved the balls of his thumbs over the backs of her hands, she gently extracted them from his, picked up her glass from the coaster on the coffee table and took a small sip of iced tea. Conversation lagged while he finished his tea, then they were silent. She shifted restlessly on the sofa.

Clay stood. "Better be going."

Amanda walked him to the door. Rousing from her nap on

36

the hearth, Bossy followed, wagging her tail hopefully until he reached down to give her a brief scratch behind the ears.

"See, I told you," her mistress said, smiling indulgently. "She wouldn't mind going home with you."

Clay didn't smile back. Pausing in the doorway, he looked down at Amanda. "There's one more thing I'd better tell you."

Dread filled her. She didn't want to hear any more bad news. Yet there was no hiding from it, so she stiffened her spine. "What is it?"

"The police are going to search Becky's apartment tomorrow, looking for clues to where she and Brad may have gone."

"Why hasn't that been done already, since she's a suspect?"

"I have searched it. The police are just getting around to it. I'm able to work on this case full-time. They're not."

"But how did you get in?"

"Professional secret."

"Well, did you find anything?"

"No. I didn't. And Brad has given up his apartment. According to the super in Becky's building, Brad moved in with her about three months ago. But maybe you knew that."

"No, she never told me he . . . Oh hell, she used to tell me everything before she got involved with him."

Clay stepped closer to her. "You're beginning to think she might have been involved in the robbery, aren't you?"

Hot tears pricked Amanda's eyes. Valiantly she blinked them back. "I . . . don't want to think that, but . . ."

"Maybe she wasn't. Let's find out. We can only do that by finding her. Will you help me?" Clay asked, his voice pitched low. "If you hear from her or if your parents do, will you let me know where she is?"

Amanda felt as though her warring emotions might pull her

apart inside. She moved her hands in a gesture of uncertainty. "I don't know if I can do that. I—I'll have to think about it."

"It might be the best thing you could do for Becky."

"And it might make me feel like a traitor!"

The muscles in his jaw tightened. He sensed the emotional conflict raging in her, and understanding it, he felt lousy. He didn't want to cause her any pain. She was a nice young woman, and he liked her, was even attracted to her. But still, the museum had hired him to recover the rubies and that was his duty. Yet . . . His gaze swept over her delicate features. He reached out to feather the backs of his fingers over her left cheek as he murmured, "I wish we could've met some other way, Mandy, instead of like this, for this reason."

Dangerous talk. And his light caress kindled wildfire on the surface of her skin. She took a backward step away from him, and he lowered his sun-bronzed hand. She wasn't up to relating to him as a woman relates to a sexually attractive man. Which he was—she couldn't deny that. "Good night, Clay," she said, her tone conveying a calm she didn't truly feel.

He hesitated a moment before giving her a slow, knowing smile. He turned and walked outside. "I'll be in touch, Mandy."

Catching her upper lip between her teeth, she closed the door and locked it, barely noticing Bossy, who nuzzled her soft nose against her knee.

Her heartbeat picking up speed, Amanda touched her cheek where his fingers had lingered.

CHAPTER THREE

"Oh, the blue looks so good on you, Benjamin," his mother said, examining her son as he came out of the dressing room. "But I want you to try on the gray one too."

The nine-year-old grimaced as if in dire pain and scratched his freckled nose. "Aw, Mom, I'm tired of trying things on."

"Have a little patience," his mother cajoled. "You want a nice suit for special occasions, don't you?"

"I guess so." Benjamin didn't sound all that enthusiastic.

Suppressing a smile, Amanda led the reluctant young man back to the dressing room. She handed over the size ten gray suit and whispered conspiratorially, "It's almost over. This is the last one that'll fit you."

Grinning, Benjamin stepped into the small space. She closed the latticed door for him.

"Call for you, Amanda," her clerk, Betsy Ann, sang out from the back of the store. "Can you come?"

"Right there. Excuse me, please," Amanda said to Benjamin's mother. "Betsy Ann will take care of you for a few minutes."

Hurrying into her small office, she picked up the receiver and said hello. The deep voice that came back was instantly recognizable and there was a catch in her breath for more than one reason. "Oh, it's you, Clay . . . hi."

He got right down to business. "I need to talk to you again. How about tonight over dinner?"

That sounded cozy. Maybe too cozy. She hesitated a few moments. "I don't know if . . ."

"We do need to talk. And we both have to eat anyway, so just say yes. It's a very easy word to say."

"Okay then. Yes," she agreed, smiling at his coaxing tone. "What you have to talk to me about—it's important?"

"I think so. I'll pick you up at your place. About seven all right with you?"

"Fine."

"See you later, then."

After saying good-bye, he hung up, leaving her holding the phone and wondering if he had more bad news for her. Becky had certainly complicated more lives than her own when she had skipped town with Brad Charles. But the deed was done and Amanda had no choice except to roll with the punches as long as they kept coming. Replacing the receiver, she brushed her hair back from her forehead and headed back to her customers, trying to put Becky out of her mind for the time being.

Benjamin's mother had chosen the suit she wanted for him. It was the one he had liked best from the beginning, and he gave her a slightly exasperated look when she decided on it.

"Mom, that's the one I tried on first but you said that tan color would show dirt too much and you made me try on all those others," he complained, scratching a mosquito bite on his arm. "Now I'm all hot and itchy."

"And it's all my fault, I know," retorted his mother good-naturedly, exchanging a grin with Amanda. "But you'll live, dear. Just have a little more patience. All we have to do now is let one of these ladies pin up the pants legs so they can be hemmed. Then we'll pick out a couple of shirts and ties."

Benjamin groaned. "Can't you do that while I go next door to the video arcade? They got the new Dragon Blaster game over there and I've never played it before."

The woman gave a resigned nod. "Go on, then, but if you don't like the shirts and ties I buy, don't blame me. You have some money?"

"Wait," Amanda interceded, reaching into an odds and ends box beneath the counter. She handed the boy some arcade tokens. "Have a few games on me, and watch out for the trolls. Those little devils are sneaky."

Benjamin was surprised. "You mean you've played Dragon Blaster?"

"A few times. I sneak away from Betsy Ann once in a while and go over to the arcade."

It was obvious she had moved up several notches in his estimation. "Trolls, huh?"

"And when the game first starts and you're going across the drawbridge into the castle, watch out for the monster in the moat."

"Hey, thanks," Benjamin said, fidgeting while Betsy Ann pinned up the trouser legs.

His mother smiled wryly at Amanda. "You speak his language. I'm afraid most of what he tells me when he comes home from an arcade is Greek to me."

"I know. So many of the kids that come into the store were talking about video games that I decided to see for myself what all the excitement was about. Some of them are fun. And, I have to admit, a little addictive."

"I'll say," Betsy Ann piped up. "She got hooked on one of them—Moon Marauders or something like that—and used to go over there every day to play it."

"But I finally broke the habit," Amanda lightly reminded her. "No harm done."

The motherly clerk shook her head. "Lots of quarters down the drain if you ask me."

Amanda gave Benjamin a secret wink.

He winked back.

At precisely seven that evening, Clay knocked on Amanda's door. When she answered, his gaze swept over her from head to toe. Her silky midnight-blue dress accentuated the color of her eyes and brought out the glossy highlights of her reddish blond hair. The skirt flared out in soft gathers from her trim waist and the bodice clung to the curve of her breasts while the short petal sleeves draped her lightly tanned upper arms. She was always attractive but tonight she was a knockout.

"You look great," he said with unabashed admiration. "I like you in that dress."

"Thank you," she replied, more pleased than she should have been by his compliment and trying not to show it too much. "Come in. I only have to get my purse, and then we can go."

As Clay stepped through the doorway, Bossy careened into the living room from the hall, her back paws skidding on the hardwood floor as she rounded the corner. Whimpering a welcome, she wagged her tail riotously and flung herself at Clay, her front legs hooking over his elbows.

"Down, Bossy," Amanda chided, snapping her fingers to emphasize the command. "You know you're not supposed to jump up on people like that."

"No problem," Clay said, smiling as the dog reluctantly returned to all fours. "At least she didn't give me a sloppy wet kiss."

"She's not a licker, like some dogs. In fact, you have to ask her for a kiss. She's very picky about who she gives kisses to."

Clay's eyes narrowed but there was a trace of a mischievous

42

glint in their depths. "I have a feeling she's a lot like her mistress in that respect."

"As a matter of fact, she is," answered Amanda dryly. "I *am* choosy about who I kiss." When Bossy nudged Clay's right hand with her nose, begging for her back to be scratched, Amanda gently directed her beyond the fireplace to the soft gold plush throw rug. "Go lie down. I'll be back soon. You have plenty of food and water in your bowls, and you can get out through the basement if you need to."

"Would you like to leave her a phone number where she can reach us?" Clay teased as he and Amanda left the house. "I've noticed how much you talk to her."

"Why would I have her if I didn't want to talk to her? She's my faithful companion, my friend."

"Lucky Bossy," he murmured, lightly cupping her left elbow in his right hand when they crossed the small porch and went down the three steps to the walk. "Do you think you and I could be friends, Mandy?"

Glancing sideways at him, she longed to say yes. But circumstances prevented that. Instead, she shrugged. "I'm not sure we can be friends in our situation. I'm trying to protect my sister and you're trying to pin a robbery on her."

"No I'm not. It's my job to recover the Shalimar collection, that's all," he told her, releasing her arm. "And for your sake and your parents' and Becky's, I hope I'll find evidence that proves she had nothing to do with the heist."

"But . . . but still you think she did?"

"I hope she didn't," he reiterated. "Believe me, Mandy, I don't get any pleasure out of upsetting you and your family."

She did believe him. He sounded so sincere that she couldn't possibly doubt him. Yet his words didn't really change anything. They were at cross-purposes, no matter what he said. At this moment, Becky was his prey and

Amanda was her sister's protectress. Her involvement was emotional; his, professional. And never the twain shall meet. That thought made her feel sad somehow but she couldn't voice what she was feeling. She said nothing at all until they were halfway across the lawn and she first noticed the green vintage automobile at the curb.

"Oh dear," she murmured, bringing forth a wry smile. "My blue dress is going to clash with your car."

"No, it'll make a nice contrast," Clay replied, opening the passenger door and taking her hand as she stepped onto the running board that swept elegantly down from the front fender. Then he walked around the front of the car, folded himself in beneath the wheel, and started the engine. "Hold onto your hair, it's going to get whipped around a little."

"I don't mind. I can give it a quick combing when we get to the restaurant," she assured him as they took off down the street. "This is terrific. I've never ridden in a '37 Jaguar before."

He glanced over at her. Her hair was streaming back from her shoulders, and she was smiling. He wanted to reach over and touch her, but he didn't. The timing was wrong.

Eyes turned as they drove on. Amanda waved to a neighbor, then smiled over at Clay. "This car's a real attention-getter, isn't it?"

He pretended to be hurt. "I always thought people looked at me when I went by because I'm so devilishly handsome."

"And modest," she added, laughing. Wind swirled her hair around her face. She tried to smooth it back but the attempt was practically useless. Finally she just let it blow. It was rather messy by the time they reached the Monticello Inn on Jefferson Street, and she slipped into the restroom to comb it. After they'd been seated at a quiet corner table and had ordered drinks and surveyed the menu, she looked across the floral centerpiece at Clay.

"What did you want to talk to me about?"

"It's nothing specific. I . . ."

"You made it sound important when you phoned."

He gave her a slow smile and shrugged. "I wanted to make sure you'd have dinner with me so we could relax while we talked. I'd like for you to tell me everything you can about Becky, without you feeling like I'm grilling you."

She toyed with her linen napkin. "As I told you, Becky's sort of naive. Not dumb—I don't mean that. In fact she's very intelligent and always did well in school, but she's unworldly. She didn't move into her own place until late last year, and at first she was homesick. I think she might have moved back in with Mom and Dad if she hadn't met Brad. That changed things—she wanted to spend most of her time with him. But except for that, she seemed like the same old Becky to me."

"In other words, she didn't suddenly become a sophisticate?"

"No." Amanda smiled fondly. "I doubt Becky could ever become super sophisticated. More independent, yes, but never a jet-setter type. In a way, she's a little shy."

"Before Brad, had she ever been seriously involved with anyone?"

"She dated, but no one special."

"And how about you?"

A puzzled frown nicked Amanda's forehead. "How about me?"

"Have you ever been seriously involved with anybody?"

"I don't see what that has to do with Becky."

"It doesn't. I asked because I want to know the answer for personal reasons," Clay said, his eyes holding hers. "Have you been?"

"No, not really," she murmured, then took a small sip of the drink she'd just been served. "When I was seventeen I thought I was in love for a lifetime. He was the high school track star. I'm not sure I can count our relationship as serious. We were a couple of kids."

"And what happened to the everlasting love?"

"It cooled down day by day. After about three months, I was beginning to wonder what I'd ever seen in him. He felt the same about me." A reminiscent smile graced her lips. "Just another case of puppy love. We both lost interest and went our separate ways."

"I had a high school sweetheart too. Martha Jean Beckman. Wonder whatever happened to Martha Jean," Clay said whimsically, but his gaze never left Amanda's face. "I assume you're not involved with anyone now either."

"I—no. Look, maybe this conversation's getting a little *too* personal," she suggested softly, taking another quick sip. "You wanted me to talk about Becky. Okay, she and I are close. We were closer before Brad came along. We shared almost everything in our lives with each other. If Becky had problems, she'd come straight to me."

"Did you go to her with yours?"

"Not so much. I'd rather solve my problems by myself, but she always needs someone very supportive to offer her advice."

"And maybe somebody more dominant?" questioned Clay, his large hands cupping his glass. "Brad may have used that to take advantage of her."

Amanda nibbled her lip. "It's beginning to look that way, isn't it? If only Becky was a little more worldly . . ."

"You mentioned your parents have been rather overprotective of her since she was sick as a child."

"Yes. Daddy still calls her 'baby,' and treats her like one half the time."

"I think maybe you resent that."

"You're very perceptive. I do, a little," she answered honestly, pleating her napkin. "They've always acted like she's a fragile piece of glass that I was responsible for whenever we went to school or anyplace else away from them. So I feel more than a year older than she is, and sometimes she gets on my nerves. But of course all siblings have their differences. I imagine you've had a few with your brother and sister."

Low laughter rumbled up from deep in Clay's throat as he nodded. "My mother says I tried to strangle my new little sister when I was three, and wasn't much happier about my brother, who came along a year later. We all act civilized now, but we didn't as kids. We squabbled, fought, and bickered. Indulged in petty jealousies."

"I'm not jealous of Becky. I used to be sometimes. I'd feel sorry for myself and decide she was the beloved princess while I was poor Cinderella," Amanda wryly admitted. "But now, I'm glad they didn't pamper me as much. Maybe if they had encouraged Becky to be more independent sooner, she wouldn't have been naive enough to fall for a man who'd lie to her about his name."

"Parents make mistakes too."

"I know. Don't get me wrong—I don't blame my parents for Becky's getting involved with Brad but . . . Ah, well, raising children can't be easy."

"My mother would agree with that. She has some stories to tell about our childhood."

Amanda's answering smile slowly faded, and worry settled over her face. "If you do find Becky and—and if she did have something to do with stealing the rubies, what . . . will happen to her?"

"She'll be charged, then tried. If she's convicted, her sentence could be lengthy."

"Oh my God, this is horrible." She briefly closed her eyes, shaking her head. "It's unreal."

He moved his hand across the tabletop to cover hers. "I'm sorry, Mandy, but I didn't think you'd want me to lie."

This time she left her hand where it was, oddly comforted by his touch, though not very. She looked at him again, her blue eyes intent. "You're determined to find her?"

"I'm determined to recover the rubies."

"All right, then, if you found her and she gave the rubies to you—if she has them—would you . . . let her go?"

He clenched his jaw. "Mandy, that's a question I can't answer."

"Why not? *Could* you possibly let her get away?"

"Get away to what? To running scared the rest of her life? Hiding? Never being able to come home again? You don't want that for her."

Amanda felt like crying. Hot tears welled up in her eyes, slightly blurring her vision. "No, I don't want that for her but I don't want her in prison either. If she was involved in the robbery, Brad coerced her into doing it. She made a mistake."

"The authorities probably won't consider a mistake of the heart a good excuse. The law—"

"I know, the law is for everyone, but it's hard to see things objectively when it's your own sister who might wind up in jail."

There was really nothing Clay could say. He simply stroked her slender fingers and wished it were in his power to change the situation.

Sighing, Amanda returned his gaze. "Well, it's possible she's going to need a very good lawyer, isn't it? Do you know any?"

"A few. I'll give you their names later. Right now, I have one more question to ask. I have a hunch Becky and Brad left the country, but if not, is there any place you can think of she might have gone to get out of sight? Some secluded area she's always liked?"

"No, I don't—" Amanda began, but stopped short, remembering just such a spot. But she was unwilling to tell him about it and had to force herself not to avert her eyes as she lied, "I can't think of anyplace."

His expression indecipherable, he regarded her face for several long moments before giving a quick nod and releasing her hand. "Okay. Would you like to order now?"

"I guess so."

"We'll talk about something else and give you a chance to regain your appetite."

She produced a weak smile. "I'm not the jolliest of companions, am I?"

"I'm not complaining."

"You're being gallant."

"Just one of my fine qualities," he replied with a wink as he beckoned their waiter. After ordering the broiled salmon she had chosen and steak for himself, he kept his promise and turned to a different topic of conversation. "Tell me about your business."

"I love it."

"I already got that impression. But it must keep you hopping since your father retired."

"Semiretired. I was surprised when he decided to slow down, even though his doctor had advised him to take things easier. By then I was already managing the downtown store. He offered the other one to Becky but as I said, she wanted to work at the museum. Maybe she'd be better off now if . . ."

Leaning across the table, Clay pressed a finger against her

49

lips. "We're not getting back into that discussion. We're going to have a relaxing dinner."

As it turned out, they did. The food was excellent, the talk scintillating. Amanda enjoyed being with him. He had many interests and a warm sense of humor. After he pressed to hear more about her life, she told him some of the details involved in running a children's clothing business, mentioning some of the more exciting buying trips she had taken. He eyed her suspiciously.

"All you've told me about is the business. Are you a workaholic?"

"No. I love my work, but it's not everything to me. I do lots of things during my free time. I—"

"Wait, let me guess," he cut in, his smile teasing. "I bet you're going to say you take aerobics classes."

She laughed. "Nope."

"Then you must be the only young woman in Richmond who doesn't."

"I'm sure there are some others besides me. I do swim whenever I get a chance, and my gardening gives me plenty of exercise."

"I noticed all the flowers in your yard. They're pretty."

"You should see the vegetable garden out back. I've had a lot of luck with it this year. Say, would you be interested in some green peppers? They're going wild."

Watching her closely, liking the way enthusiasm lit her features, he nodded. "I can take a few off your hands if you have too many."

She raised her eyes heavenward as if to say 'too many' was a gross understatement.

Time zoomed past. Taking her turn as questioner, Amanda found out more about Clay. He told her about some of the wackier cases he had handled; making her laugh often, he kindly refrained from mentioning any other jewel capers he had solved.

"What made you decide to become a private investigator?" she asked after a while. "Did you get hooked on detective novels when you were a kid?"

"When I was a kid? I'm still hooked on them. But it was my uncle who influenced me the most. He's an investigator, and I thought it must be an exceptionally exciting profession."

"Is it?"

"Not exactly the way I thought. There's a lot of tedious legwork involved, tracing down leads," Clay told her. "But I enjoy trying to put pieces of a puzzle together."

"Are you a workaholic?" she asked, wryly throwing his question back at him. "You haven't told me much about yourself besides the fact that you like detective novels. You must do more than read."

"I play lousy tennis and a pretty good game of handball. But I also like getting inside people, professionally or personally, and finding out what makes them tick. What makes you tick, Mandy?"

"Nothing unusual, I suppose. I'm just your average person."

"No, you're something special." His voice lowered. "You—"

"There are people waiting for a table," she hastily interrupted, glancing away from him at the foyer, her heart seeming to do a silly little somersault because of his words. "Maybe we should go."

A tiny knowing smile tipped up the corners of his mouth as he called for the check.

Outside in the '37 Jaguar Clay pulled away from the curb and started down the street, then looked at her. "It's a cool breeze. I can pull over and give you my jacket if you want it."

"Oh no, this is perfect," she assured him, lifting her face to the star-sprinkled sky and allowing her hair to fly around willy-nilly. "I've only been in a convertible once and never in a vintage roadster. I'm just fine. It's fun."

The vapor streetlights turned her blue dress to lilac and changed her eyes to a deep violet hue. Once again Clay wanted to reach over and touch, at least take her hand in his, and he might have if a quickly switching stoplight hadn't robbed impetuosity from the moment by making him shift gears. They said little during the fifteen-minute drive to her house. He walked her to the door, smiling when she unlocked it and Bossy greeted them with joyous whimpers, her tail wagging a mile a minute.

Politely, Amanda asked him in for coffee. He accepted and she soon carried a tray bearing two steaming cups into the living room. "Cream? Sugar?"

"Black, please."

"That's simple enough." She handed him the cup and saucer, pretending not to notice when the tips of his lean fingers brushed against hers during the transfer. But she couldn't quite suppress the shiver that ran over the surface of her skin with the brief contact, and she mentally chided herself for being so aware of him physically.

Clay lingered over coffee as long as he possibly could while they talked of inconsequential matters. Yet he sensed her discomfort, and finally he rose to his feet.

She watched him stand up, saw the flexing of his thigh muscles through his trousers. Warmth rushed over her. She called herself a fool. To be thinking of him that way . . . it was crazy.

When she walked him to the front door, he meant to say a simple good-night and leave. But as he turned toward her on the threshold, her lovely blue eyes met his and his self-control snapped. Her reddish gold hair was tousled from the ride. Lamplight cast a soft satinesque glow on her smooth skin. He spanned her waist with his hands and drew her slowly, inexorably, to him, whispering gruffly, "I've been wanting to do this all night."

"No! Clay, don't!" she protested. "No. Stop." She sounded less than convincing even to herself as he repeatedly kissed the arch of her eyebrows, her lashes, her high cheekbones, then the corners of her mouth. Still, she tried to fight the growing weakness in her legs and the sensual excitement that rocketed through her. She tried to step back, pressing her palms against his broad taut chest, but he held her fast, the heat emanating from him seeming to radiate through her flesh. She shook her head. "Clay, no, this is . . ."

"What we both want," he finished for her, supplanting her words with his own, his arms going round her. "You know it is, Mandy."

The way he said her name, almost as reverently as a prayer —that was her momentary undoing. She ceased her struggles as he kissed her fully on the lips, his own lips warm and gently insistent.

She tasted like honey. He felt the softness of her uplifted breasts yield to his harder flesh. He kissed her again and again, groaning softly with satisfaction when she wound her slender arms upward around his neck, kissing him back.

She felt almost dizzy. She'd been kissed before, many times, but never with such abruptly passionate intensity. As his hands rambled over her back to her hips, she trembled. Her lips parted eagerly beneath the persuasive onslaught of his, but when the tip of his tongue sought to open her mouth, her brain reawoke and clanged out a danger signal. She came to her senses and thrust away from him, murmuring, *"No.* I mean it, Clay. This doesn't make sense."

"Yes it does," he whispered, his breathing labored. "It does make sense."

"Not to me." She squared her shoulders. "You're going after my sister, and I have to try to protect her. That makes us enemies."

"We'll never be that. More likely lovers."

She retreated, moving his hands aside as he reached for her again. Part of her longed to go back into his arms; another part told her she didn't dare risk it and that was the instinct she had to trust. Sheer self-protection made her ask coldly, "Do you get involved with some woman during every case you take on?"

A flash of impatience narrowed his eyes. "What do you think?"

"If I knew I wouldn't be asking. Do you?"

"I think I'll let you figure that one out for yourself," he answered, his words clipped as he stepped out onto the porch and closed the door behind him. He walked to his car, cursing himself for rushing her. He hadn't meant to, but somehow libido had overwhelmed patience and he had needed like hell to kiss her. He lowered himself into the driver's seat, knowing he would have to proceed with the utmost caution and finesse from now on.

In the house, still standing by the front door, Amanda heard him start the Jaguar's engine and pull away down the street. Her hands shook slightly as she touched her heated face, and it took all the willpower she could muster to put things in some sort of perspective. All right, Clay Kendall was an exciting man; she was attracted to him; she liked the way his warm firm lips and caressing hands made her feel. But she couldn't let him affect her like this. He was just another magnetic man. Wasn't he? Of course he was. And she had something far more important to consider than her natural female response to him.

Pushing him as far back in her mind as she could, locking the door on thoughts of him, she went to the phone, called Betsy Ann, and explained that she needed her to manage the store alone the next day. There was someplace Amanda had to go.

CHAPTER FOUR

The pale gray fingers of dawn spread open in the sky the following morning while Amanda finished dressing. After her second cup of coffee, she led Bossy into the backyard, making sure her food and water bowls were full. "I'll be back as soon as I can," she told the dog, rubbing her soft black nose. "You be a good girl, now."

Amanda went back inside, crossing the small house and sweeping up her purse and a road map before she walked out the front door, locking it after her. She headed toward her car, but as she passed the large maple tree in the yard, Clay suddenly stepped out from behind, catching her completely off guard. She gave a soft cry of alarm and pressed her hand against her chest.

"What in the world?" she exclaimed, taking a deep breath. "You nearly scared me out of my skin. Don't sneak up on people like that."

"Sorry. I didn't mean to startle you."

"I can't imagine what you're doing here this early in the morning."

"Can't you, Mandy?"

"No. Why are you here?"

He looked at the map she carried, then back at her face. "It's too early to leave for the store. Planning to go somewhere else today?"

Clamping her lips together, she shook her head.

"Mandy, I know better," he persisted, his deep voice smooth and soft. "Last night, I could tell you thought of a place where Becky might have gone. And that's where you're heading right now, isn't it?"

"You're spying on me again and I don't appreciate it," she said curtly, the nape of her neck getting hot. "I see you came in your spymobile, not the Jaguar, so I wouldn't notice you were out here watching me. What a cruddy thing to do, Clay."

"You didn't give me any other choice. I asked you if there was someplace Becky might go but you said you had no idea. You weren't telling me the truth, Mandy."

"So you decided to start watching me again. Wonderful. Have you been out here all night, playing detective?"

"I'm not playing," he said, the words more hard-edged. "I got here about four thirty, just in case you decided to get an early start. When I saw your lights come on, I got out of the car and walked up into the yard. Now why don't you tell me where you think Becky might be?"

"Why didn't you just follow me and find out?"

"Because I don't want to do it that way if I don't have to. I'd rather have your cooperation."

"You're asking for a lot."

"I know I am." He stepped closer to her, his expression gentling once more. "So what happens now?"

Confusion warred with the angry defiance flashing in her eyes. "I guess I'll go to work today after all."

"I don't think you can do that. Now that you've thought of somewhere Becky could be hiding, you can't just forget it. You can't not check it out."

"Well, I can't just lead you straight to her either. If she's there."

"Maybe I'm wrong about her. Maybe you're right," Clay softly suggested, reaching out to touch a tendril of her hair. "If we find her today, we'll know the answer to that question. And it has to be answered sooner or later anyhow. Mandy, if you give me a chance to talk to her she may be able to explain everything and convince me she's innocent."

"I wish I could believe that might happen, but I'm not sure anymore," Amanda murmured, the admission difficult, heart-wrenching. "You and the police are so convinced she had something to do with the robbery and . . . and it does seem like all the evidence points right at her."

"I'm afraid it does."

"But if Brad forced her to help him, even threatened her maybe . . ."

"Let's find out what we can. Let's go look for her. Tell me where you were planning to go and we'll go together."

"Oh hell, I don't know what to do now," she said, her tone tortured. "I do want to talk to her. I need to. Mom and Dad are so worried but . . ."

"Where do you think she might be?"

"Lake Norman in North Carolina," she answered dully, knowing he was right—she had to go and check out the possibility. "Our aunt and uncle have a cabin there. We used to go with them once in a while, but that was a long time ago and Becky might not think of the place. I've even forgotten exactly how to get there."

"I know the way. We'll go in my car," he said, taking her agreement for granted and cupping her elbow in one hand to escort her to the curb.

They drove southwest, heading toward the state line. The day promised to be a hot one. The sun beamed down strong and bright. Puffy white clouds marbled the blue sky. It was a lovely morning but Amanda couldn't fully appreciate its beauty. She was anxious. Afraid they would find Becky, afraid they wouldn't. Afraid that if they did all her worst fears would be realized. Clay turned on the car stereo and played soft, calming music that helped her relax a little. They talked occasionally, always sticking to impersonal topics, but even interesting conversation didn't help her much. She thought the trip would never end.

Clay glanced over at her often, understanding her tension. There was nothing he could do to ease it and he regretted that. But some things in life can't be changed—or controlled. And the moment Becky allowed Brad to become the dominant person in her life, she had set off a chain reaction that would likely end in big trouble for her and her parents and Amanda. It was a shame she had let herself be led so far away from the values she'd grown up with. He wondered if she was already regretting it. From what Amanda had told him, he suspected Becky wasn't a very strong-willed individual. Wherever she was right now, was she scared? Probably so, Clay thought. It was sad.

Amanda tensed in the passenger seat when they veered off the highway on to the road that led to the lake. Some of the landmarks were familiar and she began to get her bearings as they passed a small grocery store. "Well, this is it," she said, looking at Clay while clasping her hands together tightly in her lap. "The cabin's on the west shore. Take the next right. I think it's a couple of miles, three at most. I'll recognize the driveway."

Knowing she was in no mood to talk, Clay silently followed her directions. The next few minutes seemed long even to him, so he could well imagine what she must be going through.

She spoke at last, her voice shaky. "See those two gigantic oaks up ahead on the left? The driveway's between them. It curves to the cabin, so you can't see the place from here, but this is it."

Clay slowed down, turned in, and followed the tree-lined lane. Gravel scrunched beneath the wheels and intermittently peppered the undercarriage. Through openings in the foliage, he glimpsed the shimmering surface of the lake, and when he shut off the air-conditioning and rolled down his window he felt a cooling breeze that drifted inland from over the water. "Nice place."

"I used to think so. We'll see if I still feel the same after today," was her strained answer. She sat practically on the edge of her seat, looking straight ahead. They rounded the curve. The cabin was directly before them, weathered cedar, tranquillity itself. There was no car parked beside it, but that didn't necessarily mean anything. The moment Clay braked to a halt and cut the engine, she was out of the car, no longer able to stand the dreadful suspense.

Clay followed her to the door. It was locked. "They might have just gone out for a while," he reminded Amanda. "We'll have to go in through a window to see if there's some evidence they're staying here."

"No, there's a spare key. At least there used to be. Aunt Julie hid it on a hook under the eaves. Here." She handed it to Clay, deciding her fingers were too trembly to guide it into the keyhole.

He unlocked the door and opened it slowly, making no noise whatsoever. He stepped across the threshold first, Amanda trailing close behind him. Inside the main room, it was hot and stuffy, the air stale. Their entrance stirred up tiny dust motes that danced in the ray of sunlight streaming in through a side window. Everything was tidy and in its proper place. Even the magazines on a low table were neatly arranged. Clay strode into the kitchenette and opened the refrigerator. Except for a bowl of soft margarine, it was empty.

He relaxed. "I'd say nobody's been here for a couple of weeks, judging by the fine layer of dust on everything. Looks like we came on a wild-goose chase. The search goes on."

Standing on a hooked rug in the center of the room, Amanda rubbed her brow and released a slow, tremulous breath.

Clay went back to her. "Was that a sigh of relief?"

She spread her hands, uncertain. "In a way, I'm disappointed Becky and Brad aren't here. I've had enough of this mess. Not knowing what really happened is driving me nuts and I want it to end. But, in another way, I guess I'm glad we didn't find them. If the truth turns out to be bad news, I don't know if I want to have to handle it."

He nodded, the expression that settled over his features conveying complete understanding. "Well, you don't have to face that moment yet. We're looking in the wrong place."

His coal black eyes held hers and she felt a rush of excitement when he moved nearer. But she fought against it and spun around on one foot to hurry away from him, beyond his reach. "It's stifling in here," she said, unlatching the sliding glass doors that opened onto the porch overlooking the lake. She stepped out onto the wood planking and went to lean against the rail. "Ah, this is much better. I feel like I can breathe again. And the water looks so cool."

"Yes," Clay agreed, joining her at the railing. "It does look cool. You told me you like to swim. Want to take a dip?"

Enthusiasm lit up her eyes, then died away as she gave the suggestion further thought and had to shake her head. "I'd take you up on that if I could but I can't. No bathing suit. You don't have one either."

"Don't let a minor detail like that get in our way," he re-

61

plied, a lazy grin tipping up the corners of his mouth. "I wouldn't mind going skinny-dipping."

"I'm sure you wouldn't," she retorted, her answering smile wry as she started back inside. "But you might as well put that idea right out of your mind."

"Spoilsport."

"No. Just wise."

"Mandy," he muttered gruffly, catching her by the hand, drawing her back to him, slipping an arm around her waist. Before she had time to react, he lowered his head, traced her lips with his, then took coaxing possession of their sweet softness.

Taken by surprise, she acquiesced for several delightful moments. His kiss was electrifying and sent volts of sensation rioting through her, arousing every nerve ending. His firm lips captured hers tenderly yet with undeniable demand. He tasted of mint. When his other muscular arm glided around her, his embrace tightening, her fingers clutched his shirtfront and she swayed against him, eagerly returning his deepening kiss.

In the branch of a sycamore that hung over the cabin roof, a mama bird began to squawk, loudly scolding a squirrel that ventured too near her nest. Her strident noisy protest awakened Amanda's consciousness, thrusting her back into reality with a jolt. Amazed at her volatile response to Clay, threatened by it, she pushed away from him, dragging her lips from his, her breathing quick.

"No, Clay," she whispered. "I told you last night that I don't want to get involved like this. I *won't* get involved."

"Won't you?" he quietly challenged, imprisoning her gaze. "You may think you don't want to, but some things are inevitable, Mandy."

"*We're* not!"

"You're wrong."

"Do you think you're irresistible or something?" she countered, her own conflicting feelings for him putting her on the defensive. "Well, you're not! Who do you think you are?"

"Bond. James Bond," he answered, sounding incredibly like Sean Connery.

She tried her best not to laugh but couldn't help herself, and shook her head at him admonishingly. "You're an impossible man."

His broad shoulders rose and fell in a casual shrug. "No, I'm not. But you've called me a spy more than once, so I might as well pretend I'm the very best."

She felt a sharp little catch in the area of her heart. She had never before realized how sensuously exciting a man's sense of humor could be, but now she knew, and when he pulled her back into his arms she was unable to resist him.

"Mandy," he whispered gruffly, cradling her neck in one hand, tilting her face up. His lips claimed hers, devouring their tenderness as he pressed her slender shapely body against the long length of his. "Not only is James a superspy, he makes women swoon."

"I've never . . . swooned . . . in my life," she managed to answer between his feathering kisses.

His lips parted hers and lingered long upon them. "Feeling faint yet?"

"Not a bit," she murmured, feeling his mouth curve into a smile against her cheek. "You might as well give up. I'm not a swooner."

"Hmm, must be losing my technique."

"I think you know exactly what you're doing. You're trying to woo me with humor."

"And am I succeeding?"

"Clay . . . I . . ."

"Relax," he softly coaxed, running his fingers through her

hair, cradling the back of her head as his lips sought hers once more.

A thrill too pleasurable to be denied rushed through her and she wrapped her arms around him, pressing closer. Although a breeze off the lake caressed them, she felt exceedingly warm. A deep, plunging tremor radiated from her very center as he gently pushed the tip of his tongue into her mouth. Breathless, she drew it in deeper, over her own.

"Sweet. You're so sweet, Mandy," he murmured huskily many delightful moments later. Kissing the smooth column of her neck, he brought his hands down her back to clasp her waist, then skimmed them slowly back up. His palms cupped the straining sides of her breasts and he could feel the heat of her flesh emanating through the sheer fabric of her bra and her thin cotton blouse. With light fingertips she caressed the rims of his ears, toying with the lobes, and fiery desire sped through his bloodstream to gather achingly in him. Widening his stance, he held her tighter against his hard thighs.

Encountering the undeniable proof of his passion, Amanda realized she had to call a halt. Here was no seventeen-year-old track star who would be content with a few wild kisses. Clay was an earthy, sensual man, and if she let this go on any longer he would want much more than she was willing to give. For his sake and her own, she turned her head to one side to escape his lips and shook her head. "I told you I don't want to get involved like this."

"I think it's too late," he whispered. "We're already involved."

"We'll just have to get uninvolved, then."

"It's not that simple." Holding her away from him, he looked into her eyes. "How can we stop being attracted to each other? We can't. And you enjoyed the last few minutes as much as I did, didn't you?"

"I . . . maybe."

"Didn't you?"

"Well, yes, then. But—"

"Mandy, we're both adults."

"But one of us is not consenting."

"You sure?" he questioned provocatively, playing with tendrils of her hair. "It's a slow, lazy day, just perfect for—"

"No."

"The lake looks so cool," he continued. "And we're all alone in a secluded cabin in the woods. You have to admit it's a romantic place to—"

"*No.*"

He threw up his hands with an indulgent smile. "Well, you can't blame a man for trying."

"And you can't blame a woman for being cautious."

"There's such a thing as being too cautious though. I'll have to see what I can do about freeing you of some of your inhibitions."

"Come on, James Bond, let's get out of here," she said, shooting him a tolerant grin before walking back into the cabin. "I don't know about you but I'm ready to find a place for lunch."

After locking up and replacing the key on its hook under the eaves, they walked to the car.

"There are some small towns around the lake," he said as they got in and buckled up. "I'm sure we can find a restaurant in one of them."

"Let's try to find one fast. I'm starved. I had to get up so early that I only wanted a slice of toast for breakfast," Amanda explained. She looked quickly at him. "And you . . . You got up at four o'clock, so I bet you haven't had anything to eat since—"

"Dinner last night."

"You must be hungry, then."

"Haven't you heard my stomach growling?"

"Is that what that was?" she drawled, amusement sparkling in her eyes. "I thought maybe there was a bear loose in the woods somewhere."

Clay laughed.

The restaurant they located was actually a mom-and-pop café, but the hamburgers they ordered turned out to be thick and juicy and delicious. Amanda passed up the french fries when ordering but soon began casting covetous glances at the ones on Clay's plate. Noticing, he shared them with her. Unrushed, they enjoyed the meal, talking between bites. When they had finished, the rail-thin waitress-cashier bustled back to the table with a smile.

"Get you folks dessert?" she offered. "We've got fresh apple pies today—baked them myself. And I'm not ashamed to say you'll never taste any better. How about it?"

Clay nodded. "You talked me into it."

"No thanks," Amanda said. "It sounds delicious but I'd better skip it."

"I shared my french fries with you, but there's a limit," Clay teased. "You'll have to get a slice of pie if you want any."

Amanda wrinkled her nose at him. "I promise I won't ask you for even one tiny morsel."

"Honeymooners?" the waitress piped up, beaming down at them. She was a motherly woman and appeared to be in her early fifties.

Amanda shook her head. "No."

"Yes," Clay said simultaneously, straight-faced.

"We're not honeymooners," Amanda had to tell the woman while she nudged Clay's shin with the toe of her shoe under the table. "He just likes to kid around."

"Well, I'm good at sizing people up and I'm sure surprised

66

you're not newlyweds," the waitress said. "You've been smiling a lot and acting like you get along so well, the way people just married do."

When she left to get the pie, Clay leaned over the table to murmur, "See, there's someone else who thinks we should be —er, closer."

He might as well have said lovers. The intimation was not lost on Amanda. She decided to ignore the remark altogether, but even as she maintained a suitably bland expression, he could see the corners of her mouth twitching in her effort to fight back a smile.

On the road again ten minutes later, they made good time. She offered to take a turn driving but he assured her he wasn't tired. When she slipped off her shoes, tucked her feet up on the seat beside her and shifted into a comfortable position, he nodded his approval. "It's good to see you relax. You were so tense this morning."

"The unknown is scary. Now I can relax a little, but I feel sort of guilty about it."

"Why?" Turning his attention from the road to her, he scrutinized her face, his dark eyes narrowing. "You have nothing to feel guilty about."

"Don't I? I'm not so sure. Becky's in serious trouble and I need to talk to her. But here I am, almost relieved we didn't find her today."

"You're doing everything you possibly can to help her, Mandy."

"Which amounts to absolutely nothing."

"Not true. You even asked me if I'd be willing to let her get away if I find her."

"H-have you thought any more about that?" she asked gingerly, catching her upper lip between her teeth. "I mean, do you think you might be able to let her go?"

"I'll cross that bridge when I come to it."

"Does that mean you might?"

"I doubt it," was his candid answer. "If people break the law, they have to accept the consequences."

"What a noble thought," she said, unable to veil her sarcasm. "Too bad I can't quite buy it. Why are so many real criminals running around loose? The crooked government officials in high office? Mafia bosses? If they don't have to accept the consequences of their actions, why does Becky have to be punished for falling in love with the wrong man?"

"Because they have power and she doesn't. It's ugly and unfair but it's that simple."

"Terrific," she mumbled. "Whatever happened to democracy?"

"We're getting there. We have our setbacks but most of us want to keep going forward. You know that, but right now you're so worried about Becky's problem you can't think objectively. Maybe you should try to back away from the situation and ask yourself a question: are you your sister's keeper?"

"*Yes!* Yes," she repeated less stridently. "I've always been."

"Then maybe it's time for a change. You can't live her life for her, Mandy. She's a grown woman who has to make her own decisions, right or wrong. And when she's wrong, you can't always rush to the rescue and make everything right again. It's all right to love her, to worry about her, but you have a life of your own. You can't dedicate it to her happiness. She's going to have to find that by herself."

"Oh, Clay, you're giving me logic, but emotions are involved here. I've always felt responsible for Becky, and that's a hard habit to break."

"Damn it, I shouldn't have said anything. You're all uptight again," he murmured. His right hand, which had rested over her seat, dropped down to curve around her neck. "Forget I mentioned it for now. You can think about it later."

His long, lean fingers kneaded the tension-tight tendons of her nape, and his gentle massage slowly allowed her to relax so much she actually drifted into a doze for a while.

When they turned onto Amanda's street she saw her parents' car parked in front of her house. "Stop!" she softly cried out, clasping Clay's right forearm, gasping with relief when he immediately pulled over. "Mom and Dad are at the house. I'll get out here. If they see me with you I'll have to tell them Brad lied about his name and they'll go out of their minds worrying about Becky."

Clay nodded understandingly as she opened the door and started to get out. "I'll be in touch."

She nodded back, sure he would.

Her parents jumped up from the sofa the instant she opened the front door and entered the house. Both looked older to her than they ever had.

"Thank God you're home!" "We were about to call the police!" Their voices intermingled as their words poured out.

"What's going on?" Amanda asked. "Why are you so upset?"

"Why? Because your car was here but you weren't. You told us to come pick some tomatoes, but when we got here we found Bossy in the backyard looking like it's the end of the world," her father explained gruffly. "When we called Betsy Ann, she said you weren't coming in to the store at all today. First Becky disappears and then you seem to. Where have you been?"

"I'm sorry, I should have told you I had to go to Greensboro for a meeting with a wholesaler. And Barbara—I've mentioned her to you, the friend I met swimming at the Y last winter—she had to go to Greensboro to see her aunt, so we flipped a coin, took her car, and shared the cost of the gas," Amanda lied, knowing Barb would agree to back up her story if asked. "She let me off at the corner. I'm sorry you've been worried about me, but I knew you had my spare key, so you could let yourselves in."

Her parents seemed satisfied with her explanation. She went to them, giving both a reassuring kiss and a hug. She hated lying to them but it seemed necessary.

Two days later, Amanda had news for Clay. It wasn't much; perhaps that was why she was willing to share it with him. She called him from home, but he wasn't in. Leaving her name and number with his answering service, she suggested he return her call if he had a chance.

Her message surprised him. They hadn't talked since the trip to the lake and under the circumstances he could understand why she wouldn't be the one to get in touch. Now that she had, he gave her message top priority. He picked up the phone, started to punch her number, then paused a moment before putting the receiver back. A phone call was too impersonal. He would drive over to her house instead.

When Amanda answered the knock on her door and found Clay standing on the small front porch, her heart rate picked up some speed. He seemed to have a talent for catching her off guard, but she managed to give him a casual greeting.

"I got your message," he said, taking in the cut-off jeans and tank top she wore. "I assume there's something you want to talk about."

"Yes, but you didn't have to come all the way over here. You could've just called me back."

"You promised me some green peppers from your garden, so I decided to drop by and pick them up. Maybe you'd rather I hadn't come?"

"No, I didn't mean it that way. I just didn't want you to be inconvenienced."

A wry smile moved his mouth. "You sound like a polite stranger. I think we're past that stage, don't you?"

"Come in," she invited, without answering his question. Motioning him to the sofa, she hooked her thumbs in her back pockets. "Can I get you some iced tea?"

"Maybe later. Come sit down, Mandy. Tell me what you want to talk about."

"It isn't much really," she began to explain, settling on the cushion next to him. "It's good news, but it won't be too much help to you. I got a note from Becky today. So did Mom and Dad. Both of them were postmarked New York City, but she wrote that she and Brad were about to leave town."

"What else did she say?"

"Just that she was happy and didn't want us to worry about her. That's asking a bit much, I think. At least she finally got in touch."

"Obviously she didn't mention the Shalimar rubies?"

"No."

"That's a revealing omission."

"Revealing?"

"Think about it, Mandy. If she wasn't involved in stealing them, she's surely heard about the robbery—it's been such a big story she couldn't have missed it. It would be natural for her to mention the theft in her letter. After all, she worked in that museum. She'd be interested."

"I hadn't thought about that," murmured Amanda. "But it's not exactly hard evidence."

"No, but it's certainly suspicious."

"I guess," she half conceded, looking at her hands lying in her lap. "Well, Mom and Dad feel a little better because they heard from her—not much, but a little's better than nothing.

But Clay, knowing where she was three days ago can't help us find her now."

"There's a man who does some investigating for me in New York. I'll have him check out the forgers he knows and show them Becky's and Brad's pictures. Maybe one of them did some false ID and passport work in the past week or so and will be willing to talk."

"Becky has a passport. But I guess you're saying she wouldn't risk using her own."

"Exactly."

"Don't mince words on my account," she snapped sarcastically.

"Mandy, you don't want me to lie to you," Clay said, regretting the pain he'd detected in her voice. "I'm not deliberately trying to hurt you or your sister. I just have a case to solve."

She realized that. The more objective part of her mind even accepted that what he said was true—he didn't want to hurt anyone. But she and her family were likely to get hurt anyhow and sometimes it seemed easy to blame him for that. It wasn't fair but she couldn't help it. At that moment, however, she pushed aside emotion in favor of logic and a practical question. "What makes you think Becky and Brad left the country?"

"They'd probably be safer selling the collection in Europe, where there are plenty of potential buyers."

"Do you think your man in New York will find out anything?"

"I won't lie to you about that, either. I figure he has half a chance," Clay admitted. "He doesn't know that many forgers, so he'd have to get mighty lucky to find the one who did the work, and to find he's willing to talk. For a price, of course."

"How can they . . . How can anyone get the rubies through customs?"

"There's a way to smuggle just about anything."

Amanda grimaced distastefully. "Smuggling. Forgers. If you knew Becky-you'd understand how unbelievable it seems for her to be part of such sleaziness. Damn that Brad! If I could get my hands on him right now, I'd . . ."

"But you can't," Clay reminded her soothingly, covering her clenched fists with his right hand. His slow smile was one of understanding. "When I find him, though, I'll try my best to give you a crack at him."

"Promise?"

"Have I ever lied to you?"

He hadn't, as far as she knew. In fact, he was often distressingly forthright. Maybe that was one of the reasons she liked him—he wasn't a game-player. Naturally, there were other reasons too. He was attractive, intelligent, witty, and he knew how to be kind. The list didn't necessarily stop there, but she shook her head as if to reassemble her thoughts, feeling she might be wandering into dangerous territory. Especially since his fingers moving slowly over hers were creating tingly sensations that threatened to spread.

"Ready for that tea now?" she asked, unhurriedly easing her hands from his. "I could use a glass myself."

For a long moment, Clay's narrowed eyes held hers, but he nodded at last. "Sounds good." He followed her to the kitchen and leaned in the doorway, supporting himself against the jamb. "Where's Bossy?"

"She had to go out right before you came," Amanda told him, taking a pitcher of tea from the refrigerator. "She must be napping in the backyard, else she'd be scratching at the door, wanting to get back in. She's spoiled."

"I noticed," he answered wryly, watching Mandy's naturally graceful movements as she reached for two lead crystal glasses, put them on the counter, and filled them with sparkling ice cubes from the freezer. She poured the tea and added sprigs of mint. When she handed him a glass, one trim shapely arm extended straight, he discreetly surveyed her once more. Her cotton knit tank top was modest compared to many he had seen, but through the clingy material her round bosom was clearly defined. The surface of her arms and shoulders shimmered opalescently in the light pouring in the windows, and the trimness of her waist was enhanced. In a mere split second he saw all this and was aroused. What reasonably intelligent man wouldn't be? She wasn't a beauty in the strict sense of the word. Her nose was a little short and almost tipped up, snub. She was shorter than average, definitely verging on petite. But there was something about her that intrigued him. Or perhaps it was almost everything. Her lovely blue eyes were open and honest and reflected keen intelligence and compassion. And there was the promise of hot passion in her too. He sensed it simmering just beneath the surface, passion he very much wanted to ignite.

Unaware these well-hidden thoughts were passing through his head, Amanda started to lead him out of the kitchen but stopped short, snapping her fingers. "Oops, I nearly forgot," she said, setting down her tea and going back to open the refrigerator again. She pulled out the vegetable crisper, which was laden with ripe red tomatoes, shiny peppers, and fat radishes and slender carrots. Opening a large paper bag, she gave him a generous number of each, gently packing the produce until the sack was full nearly to the brim. Grinning, she lifted the bag and handed it to him.

He pretended to stagger under its weight. "How am I supposed to eat all this?"

"Be a sport and take it off my hands. Give some of it away.

But if you like stuffed peppers, be sure to make some with these. Like the lady in the café near the lake, I'm not ashamed to say you'll never taste any better. They're organically grown and they're delicious. Wait and see."

Smiling at her exuberance, Clay returned with her to the living room. After carefully setting the heavy sack on the floor, he sank down onto the sofa next to her and relaxed, stretching his long legs out before him. He took a long appreciative swallow of the tea and nibbled one leaf of the mint sprig, allowing his eyes to drift over her as she curled up sideways, facing him.

Recognizing the desire conveyed by his look, she took a hasty sip of tea. "Mmm, this hits the spot. It's been another hot day, hasn't it?"

"Yes," he answered, noticing the coaster on the lamp table at his end of the sofa. He put his glass down on it and turned back toward her. "But it's going to get even hotter, Mandy."

He took her glass, disposed of it, and taking hold of her left hand, lifted it to his lips. He took her breath away as his tongue flicked lazily over the very center of her palm, and when his teeth nipped the soft mound at the base of her thumb, her response was electric, surging through her in a wild unstoppable current. A swift gasp escaped from between her parted lips as Clay kissed the frantically beating pulse in her wrist. When his mouth grazed upward along the sensitive inner planes of her arm, she couldn't bring herself to stop him. His warm breath fluttering over her skin kindled blazing fires she couldn't douse. In that moment, her heart and body ruled her head. Sensual pleasure held sway. She tangled her fingers in the thick vibrant hair grazing his nape while his big yet gentle hands spanned her waist.

Her response intensified the passion that throbbed through him. He showered kisses across her shoulder to her creamy neck, finding the racing pulse in her throat as he nibbled at it. He inhaled the faint fragrance of her spring flower perfume. She smelled delicious and tasted even better. He couldn't get enough of her.

"Mandy, I want you," he growled, pulling her to him, tightening his arms around her. "*Need* you."

She, who had never come close to fainting in her life, felt incredibly light-headed now, all the more so when his minty-fresh mouth descended on hers, opening her lips wider apart with rousing insistence. Her tongue met the tender invasion of his, and both entangled in an erotic dance.

It was happening so fast she could build up no resistance. He cupped the weight of her breasts in his palms, then with deft swiftness pulled the thin shirt over her head. She moaned softly, on fire, as his fingers moved in slow concentric circles over her bared breasts, probing her resilient flesh as he sought the summits.

Her hot nipples swelled to his touch, and he caressed them to aroused nubbles, stroking and rubbing. Her skin was like satin, and he ached to take complete possession of her as her feverish fingers scampered along his spine. Shuddering with pulsating sensation, he bent her backward slightly over his supporting arms, covering her sweet mouth with his, plundering its softness.

She kissed him back, enjoying the tender mastery of his lips and hands. Inhaling the faint lime scent of his after-shave, she buried her fingers in his hair.

Senses inflamed, he lifted his head to gaze down at her rapidly rising and falling rose-tipped breasts. Firm and full, they beckoned his mouth. He leaned down to trace his tongue along the scented valley between them.

Pleasure came alive in her, too intense, and fraught with danger. Her self-control was slipping badly, but she made a herculean effort to regain it. When he feathered his lips up over the rise of her left breast, grazing the aroused nipple, excitement rushed through her, but she made herself resist it. Stiffening, she shook her head and raised his. "Don't," she breathed. "This all happened too fast and it has to stop now."

"Why?" he asked hoarsely, gazing down at her flushed face. "We both want—"

"I don't."

"What are you afraid of?"

"Nothing." Which wasn't strictly the truth. Deep inside, she was worried she might become too fond of him and let things get totally out of hand. He was a likable, sexy man, but she couldn't tell him that. There was, however, a truth she could tell him. "I just don't believe in casual . . ."—she searched for the right word—". . . affairs."

"Don't you mean casual sex?"

"All right, if you want to be blunt about it, yes. That's what I mean."

"Have I suggested I want a one-night stand?"

"No, but—"

"Then don't assume I do," he interrupted softly, catching her chin between thumb and forefinger. "How can you believe that's all I want?"

"How should I know what you want?" she questioned quietly, nearly transfixed by his black eyes. "I don't really know you very well."

"You know me better than that."

She thought she did. But Becky had thought she knew Brad, too, and look where it had gotten her. Amanda didn't want to make getting involved with the wrong man a family tradition, and under the circumstances, her getting involved with Clay would surely be a mistake on a grand scale. If Becky had never met Brad, if she had never been implicated in the robbery, if Clay hadn't been hired by the museum to recover the rubies . . . So many ifs. If the two of them had met socially, perhaps, and the specter of her sister's trouble had never come between them, things might have been different. And one day, after this investigation was behind them, maybe she and Clay could rekindle the feelings they'd allowed to surface. As it stood now though, she wasn't at all sure they could develop and maintain the kind of meaningful relationship she would want with him.

Her silence dragged on, defusing his desire. Letting her go, he raked his fingers through his hair and watched with a rueful expression as she hastily slipped her shirt back on. "Okay, Mandy," he said evenly, rising and heading for the front door. "If this is the way you want it."

"It's the way I think it has to be."

"If you change your mind, let me know."

She almost changed it then and there but fought the temptation. Still, as he opened the door, she hated to see him go. Spying the paper bag on the floor, she jumped up to carry it to him. "Don't forget your peppers."

This time it was his silence that created the tension between them. He turned and left without another word. She closed the door after him and leaned back against it with a heavy sigh.

Thursday evening, Clay phoned Amanda at home. The instant she heard his voice, she tensed with anticipation. She hadn't heard word one from him since Tuesday, and the very fact that he was calling now must mean he had something to tell her about the case—about Becky. Swallowing hard, she wasn't sure she wanted to hear it, but since in fact she had no choice she took the initiative, inquiring, "Your man in New York found out something?"

"Nothing came of that. But I do have a lead," he told her, his voice low, his tone even. "Seems the Shalimar rubies have turned up in Bermuda."

"H-how do you know that?"

"I have a few connections. I'm taking the nine ten flight to Bermuda tomorrow morning to check it out."

He didn't seem inclined to elaborate, and she didn't press him. Instead she asked, "And to find Becky and bring her back?"

"I've told you, my job is to recover the rubies."

His answer didn't reassure her. Worry caused a choking knot to form in her throat. If he found Becky and Brad, *if* they did have the rubies in their possession, what would happen then? She had an idea: Clay would turn them over to the authorities. They'd be extradited and brought back to the States under arrest, quite probably handcuffed. Becky would be so horribly scared. Tears welled up in Amanda's eyes. Becky was her little sister, much loved even if she had made a stupid mistake, and there must be some way she could help her. Yet she couldn't think of a thing she could do. Feeling utterly helpless, she dropped into the chair beside the telephone stand. Gnawing her lower lip, she rubbed her forehead with stiff fingers. Clay said nothing more and she felt compelled to speak. "Thanks for telling me what's going on."

"I thought you had a right to know."

She released her breath slowly with a soft hitching sound. "Well, thanks again."

"It's the best I can do, Mandy," he said, the tone of his deep voice lowering before he broke the connection.

The dial tone buzzed stridently in her ear. Dropping the receiver into its cradle, Amanda leapt to her feet and paced back and forth across her living room. But she soon came to an abrupt halt. A spark of pure inspiration illuminated her eyes and brightened her features. Maybe there was something she could do after all! She rushed back to the phone and slapped the directory open to the yellow pages. With one finger beside the first number in the appropriate listing, she quickly jabbed the buttons of the telephone, knowing she might have to make several calls to gain the information she sought. After that, she'd have to call Mom and Dad, a considerably more difficult task. But she'd accomplish it. She had to.

CHAPTER FIVE

The next morning, Amanda stepped up beside Clay at the counter in the boarding lounge. Before he noticed her she glanced at the boarding pass being handed to him. "Oh, you're just across the aisle from me," she announced, smiling innocently as he turned his head. "Too bad we can't sit together."

He stared at her, surprised and perplexed. "Mandy, what are you doing?" he began. Then he saw her tote bag and suitcase. His jaw set. "What *are* you doing here?"

"I'm going to Bermuda with you."

"Like hell you are!"

"Oh, but I am. You told me last night what time your flight was leaving so I called the airlines to find out which one scheduled that flight, reserved a ticket, and here I am."

"Wrong," he answered sternly, gripping her left elbow. "You're going home where you belong."

She gave an adamant shake of her head. "Oh no I'm not."

"Damn it, Mandy, what are you trying to prove?"

"I'm not trying to prove a thing. I'm just going with you."

"That's impossible," he said tersely, moving her away from the counter and out of earshot of the curious agent. His narrowed eyes imprisoned hers. "I'm not letting you go with me."

"I don't see how you can stop me. I have a passport and

81

you don't even need that much to travel to Bermuda. And my ticket's paid for, so you can't make me stay here."

Impatience passed over his face. "This is ridiculous. What good can you do in Bermuda?"

"You're tracking down my sister," Amanda answered simply. "If you find her, I want to be there. I can help her."

"When's she going to start learning to help herself? You can't baby-sit her forever. Even you said you were getting tired of being her protectress."

"I know what I said, but this is different. She's in real trouble this time. What do you expect me to do? Desert her?"

"I expect you to have some sense and give up this silly notion," Clay growled, his gaze impaling her. "Do your parents know what you're doing?"

"They know I'm going to Bermuda because you think you might find Becky and Brad there. I had to tell them so Dad could take over at the store while I'm gone."

"But they still don't know the whole truth about Brad, do they?

"If they did know, do you think they'd encourage you to confront him? Good God, Mandy, he's a thief, and criminals don't like getting caught. He's not going to surrender to me or the police or anybody else without putting up a fight and trying to escape. And if you get caught in the middle of something like that you could get hurt."

With her free hand she dismissed his warning. "Oh, I don't think Brad's the violent type."

"Oh you don't?" Clay muttered through clenched teeth, his voice edged with sarcasm. "And how would you know anything about people like this? You've never dealt with them. I have. Some of them can be very dangerous."

"If Brad is, then Becky needs my help even more."

"You're not being reasonable, Mandy."

"I think I am."

"Just forget it," he softly commanded, tightening his fingers around her upper arm. "The discussion's over. You're not tagging after me in Bermuda. Even if you do go, I'll lose you as soon as we get there."

"I won't let you. If you won't cooperate, I'll just have to follow you around. You've followed me often enough, so I won't feel bad about it."

Clay uttered an explicit curse. "I never realized you're such a stubborn—"

"No name-calling," she hastily interrupted, regretting his negative reaction, though not surprised by it. She had come prepared for a battle of wills and determined to win. She *was* going with him. "You're right," she admitted. "I can be stubborn, so you might as well give up trying to change my mind."

Anger glinted in his eyes. "You're forcing me to be blunt. I don't want you getting in my way. I'm not going to put up with your interference." He glanced at his wristwatch and back at her, his expression gentling somewhat. "We're supposed to take off in ten minutes. You know this is a crazy idea, Mandy. Go home."

"No."

"Damn it, woman, you—"

"I don't like being manhandled," she snapped as his fingers pressed deeper into her flesh. Patience wearing thin, she snatched her arm free of his grip. "Let me go. The cave man act doesn't suit you."

"I'd like to turn you over my knee."

"Don't try it."

With a few words she wouldn't have cared to repeat, he strode away from her, past the counter and into the seating area. Watching him go, she nibbled her lower lip an instant, then thrust her chin out a little and followed.

After a delay of approximately thirty minutes they were airborne, climbing in altitude. When the plane leveled off and the seat belt signs went dark, the flight attendants began offering drinks to the passengers. After choosing tomato juice, Amanda heard Clay ask for coffee, and when the steward pushed the cart on by she looked over at him. He was in an aisle seat, as was she. She could easily have reached over and touched his arm to indicate she wished he wouldn't be so hostile. But she didn't reach, didn't say a word. He didn't even glance at her. In fact, his head was buried in a newspaper. Sighing, she took a book out of her tote bag and tried to read.

There was a brief layover at Newark during which Amanda trailed Clay around Terminal B, suspecting he might try to give her the slip by transferring to another flight. He didn't go near the ticket counters, however, and totally ignored her, although she was never far behind. When they boarded another plane for the last leg of the journey, they were seated some distance apart. Amanda saw him only once, when she walked back to the restroom, but she knew he could hardly get away from her at 20,000 feet. When she passed him he paid no attention.

About an hour or so out of Newark, the pilot began a slow descent. The fluffy white cloud bank beneath them thinned as they glided smoothly down and looking out the window Amanda soon saw the dark blue waters of the Atlantic gradually lightening to a jewel-clear sapphire. The waves rolled and found land, frothily lacing pinkish white beaches where sunlight glinted on the sand. As she heard the hydraulic whine of the wheels going down, she glimpsed the lush island, bejeweled by the white roofs of the houses. They landed with a light bounce and swept along the tarmac before coming to a complete halt at the terminal building.

Amanda disembarked before Clay and waited for him in the luggage claim area. She had already picked up her canvas suitcase, so she was ready to follow him after he claimed his own brown leather bag. He moved away from her, his strides long and fast. Then he stopped short, turned, and came back, his expression somber as she looked up at him.

"Mandy, stop this nonsense," he said, his tone compassionate. "Take the next flight back home."

"I can't."

"You can. If anything at all happens I'll let you know."

She shook her head. "That's not good enough."

"But—"

"You wouldn't desert *your* sister if she was in the trouble Becky's in, would you?"

"No, but that's beside the point," he countered. "I have a lot of experience with this kind of thing and you don't have any. You know nothing about investigative work or the kind of people I have to deal with sometimes."

"Teach me, then," she softly requested, looking into his black eyes. "Make this easier for both of us and let me help you find Becky if she's really here."

There was no reasoning with her, and Clay knew it. He felt like grabbing her by the shoulders to try to shake some sense into her but that would accomplish nothing. She'd made up her mind. But he'd made his up too. Biting back the words he wanted to say, he turned around and walked away again.

She kept him in sight as they passed through the terminal and walked out into bright sunshine. Wasting no time he hailed the closest taxi and she quickly beckoned the one pulling up behind his. Politely declining the driver's offer of help with her luggage, she tossed her suitcase and tote bag into the backseat and climbed in after it.

"Where to, ma'am?"

"I'm not sure yet," she admitted, smoothing the skirt of her cream-colored suit. "Just follow that cab in front of us, please."

"Are you joking, miss?" the driver asked with surprise, his accent slightly British. "You don't really want—"

"I want you to follow that taxi."

Lifting his cap, he rubbed his head. "Do you mean the one the gentleman just got into?"

"That's it. Don't let it get away from us."

"Nobody's ever asked me to follow another taxi before. Life's pretty quiet here. What's this about, miss, if you don't mind me asking? Man trouble?"

Amanda smiled ruefully. "I guess you could say that."

"Well, I'll do my best," the crusty man promised. "I'm a romantic, my wife says, so I'll do anything I can to help the course of true love."

Amanda could have kissed him for his willingness to cooperate. She had no intention of dashing his romantic misconception about what was going on.

Up ahead, Clay turned to look out the back window, the angular lines of his face tensing as he saw Amanda talking to her driver. "Lose the taxi behind us as soon as you can. Long before we get close to the Windsor Arms Hotel," he instructed his own driver, swearing inwardly.

The driver's dark brown eyes shot up to the rearview mirror. "You've obviously never been to Bermuda before, sir."

"I've been here."

"Then you must know we have a strict speed limit. This isn't an American city," he declared with unequivocal pride. "We don't have high-speed chases here, like you see on the telly."

"I'm not asking you to break the law. But if you can take some shortcuts and lose that taxi . . ."

86

"I'll try my best, sir."

As it turned out his best wasn't good enough. Amanda's driver, spurred on by romantic thoughts, kept up with the taxi in front of him. The winding road passed beaches sparkling under the sun and exquisite coves dotted with windswept sailboats. Amanda kept one eye on the scenery and the other on the car ahead, never forgetting her mission despite the verdant beauty of the island. Her cab easily kept pace with Clay's even though it took a sudden right turn on to a narrower road lined with stone walls. In Bermuda as in England, cars use the left side of the road. Amanda was just about becoming accustomed to traveling in what was to her the wrong lane when the hotel came into view. She took a quick breath, dazzled by its loveliness. A sprawling gray stone edifice, it was a gem mounted on a background of lush greenery, its beauty almost understated, making it all the more lovely. The sun shimmered on the mullioned windows. Beyond the hotel, the sea sparkled and an accessible beach fringed the grounds in pale coral-tinted sand.

"Sorry, sir, but I did tell you I probably couldn't lose them," Clay's driver said, braking to stop before the hotel's entrance. "That's Henry driving the other taxi and he knows every inch of these islands like the back of his hand."

"No problem. I understand," Clay said, opening the back door and getting out of the cab. After paying and tipping the driver, he walked toward the arched entrance.

The taxi Amanda rode in slowed to a stop. Tipping generously, she got out and leaned down to smile at the driver. "Thanks for your help."

Smiling back, he nodded. "Good luck with your man, miss."

"I have a feeling I'm going to need it," she confessed. Waving good-bye, she headed into the hotel lobby, admiring the red and black oriental rugs and the cedar-framed settees and chairs. Clay had chosen a very nice place to stay.

The two desk clerks were occupied with other people, so Amanda stopped beside Clay as he waited to register. "I've never been to Bermuda before," she commented conversationally. "It's beautiful, isn't it? Did you see all the flowers alongside the road on the way here?"

He stared down at her. "This isn't a sight-seeing trip. It's business."

His clipped reply immediately wiped the smile off her face. She glared icily at him. "I know as well as you do we're here for serious reasons, but that doesn't make me blind to the beauty of the place. And you can't sulk forever just because I came along with you."

"I never sulk, Mandy. I just get mad as hell," he said, his voice lowering dangerously. "Especially when somebody interferes with my work."

"But I won't interfere."

"You're already doing a fine job of it."

"What have I done?" she exclaimed. "Nothing at—"

"You're here, which means I'm responsible for your safety."

"No, you're not. I can take care of myself."

"Innocent little idiot," he said, the planes of his sun-bronzed face hardening. "I may have to deal with people who aren't like the law-abiding, church-going folks you know back home. Get in the way of some of them and they get rough. What do you know about taking care of yourself if that happens?"

"If you're trying to scare me, it isn't working."

His expression stormy, he stepped ahead of her to the desk, greeting one of the clerks, both of whom were now free.

Amanda approached the other. "I'd like a single room please."

"Do you have a reservation?"

"Well, no, I . . . do I need one?"

"I'm afraid so, miss. All our rooms have been booked," the young clerk said, smiling kindly while tucking her ebony hair behind one ear. "I wish we could accommodate you, but it's impossible."

"Um, I see," murmured Amanda. This was an unforeseen development that complicated matters, but not insurmountably. She wouldn't let it. "There must be hotels close by that still have some vacancies. Can you recommend one."

"The Pink Sands isn't here in St. George's, but it's not far away. You may be able to find a room there."

"Thank you very much," Amanda said, turning away from the desk to find Clay watching her, a room key in his hand. She looked at it. "Obviously, you did make a reservation."

"Naturally. I plan my travels. I don't take off on the spur of the moment without making arrangements."

"Is that your way of insinuating I'm irresponsible?"

"If the shoe fits . . ."

She smiled sweetly, refusing to let him provoke her.

"Not being able to get a room here could be an omen," he continued, "telling you it'd be wiser to fly home."

"I don't think so."

"Then you'll be staying at the Pink Sands. Are you going there now?"

"Fat chance," she retorted, shaking her head. "If I leave this hotel, you'll go wherever it is you plan to go, and I won't know where you are. I'll wait until this evening to get a room."

"Suit yourself, but rooms may be even harder to get then. And you might get tired of waiting around. After I drop my bag in my room, I'm having lunch."

"Great idea. I'm hungry too."

"Aren't you going to feel a little funny carrying your suit-case around?"

"I don't suppose you'd let me leave it in your room?"

"The answer's no," he said quite somberly. "Don't expect any encouragement from me."

She shrugged in reply, and watched him follow the bellman across the carpet to the bank of elevators. When the doors of one swept silently open, they disappeared inside. Turning back to the desk, Amanda gave a hopeful smile. "Could I leave my luggage here a few hours, please? I wouldn't ask, but there's someplace I have to go in a few minutes. I don't have time to get a room at the Pink Sands first."

The clerks looked at each other, showing their reluctance. "I don't know, miss," said one. "Personally, I'd let you do it, but it's not hotel policy to guarantee the security of luggage left at the desk."

"I'm sure it would be safe here," Amanda went on. "And if it isn't—I mean, if something should happen to it, I wouldn't hold the hotel responsible."

"Even so, I . . ."

"Somebody in my family is in trouble," she told the two women candidly. "I'm trying to help. That's why I can't go check in to the Pink Sands right away."

"If it's that important . . ."

"It is, believe me, and you'd be doing me such a favor."

"All right," she said at last. The other clerk nodded in agreement. "We'll keep your things here behind the desk."

After expressing her gratitude, Amanda found a brocade upholstered settee with a clear view of the elevators. For the next twenty minutes, which seemed to last hours, she waited for Clay to return, anxiously tapping her toe against the orien-tal rug. When he finally appeared, she breathed a swift sigh of relief and got up. He had changed clothes, replacing his suit

90

with gray slacks, navy blazer, and a white shirt open at the neck, attire more suitable to the tropical atmosphere. She felt overdressed in her own suit but that couldn't be helped at the moment. Fidgeting with the buttons of her jacket, she smiled as he walked toward her, but he walked right past her without a word. Taken aback, she hurried to catch up, touching his sleeve as she fell into step beside him. "You were gone so long I thought maybe you'd gone out the back way."

"I would've if I could," he admitted, his expression unyielding. "But all the exit stairs lead into the lobby, and I couldn't jump from my third-story balcony."

"A lucky break for me."

Despite her hopeful smile, he said nothing. As they walked outside through the arch, he hailed one of the taxis waiting in the flower-festooned courtyard.

"Must be checkout time. We have plenty of cabs to choose from," she chattered, following him to the nearest one. She got in with him, as casually as possible. "It's silly for us to take separate cabs to the same place when we can split the fare for one," she attempted to explain. Holding her breath, she almost flinched, half expecting an explosion.

A muscle worked with fascinating regularity in Clay's tensed jaw and his magnificent black eyes bored into the depths of hers, but finally he issued directions to the driver and they were off. Perhaps he didn't want to make a scene in public. More likely, he simply wasn't a man who could drag a woman out of a car, which is what he would have had to do. Sometimes, sheer obstinacy pays off, she thought. Amanda didn't enjoy being considered a nuisance. But what was the alternative? Helping Becky was as important to her as his case was to him. If only she could make him understand that.

The silence in the back of the taxi seemed deafening to her, and she looked out her window, trying to relax. In a crystal-clear bay, boats all colors of the rainbow bobbed in the gently undulating water. One sliced cleanly through the miniwaves, its triangular white sail stretched taut as it caught the wind. After they'd left the bay behind them they passed a cluster of limestone houses with white tiled roofs, perched on the hillside the road bisected. Louvered shutters that pushed out from the bottom and hinged at the top shaded the windows, and everywhere there were flowers. Amanda saw many sprawling bushes laden with deep-pink clustering blossoms. "Is that bougainvillaea, driver?" she asked. He said it was. "What about those big scarlet flowers? What are they?"

"Hibiscus, miss."

"And the light pinks?"

"Oleander. But if you'd like to see something even prettier, come back to Bermuda when the royal poinciana trees are in full bloom. They're past their peak now. It would be worth another visit to see them."

"I'd love to. But these flowers are lovely too," she said, glancing at Clay. "Aren't they beautiful?"

"Yes," was his brief answer.

Which didn't encourage her to try to strike up a more meaningful conversation.

The town of St. George's was a quaint old village, charming in every way, bordered by a deep harbor where a huge Swedish ocean liner was docked, its name emblazoned in royal blue letters on the gleaming white hull. Amanda was intrigued by all of the sights, including the names of some of the side streets—Old Maid's Lane, Silk Alley.

Still overlooking the harbor, near the outskirts of town, the driver stopped at Queen Anne's Inn. As she had promised, Amanda produced half the amount of the fare and tip and Clay took the money, adding it to his. Hot sunlight beamed down on her bare head as they got out of the cab, but a cooling breeze helped counteract the effects of the fierce rays. Although Clay walked fast, she kept up with him, and they actually entered the restaurant together. The inn was delightfully English with beamed ceilings and wood pillars. It had authentic pub tables and even a dart board hanging on one paneled wall. Yet the windows were wide and tall and light poured in through the panes.

A hostess met them in the foyer. "Table for two?"

"One," Clay answered.

"Oh, pity, we only have one table available. You may wait in the bar, miss, until we have another," the hostess said graciously but looked back at Clay. "Unless, you'd be willing to share your table, sir?"

"I'm starving," Amanda said out of the corner of her mouth, so quietly only Clay could hear. It was a deliberate play for sympathy and, perhaps, a resort to feminine wiles, uncharacteristic but necessary. If he had lunch before she could get a table, she'd have to leave without eating in order to follow him. And she was *hungry.* "Come on, Clay, be a sport. What harm can it do for us to share a table?"

"I don't mind sharing," he told the waitress, knowing full well he would feel like a bastard if he did otherwise—like a villain stealing crumbs from an orphan. He wasn't sure why he felt that way. After all, Mandy was a grown woman and hardly on the verge of starvation, but still . . . Accepting his fate, at least for the moment, he indicated with a gesture that she should precede him as they followed the hostess to a small table with a view of the sapphire water. She handed them each a menu and whisked away.

Their waiter appeared shortly. After ordering, Amanda added, "Separate checks, please."

Nodding, he turned to Clay and took his order. "Would you

care for anything to drink while you wait?" he asked them both.

She decided on white wine, hoping it would help loosen the knot of tension clutching ever tighter in her chest.

"Gin and tonic," Clay said. "Light on the gin."

It wasn't the most comfortable meal Amanda had ever had, far from it. She and Clay talked very little, but still she enjoyed the freshly caught red snapper. After she had eaten every last succulent morsel, she felt much better physically. Her emotions still weren't in terrific shape but that was hardly surprising under the circumstances. She swallowed the last sip of her one glass of wine.

Clay had already finished his combination of steak and shrimp, and sat watching her. Suddenly, he covered her small hand resting on the table with his. "You shouldn't be here, Mandy," he murmured. "Go home, please."

His husky voice sent a delightful shiver up her spine, and the warm touch of his fingers made her realize how very much she disliked being at odds with him. "I can't go home yet," she said quietly. "If Becky's really here, I—"

"Okay. Fine." Abruptly he released her hand.

They paid their checks and walked out of the inn. Sighing, Amanda looked up at him. "Are you going to take me with you or make me follow you?"

"Get in," he said, leading her to the taxi he had beckoned to a stop. Lowering himself onto the backseat beside her, he slammed the door after him. "We're going to see a man, and I don't want any trouble from you. Let me do all the talking."

As she readily agreed, he gave an address to the driver.

Between St. George's and the larger town of Hamilton, the road cut through limestone. Sheer rock towered overhead, boxing in the thoroughfare. Always somewhat claustrophobic,

Amanda was relieved when they left behind the tunnellike rock facings and were out in the open again.

A few minutes later their driver turned onto a private asphalt drive that wound down a hillside overlooking the ocean. Amanda's eyes widened at the grandeur of the sprawling hacienda-style house they approached. A profusion of bright flowers climbed the white walls, and stairs led down to a private beach.

"This is some place," she commented. "You gave me the impression we'd be meeting somebody in a dark room somewhere. Who lives here, anyhow?"

"Bernard Cooper," answered Clay without elaborating. Asking the driver to wait, he got out of the car.

Amanda faithfully followed him along the tiled walkway and through the front courtyard, where a fountain tinkled merrily. Tucking her clutch purse under her arm, she waited beside him as he rang the bell, which was answered almost immediately by a stiff-spined manservant who acknowledged them with the briefest of nods.

"Yes? May I help you?"

Clay stepped forward. "We're here to see Bernard Cooper."

"Mr. Cooper didn't mention he expected guests."

"No, we—"

"He's not here at the moment."

"I see. When do you expect him back?"

"Not until tomorrow afternoon at the earliest. He and Mrs. Cooper are spending the night with friends who live in Southampton."

"Would you give me the name of the friends? I'd like to talk to Mr. Cooper today if possible."

"He wouldn't want to be disturbed, sir. I suggest you call tomorrow around three o'clock."

"Until tomorrow then," Clay agreed, as the door started

closing. When he and Amanda walked back across the courtyard, he murmured almost to himself, "Bad timing."

"I thought you always planned in advance," she had to say, with a teasing note in her voice. "I'm surprised you didn't make an appointment with Mr. Cooper."

"Sometimes it's better to arrive unannounced."

"Who is Bernard Cooper? He's obviously a wealthy man. Is he one of those collectors you told me about? Do you think he might have bought the rubies?"

"That would make solving this case fairly simple, wouldn't it?" Clay said, answering her question with a question. "But simple solutions are few and far between. Maybe you read too many Nancy Drew mysteries when you were a child and they made you believe investigations are easy."

"I did read all the Nancy Drew stories," she admitted without shame. "I loved them."

"Just control your imagination. I don't need you playing girl detective on one of my cases."

"I'm not a girl. I'm a woman."

"I've noticed. 'Girl' was a bad choice of words on my part," he said dryly as they got back in the waiting cab.

Since Clay couldn't proceed further without talking to Bernard Cooper, he asked the taxi driver to take them to Hamilton. "We've got a lot of hours to kill until tomorrow afternoon," he explained to Amanda. "Might as well see as much of the island as we can."

The city of Hamilton was considerably larger than St. George's. It was a bustling little town, quaint enough to charm tourists while containing all the shops necessary to tempt them to spend their traveler's checks. Amanda and Clay ambled along Front Street by the island-dotted harbor and up and down the hilly sidewalks. He was polite but distant, causing her to become very quiet and somewhat depressed. She saw couples everywhere. Some of them looked like they might be newlyweds, while others were older, perhaps on second honeymoons. Everybody seemed to be having fun. She wasn't.

"Damn it, Becky, how did you get us all in such a mess?" she muttered under her breath.

"What?" Clay asked. "Did you say something?"

"It was nothing, really. Just talking to myself."

Nodding, he led her into a small, modest souvenir shop. "Guess I better buy something for my sister's kids. They might never forgive me if I don't. Any suggestions on what to get?"

"Maybe. How old are they?"

"Josh is five and Vicky's three."

"Um, let's see now." Amanda considered the problem, walking slowly along one aisle. "They're too young for beer mugs and wouldn't be thrilled by beach towels. Let's move over to the other side."

Clay tagged along after her, grimacing with some disbelief at the many plastic replicas of Gibb's Lighthouse. He shook his head. "I'm surprised they're trying to sell something that tacky."

A beaming smile brightened Amanda's face. "Well, I must admit I've seen better-looking replicas. Full as that shelf is, they're not selling like hot cakes, so most people must feel the same way." She stopped in front of stacks of T-shirts, which she began to look through. In a few moments, she held up a bright blue one that proclaimed in blue letters MY PARENTS WENT TO BERMUDA AND ALL I GOT WAS THIS SHIRT. "It's not exactly true but it's funny."

"Yeah, I like it," he agreed while picking up a red shirt and showing her its message with a grin. REMOVE ALL BREAK-

ABLE ITEMS—HERE I COME it warned. "This one might be more appropriate for both of them."

She chuckled. "Rowdy kids, huh?"

"I'll just say they're incredibly energetic. But we'd better go with the ones you found. If I buy these, Mom will fuss. She says I've been a bachelor too long and that I'd see what perfect little darlings they are if they were mine."

"Do you think you would?"

"Probably. I understand fatherhood changes your attitude. Besides, I'm exaggerating. They're nice kids. But are you sure they'll want something to wear for a present?"

"Oh, sure, children love new clothes. Especially T-shirts, because they're comfortable."

"I couldn't begin to guess what sizes to buy, though."

"But you've brought along an expert. Children's clothes are my business, remember?" She searched the stacks thoughtfully, her lower lip caught between her teeth. "I'll get a size larger than average five- and three-year-olds wear. It's better to have something to grow into than something that might be too little to begin with."

Finding two such shirts with no visible flaws in them, she handed them to Clay and started around to the next aisle. "But it wouldn't hurt to take them something to play with too." She chose an inflatable beach ball with BERMUDA printed all over it for Josh, and a small soft teddy bear for his sister. "There you are, T-shirts *and* toys, all easily packed in your suitcase. And I think they'll be pleased."

Since she was the expert on children and he was admittedly rather ignorant about what they might or might not like, he accepted her decision.

After leaving the souvenir shop, they went into the store next door, a more elegant establishment. There they headed in opposite directions. Amanda looked around, feeling she should buy something for her parents and Betsy Ann. But her heart wasn't truly in it. Maybe her folks wouldn't want anything from the island if she didn't find Becky while she was here. It might be even worse if we *do* find her, she thought. But maybe gifts would cheer them up just a little. She began to shop more earnestly, finally choosing a set of Irish linen dinner napkins for her mother, a pipe for her father, who collected them, and a small flacon of French perfume for Betsy Ann. While a helpful clerk tallied up the amount of her purchases, Clay joined her at the counter.

"Is the perfume for you?" he asked.

"No, for Betsy Ann, my assistant at the store."

"I can guess the pipe isn't for you and I imagine the napkins are for your mother. Aren't you buying anything for yourself?"

"I didn't see anything I really wanted."

Her purchases made, they continued along Front Street, then turned onto a tiered arcade that rose upward and was walled in by buildings on either side. It was little more than an alleyway, but not at all littered or dark. Charming shops lined both sides of it, beckoning, and from window boxes flowers of bright red, yellow, and blue spilled forth. They ventured into a bookstore with straw mats on the floor and shelves overflowing with rare and used old volumes.

"You may have to drag me out of here," Amanda told Clay inside the bookstore. "I could spend hours in a place like this."

He heeded her warning. About ninety minutes later, he stepped up beside her as she carefully perused the titles on one dusty shelf. "Find anything you want here?"

"Everything," she confessed. "I'll never decide which one I want."

"Ready to go then?"

"Yes." She preceded him out the door before noticing the package he carried. "Oh, but you bought something."

"For you," he said, bowing from the waist before handing her the brown-paper-wrapped book. "From me, since you wouldn't buy a souvenir for yourself."

Tearing off the paper, she expected to find a bland history of the island, but she was wrong. Instead, she found a Nancy Drew mystery, one of the very first in the series, a first edition in mint condition. She stared up at him. "You paid too much for this. I can't—"

"I figured it was worth the price," he softly interrupted. "Read it tonight and maybe you'll get amateur sleuthing out of your system."

"I doubt it. And the book's too expensive a gift. I can't accept it."

"Take it, please."

There was that coaxing word again, and this time she couldn't resist it. She would take the book, she decided, because he really seemed to want her to.

Later, after they returned to St. George's by bus, she dogged him to the hotel dining room, feeling foolish although she thought it was necessary. Once again, he agreed to share a table with her, but they didn't talk much. When the meal ended, they stood before the elevators, he on his way up to the third floor, she on hers to the lobby. He pushed the Up button. She pushed the Down.

"What'll you do if I check out of here tonight and go stay somewhere else?" Clay asked abruptly, his dark eyes holding hers. "You might not be able to find me, and then you'll have to go home."

"But I don't think you will check out," she replied calmly. "According to your desk clerk, rooms aren't exactly abundant anywhere on the island."

"True. So what will you do if there aren't any vacancies at the Pink Sands?"

She moved her hands in an uncertain gesture, palms up. "I'll try someplace else. If worse comes to worst, I guess I'll spend the night in the lobby downstairs."

"I doubt the hotel encourages loitering."

"Then there are benches out in the gardens. I can sleep on one of them."

"Don't be ridiculous. You can't spend the night on a damn bench," he barked, respecting her determination enough to add, "If you can't find a room, you can share mine. Number three fifteen."

She swallowed hard. "D-do you have a suite?"

"No, it's just a single room."

"Then I couldn't—"

"Yes you can." He raked his fingers through his hair in sheer exasperation. "There are two beds."

She said nothing. Elevator doors swooshed open, the lighted arrow above them pointing upward. Without a word, Clay got in, and she took the next one down to retrieve her luggage from the front desk. The night clerk appropriately asked for identification before handing over Amanda's suitcase and tote bag.

Clay's suggestion that she might not find accommodations for the night began to nag at her. Hurrying to a pay phone, she called the Pink Sands and was told all their rooms were occupied. She stood gnawing her upper lip. Not willing to give up, she phoned the following ten or twelve listings in the telephone book, but with no better luck. Over and over she heard apologetic voices explain that it was the height of the busy season and that several organizations were holding conventions on the island at that time.

Finally, she gave up and replaced the receiver. Glancing

around the lobby almost as if she expected a fairy godmother to appear magically and rescue her, she tiredly rubbed her stiff fingers over her forehead. She thought of trying to sleep on a bench in the gardens and shivered. She thought of a hot relaxing bath and a comfortable bed.

Clay had offered her that.

Yet, staying in the same hotel room with him would be like playing with fire, wouldn't it? That compelling attraction between them . . .

What should she do?

There was really only one sensible answer to that question.

CHAPTER SIX

Amanda wasn't afraid of Clay. She knew how to say no to a man. Still, it was difficult for her to knock at the door of room 315, and when he opened it a few seconds later she smiled sheepishly.

"Is the offer you made still good?" she asked. "I called quite a few hotels and they're all full."

Silently, he opened the door wider and stepped aside.

She walked in. "Thank you."

"You're welcome, although I don't know why I'm doing this," he bluntly said. "If I let you spend tonight on a bench in the gardens, I bet you'd be eager to go home tomorrow."

"But you can't be that unchivalrous, can you? Your mother raised a gentleman."

"She tried."

"I think she succeeded. Lucky thing for me," Amanda acknowledged, a little shiver dancing up and down her spine as he closed the door and locked them inside together. Being alone with him in a hotel room was unsettling, to say the least. He had obviously just taken a shower. Droplets of water sparkled in his hair and he wore only slacks. She had never seen him shirtless before, and couldn't deny to herself that she liked the way he looked in that state of undress. The muscular contours of his naked torso, shoulders, and strong arms intrigued her. In the soft light, his skin was like burnished copper—so smooth, touchable . . . inviting. Mentally, she shook her head to get rid of such thoughts. Simply allowing her mind to wander in that direction could prove dangerous, and it was crazy to ask for trouble.

Trying to be less distracted by his physical attributes she turned her attention to the room, which was lovely. Decorated in blue and ivory, it was spacious yet cozy, and the Mediterranean-style furnishing added to the appeal. And she was glad to see he hadn't lied—there were two beds.

"You take whichever bed you want," he offered, as if reading her mind. "Would you like the one closest to the balcony?"

"Oh, I don't really care. It's your room, so you choose the one you want."

"It doesn't matter to me."

"Me either. You pick."

"Just take a bed, Mandy."

"You."

He laughed suddenly. It was a pleasant sound rumbling up from way down deep as he looked at her, shaking his head. "I can't believe this conversation. What do you want to do? Stand here all night and argue about who's going to choose?"

She laughed with him. "No. I'm putting an end to the nonsense right now. You take the bed nearer the balcony. I want this one."

"I knew we could come to a decision if we really put our minds to it," he teased, his gaze roaming slowly over her as she put her bags on the carved chest at the foot of the first bed. "There are plenty of hangers in the closet if you need them."

"I do have a few things to hang up. And as soon as I get that done, I'm going to take a nice hot bath," she said enthusiastically, unlocking her suitcase and straightening to look at him. "But don't let me bother you."

He cocked one eyebrow. "You're not bothering me, Mandy."

"Just pretend I'm not here."

A wicked little smile moved his hard mouth. "Now you're asking too much. There's a limit to my acting abilities. I can't forget the fact that you're here getting ready to spend the night with me."

She felt warmth rising in her cheeks but tried to ignore her physical response to his provocative tone. "What I mean is, don't let me get in your way. If you want to go to bed now or while I'm taking my bath, go ahead and turn the lights off. I won't mind."

Still smiling, he glanced at his thin gold wristwatch atop the nightstand between the beds. "It's only a little after nine. Too early to go to sleep for me. I'm going to read awhile. That'll give you a chance to get started on your Nancy Drew."

Refusing to be baited, she simply stuck the tip of her tongue out at him and hung up her clothes, lining up her shoes on the closet floor. Next she carried her tote bag into the adjoining bathroom and removed her toilet articles: toothpaste and brush, special soap for her face, lotion for a soft dewy complexion, makeup, cologne, deodorant, shampoo, brush and comb. She arranged them neatly on the top of the vanity and walked back into the bedroom. Clay was on his bed, sitting back against propped-up pillows, seemingly absorbed in the book he held. Quietly, almost on tiptoe, she found her white lawn nightie, matching cotton robe, and a change of undies before turning back toward him, coughing softly to gain his attention. She waved her hand in the direction of the bath. "I may soak for a pretty long while, so if you need to go now, uh . . ."

He looked up, smiled, shook his head. "Not at the moment, but if there's an emergency, I'll let you know."

"Please do," she replied flatly, heading for the bathroom door. She sensed his eyes following her and suspected they held a glint of amusement.

She was right. He watched her walk away with an indulgent grin. Though he wasn't laughing at her at all, he did enjoy teasing her, simply to find out what her reaction would be. Often she was clever at turning the tables on him, which made her all the more interesting.

Amanda prolonged her bath for nearly an hour. At about ten o'clock she finally came out, feeling refreshed and much better than she would have if she'd been crazy enough to try spending the night on a bench. But when she padded barefoot toward her bed and Clay glanced up from his, she felt suddenly vulnerable in her modest yet somewhat thin gown and robe. It didn't help matters when he gave a wolf whistle.

Reaching out, he captured her by the left hand and drew her slowly toward him. "Hey, I'm glad I decided to let you stay with me," he murmured, only half joking. "You look nice. Very nice."

His gaze roved boldly over her from head to toe, and his fingertips grazing over the quickening pulse in her wrist kindled wildfire on the surface of her sensitized skin. But she rallied all self-control to shake her head disapprovingly. "You'd better go back to your reading."

"What reading?" he responded huskily, pulling her nearer the edge of his bed. "You're all I have on my mind right now."

"Then you'd better change your mind."

"Easier said than done. Seeing you like this makes me want—"

"Forget it, Mr. Kendall," she hastily cut in, afraid to hear exactly what he did want, wondering if he might be able to make her want the same thing. "Remember? We're not here on vacation. That's what you said this afternoon. We're here on serious business."

"I did say that, but I forgot to add that sometimes there's nothing wrong with combining business with pleasure."

"This isn't one of those times. Think of me as . . . um, a junior partner in this investigation. A Nancy Drew type. And you wouldn't dream of trying to seduce someone as sweet and wholesome as Nancy, would you?"

She had turned the tables again. He loved it. But he wasn't willing to let her completely off the hook just yet. Affecting a villainous expression, he leered at her. "I could toss you out of here and let you sleep in the gardens if you don't decide to be more cooperative."

Her delicately arched brows lifted. "Blackmail?"

"You got the picture, baby."

"I don't believe that for a minute," she retorted, laughing at his lousy attempt to imitate James Cagney's voice. His Sean Connery impersonation was far superior and she told him so, adding, "Besides, you're not the kind of man to resort to blackmail to satisfy lustful desires. And I know you're a gentleman at heart. I trust you."

Clay groaned melodramatically, released her, and comically smote his forehead with the heel of his hand. "That's the worst possible thing you could've said to me. How can I try to take advantage of you when you tell me you trust me? I'd feel like a cad. You've ruined all my plans."

She answered with a fatalistic shrug of her shoulders while inwardly relieved he'd let her go. The dangerous moments had passed and the need to go swiftly into his arms was subsiding slowly but surely. Her breathing began to return to normal. Forcing a merely amused smile to her lips, she moved beyond his reach and sank down on the edge of her own bed, trying not to notice the slight trembling of her hands or the faint weakness buzzing in her knees, while his obsidian black eyes continued to hold her own captive. She decided it was a great time to change the subject completely and waved one hand at the phone on the nightstand that separated her bed from his.

"I told Mom and Dad I'd call them tonight," she announced matter-of-factly. "Would you mind?"

"Be my guest," he said, regarding her with renewed respect. She was a very classy lady, one of the most intriguing he had ever met. Hot desire stirred in him once again, but he held it strictly in check. Too soon. She wasn't ready yet.

"I'll pay for the call, of course," she added, wondering what he was thinking, not precisely sure she wanted to know. "And I want to share the cost of the room too."

Clay nodded. "We'll work that all out later. We're going to have to spend tomorrow night here, too, because the last flight to the States is at two forty. We can't see Bernard Cooper until after three."

"I know, but when we do check out, I want to pay my half," she reiterated as she picked up the receiver. Within a second or two the phone at the other end of the line began to jangle in her ear. Her father answered on the third ring, and in a calm strong voice she told him she really had nothing to report as yet.

He sounded disappointed. But he also seemed somewhat relieved that she hadn't found Becky. Amanda understood only too well the conflicting emotions pulling him apart. He said good-bye and her mother came on, her voice quavering as she murmured, "You still don't know where Becky is, do you?"

"Not yet. We hope to get some information tomorrow."

"So you're still following Clay Kendall?"

"I'm keeping a very close eye on him," Amanda answered

discreetly, unwilling to lift her eyes from the top of the night-stand to see if he was listening.

A frugal woman, Amanda's mother reminded her of the cost of long distance and didn't indulge in idle chitchat.

"As soon as I find out anything, *if* I do, I'll let you know," Amanda promised as the abbreviated conversation came to a close.

"I notice you didn't mention we're staying in the same hotel room," Clay spoke up, closing his book on his right forefinger to keep his place. "Why didn't you?"

"For one very good reason. Dad's extremely old-fashioned. If he knew we're spending the night in the same room together, he just might grab a shotgun and fly down here to force you to make an honest woman out of me."

She was exaggerating. He knew it, but he played along, answering solemnly. "Then you were wise to keep your mouth shut about our being roommates."

"I thought you'd see it my way."

Getting up off the bed, Clay went into the bathroom. "Good God, it looks like a drugstore in here," he comically exclaimed. "What do you do with all this stuff?"

"I think most of it's self-explanatory. If you mean the makeup, I wouldn't travel without it. I want to look my best, you know," she called with a faint wry smile. "If it's in your way, though, just push it all into a corner."

When she heard him close the door, she hastily shed her cotton robe, slipped into bed, fluffed up the pillows, and sat back against them, demurely pulling the light covers up under her chin. He came back out as she was getting settled, and he stopped at the foot of her bed. Looking up at him, she felt her pulse fluttering as her eyes were imprisoned by his.

"You're embarrassed," he said quietly, "aren't you?"

She flipped one hand from side to side. "Not really embar-

109

rassed. But I didn't expect to have to share a room with you. It takes some getting used to."

"To tell the truth, I'm a little embarrassed myself," he announced straight-faced. "I'm a very shy, modest man and sort of afraid of women, so you'll have to close your eyes while I undress. Or we can turn off the lights."

Amanda laughed. "I don't believe a word of that. You? Afraid of women? No way."

"So I told a little white lie—but only to help you relax."

"More proof that you're a gentleman at heart," she quipped, though her gaze swept quickly over his broad tanned chest before meeting his eyes again. "Thanks for the reassurance."

"Mom would be proud of me, I'm sure," he drawled, and walked away to drop down onto his own bed and pick up his book. "Turn on the TV if you want to."

"No thanks," she murmured, reaching for the first edition he had bought her in Hamilton. She glanced through it, perusing a paragraph here and there. "This story's very familiar. I'm sure I read it when I was a kid but I can't remember how Nancy solved the mystery, so it'll be like reading it for the first time."

"Mmm, that's good," was the extent of Clay's response as he turned a page of his own book.

In the silent room, Amanda got through two chapters before her eyelids started getting heavy and her chin dropped slowly onto her chest. It had been a long, nerve-wracking day. Weariness caught up with her and soon she drifted off to sleep.

Clay noticed immediately when she stopped turning pages. Quietly he got up and walked over to the side of her bed to slip the book from her loose grip. Using a sheet from a memo pad in the nightstand drawer he marked her place and stood gazing down at her. She had nuzzled her right cheek into the plump pillow, and her silky hair curved over the left one. Her thick lashes lay in feathery crescents on her smooth skin, and her fully curved lips suddenly parted. When she moved a little in her sleep, he could see the shapely contours of her slender body outlined beneath the sheet.

Tempting. Too tempting. He wanted to take her in his arms and make wild, passionate love with her the whole night long, but knew that she would probably fight him tooth and nail if he tried to seduce her. She wasn't ready for that kind of relationship with him yet, so he wouldn't rush her. He could wait.

"Keep telling yourself that," he murmured aloud, walking away from her. After undressing and pulling on pajama bottoms, he got into bed and switched the lamp out. But sleep didn't come easily for him. It was hard to forget Mandy was only a few feet away, warm, cuddly, her skin smooth as alabaster and soft as satin.

"Well, what now?" Amanda asked after breakfast the next morning. "What are we going to do until three?"

"I'm going down to the beach," Clay answered matter-of-factly. "I don't know what you're going to do."

"That doesn't sound very friendly."

"I still think you should fly home and leave this to me," he explained as they left the hotel dining room. "Let me handle everything, Mandy."

"I can't. And if you were me you'd do the same—try to protect your sister."

"Sure, but I have experience in situations like this, while you—"

"Clay, no more sermons. My mind's made up."

"I'm as strong-willed as you are, Mandy."

"I don't doubt it. But I followed you here and now you're

stuck with me. And be honest. I haven't gotten in your way, have I?"

"We haven't done anything yet," he reminded her, intently regarding her upturned face. "But you'd better not cause me any trouble when I talk to Cooper later."

"Come on, be a sport. Give me a chance. I might even be able to help you with this case."

"Should've made you spend last night outside on a bench," he grumbled, jabbing the Up elevator button with his right index finger.

"I think I'll go swimming with you," she softly said. "That is, if you don't mind me tagging along."

"My minding hasn't stopped you so far."

The words were harsh, but his tone took some of the edge off them. He sounded more resigned than angry, and rather illogically, that very fact aroused some suspicion in her. Maybe he was hatching some kind of plan to give her the slip before meeting with Cooper. He might arrange to meet Cooper someplace besides the man's house. It was a possibility she'd be wise to keep in mind.

When the elevator arrived she started to step inside, but stopped short with a snap of her fingers. "One minor detail I forgot. I didn't bring a bathing suit with me. But I can buy one in that little shop off the lobby. It won't take long."

Clay nodded. "I'll go up to the room and get ready."

As he turned away, she reached out to touch his arm, causing him to hold the elevator doors open with his hand. "One question," she began, a puzzled frown knitting her brow. "Why is it so important for us to see Cooper before we do anything else? Instead of swimming, shouldn't we try to find Brad and Becky?"

"That would be like searching for a needle in a haystack. If they're in a hotel, they're certainly not registered under their real names, and they could even be staying in a private home. Bernard Cooper's our best chance to locate them and find the Shalimar collection."

"*If* they're the ones who have the rubies."

Clay vanished behind the closing elevator doors.

In the crowded shop there was only one clerk, who flitted from customer to customer, trying to help them all at once. Amanda was fine on her own. She found three swimsuits with possibilities on a corner rack but had to wait for her turn in a changing room before trying them on. At last she chose the suit she liked best, paid the busy clerk, and hurried upstairs to the third floor. Clay's door was unlocked but the room was empty. There was a note propped up on the dresser, which simply said, *meet you on the beach.*

But would he be there? What if . . . She rushed out onto the balcony, discovering the beach wasn't close enough for the people on it to be recognizable.

"Ninny," she mumbled, knowing she would want to kick herself if he had indeed gotten away. She'd have to be lucky to find him before he saw Cooper. In fact he'd make that a near impossibility by evading her at every turn. In his profession, he'd know all the tricks. There was only one thing for her to do: get down to the beach and hope the note he had left didn't prove to be a lie.

Ten minutes later, Amanda followed the winding path that led down from the hotel. She set off across the sand, which quickly filled her sandals. Kicking them off, she carried them past the elegant little gazebo housing the bar to the roofed pavilion, where she got a towel from an attendant. She thanked him, pushed her sunglasses up on her nose, and carefully surveyed the beach. Clay was nowhere to be seen. Her heart plummeted, but she didn't give up. Shading her eyes with one hand she looked out over the sun-gilded water, then breathed a great sigh of relief when she saw Clay swimming with sure, strong strokes out beyond the gentle breakers.

The sand was hot on the soles of her feet as she walked to the far end of the beach, stopping a few feet from where the shoreline became rocky and pointed a stony finger into the sea. After spreading her towel, she sank down cross-legged on it. The sun was blazing hot on the top of her head, but a brisk salt-scented breeze counteracted the effects of the rays and made the day thoroughly pleasant. The faint fragrance of bougainvillaea scented the air. Cotton-ball white clouds speckled the azure sky, and Amanda watched their slowly shifting patterns for several minutes before she stretched out and turned onto her stomach. Resting her chin in cupped hands, she inspected the pink-tinged sand and spotted a tiny ruffled yellow shell that had once been half the home of a minute ocean creature. It was unbroken and lovely. She placed it on her towel and began adding others to it, some shimmering white, a few pink, a couple pale green. Sweeping her fingertips through the sand, she found many perfect specimens and knew how beautiful they would look in a clear glass cork-stoppered bottle when she took them back home.

Her search continued until something nudged her left leg. Suddenly in shadow, she turned over halfway and saw Clay lightly graze the toes of his right foot over her calf once again. She took a swift short breath as her eyes wandered up along his long muscular legs and over the white trunks that accentuated the dark skin of his flat midriff and wide chest. She smiled faintly.

He grinned. "What are you looking for in the sand? If it's pirate treasure, there must be a better way to dig for it."

"No treasure. Just seashells. Very little ones," she said, showing him the small pile she had made.

He dropped down on his knees on the towel beside her to look. "They're pretty."

"Yes."

"I came on down to the beach because I thought you might be one of those shoppers who takes forever to decide what to buy."

"No. That's not what took me so long. The shop was just full of customers."

He carefully inspected the strapless maillot swimsuit she wore. Aquamarine, it matched her eyes precisely and molded her curvaceous body, covering but not concealing feminine lines. He grinned once more. "I hoped you'd buy a bikini."

"I liked this. Don't you?"

"Oh, I'm not complaining. This one certainly clings in all the right places."

"How's the water?" she asked, deciding not to outwardly react to his comment. "Is it warm?"

"Perfect. Come on," he said, standing to pull her up by one hand. He chased her across the beach into the swirling foamy surf. Laughing, she dived over an incoming wave, trying to escape him, but he soon caught up, grabbed her left ankle and pulled her back toward him. They bumped together, legs entangling.

His hair-roughened skin grazed against hers, setting off tingling sensations that scampered over her nerve endings. A great desire to wrap her arms around his neck and kiss him washed over her momentarily but she suppressed it. Life was already complicated enough. Giving him a playful splash, she swam away again and this time he decided to let her go—for the moment. She had told him she enjoyed swimming; now he could enjoy watching her as she glided through the water. A strong swimmer, she was graceful and confident, unafraid to go out some distance from the beach. Of course beyond the breakers, the ocean was calmer, and with his steady crawl he didn't let her get far away from him.

Amanda was exhilarated. The ocean always excited her—its vastness, its beauty, its latent danger. Every time she stepped into the waves, she remembered she was sharing the same body of water with whales and dolphins and mysterious sea creatures. There was no barrier between herself and them, except distance. Perhaps it was childish to be beguiled by such thoughts, yet it was irresistible.

Amanda suddenly squealed. At the very instant she had thought of sea creatures, something clamped her ankle. It took her a panicky second to realize it was only Clay, after her again.

"You!" she gasped, half floundering. "What lousy timing. I was just wondering if some stupid shark might come in this far, and you grab me!"

"Sorry," he said, and dunked her without ceremony.

She held her nose as she went under, then she surfaced, pretending to splutter indignantly. Bent on revenge, she maneuvered around him, finally gaining a position where she could clasp her hands over his shoulders, thrust out of the water, and push down with all her might. He didn't meekly surrender. Stronger physically, he dunked her again and she resurfaced more determined than ever to get back at him, no easy task, since she was giggling. At last, however, she resorted to tickling his sides in order to gain the advantage and push him under. Mission accomplished.

He came up grinning and with a toss of his head flung back the hair that had fallen forward across his forehead. Mischief written all over his face, he drove through the water to her. He could easily have dunked her again, but didn't. Instead, he simply looked at her as they faced each other treading water. He had never seen her so at ease, so relaxed, so much her true self. The sheer joy of life shone in her, illuminating her delicate features and glowing in those eyes that matched the incredible blueness of the sea. Sometimes, she could be self-contained, even cool. But that wasn't the real Mandy, he knew it. This was the real Mandy: earthy, fun-loving, bold. *Desirable.* Hot passion stirred in him, and he murmured, "You *are* lovely."

"Flatterer," she said lightly, though the rough tenor of his deep voice made her heart hammer in response. She shook her head. "I must look a mess. My hair's wet and stringy and most of my makeup's washed off."

"You look like a child of nature, a mermaid," he persisted, before allowing a quirk of a grin to touch his lips. "I bet you used to be a real tomboy."

Making a funny face, she lifted her eyes heavenward. "So it still shows, huh?"

"Do you mind if it does?"

"I don't. But Mom probably wouldn't be pleased to hear you say that. She always told me I shouldn't be so rowdy, that I should try to be more ladylike, like Becky."

"Just goes to show mothers can be wrong sometimes too," Clay said. "Surely she didn't want you to sit in the house and do needlework or bake cookies?"

"No. Of course she wanted us to be active, but she thought we could do that without risking life and limb climbing trees, which I did every chance I got. Or playing baseball with the neighborhood boys—and I did that every time they'd let me in a game. Becky always stuck to jumping rope or hopscotch, much more ladylike endeavors."

Clay's black eyes narrowed. "But look who's in trouble now. Not the tomboy. No, it's Becky, the little lady, who's gotten herself into one hell of a mess."

117

Anguish mantled Amanda's features. Her eyes fell, and she stared at the gently undulating water between them.

He cursed himself. She was already hurt and he had deepened the wound with careless words. "I'm sorry," he whispered, lifting her small strong chin with one forefinger. "That was a rotten thing to say."

"Yes. Yes, it was."

"Forgive me?"

"I'm not sure," she replied, and swam away.

He allowed her to go, wanting to give her time to compose herself, to relax and face the situation with perspective while pardoning him for his loose tongue. After waiting more than twenty minutes, he approached her once more when she was floating idly on the surface. After giving her fair warning, humming the distinctively recognizable musical beat from the movie *Jaws*, he dunked her once more and was pleased when she came up laughing in pursuit of him.

Tired out by the roughhousing after a while, Clay suggested snorkeling as a less strenuous activity, then added, "If you don't mind a late lunch."

"No, I don't mind a bit. I think I could stay here forever," she admitted, smiling up at him. "This is fun."

After renting face masks and snorkeling equipment from the attendant, they paddled side by side out alongside the fingerlike reef. Lying facedown in the water, Amanda felt at peace, bobbing along in the mild waves. Below her fish darted, some striped, some spotted, all colorful and smooth and graceful as ballerinas. Occasionally a crab lumbered across the sandy bottom, its gait lurching and awkward, but she was no less intrigued by the clumsiness of crabs than the finesse of the waltzing fish. And she knew Clay was beside her. Glancing sideways she could glimpse his long lean brown body when he moved a short distance ahead of her. Always she could feel the underwater ripples as he slowly paddled.

For a while, Amanda was conscious only of the wildlife below her and the swaying fronds of fringed seaweed. Becky and all the trouble she was in mercifully forgotten, she welcomed the respite from worry, unexpected and unasked for though no less precious. And when Clay tapped her shoulder, giving her the thumbs-up, she surfaced reluctantly, knowing the peaceful interlude was over. It was reality she had to face now.

They swam toward shore, letting the waves carry them in to the beach. After they gathered up towels and belongings, she gazed back out over the open sea.

"I've never seen water this blue. And clear, like glass," she said softly. If only she and Clay were on the island for a different reason. If only they could truly relax and enjoy each other and the beauty around them. If only Becky didn't stand between them. . . . *If only*. So many ifs. Moistening her dry lips with the tip of her tongue, she looked up at him, meeting his coal black eyes. She sighed. "I wish . . ."

"So do I," he muttered perceptively, brushing the back of his hand briefly against hers as they walked through the damp sand together. "But life's not so simple, is it?"

"No easy answers," Amanda had to agree, depression crawling over her with the admission. Becky's trouble colored everything between them. No matter what pleasant moments they shared, they were, in a sense, enemies. And she wished with all her heart they didn't have to be.

CHAPTER SEVEN

By the time Amanda and Clay reached the third floor, her spirits had risen a little. When he unlocked the door to his room she glided inside first, managing a cheeky grin as she looked back at him.

"The water was awfully salty, wasn't it? And I feel like I have a ton of sand in my hair. I know we both want a shower, but I think I'd better take mine first," she told him candidly, "because if I let you go ahead of me, you might get dressed and take off before I can get out of the bathroom."

He shook his head. "What good would it do for me to try to give you the slip now? You know where Bernard Cooper lives. You could follow me there."

"But I can't be sure you won't ask him to meet you someplace besides his house."

"I doubt Cooper would be that cooperative."

"Even so, I'd rather be safe than sorry. I know it's pushy of me to insist on taking my shower first. After all, this is your room, not mine. But I can't take a chance on you sneaking away."

He drew in a deep breath, then let it out. "I guess I could call security and tell them my room's been invaded by a beautiful crazy woman who refuses to leave."

"You could, but I don't think you will."

"What if I did?"

"I guess I'd just have to tell security that you and I had a lovers' quarrel and that you're trying to get me thrown out of the hotel for revenge."

He had to smile a little. "You'd really do that, wouldn't you?"

"If I had to."

"Go. Take your shower," he commanded wryly, walking across the room and out onto the balcony as she gathered up some clothes and went into the bathroom. Leaning against the high railing, he rested his chin on steepled fingers and chuckled to himself. He had to admire her tenacity.

After finishing in the bathroom, Amanda styled her freshly washed hair with a blow dryer while Clay showered. When she was satisfied with the way it looked, she patted a trace of translucent powder on her face and applied rose-colored lipstick that matched the tiny stripes in her sundress. She was ready to go when he left the bathroom, buttoning his shirt, and since they were both hungry, they decided to lunch at the hotel and not waste time deciding on an outside restaurant.

It was a few minutes past three when they finished their meal, so they immediately took a taxi to Bernard Cooper's miniestate. The same stiff manservant answered the bell, and he positioned himself in the doorway, seeming to look down his pinched nose at them.

"You were to call first, sir," he announced regally.

"I want to see Mr. Cooper in person," Clay replied. "I assume he is here today."

"He's in, but I don't know if he will see—"

"Who is that, Judson?" a booming voice with a crisp British accent called from inside the house. "Visitors?"

"Yes, Mr. Cooper but—"

"Well, show them in."

Looking less than pleased, Judson ushered Amanda and

Clay into the marble foyer, where they were soon greeted by a bear of a man clad in bright red sports pants and a white knit golf shirt. Although they were perfect strangers, he smiled beamingly at them, beckoning them into a room on the left.

"Come in, come in," he invited heartily. "I wager you're here on behalf of some charity or another. Am I right? Well, I don't mind. Always like to do whatever I can for a good cause. And you must excuse Judson. Afraid the old boy's a bit of a stuffed shirt. Seems to think that's expected of an English butler. Please sit down."

Clay spoke up the instant he was allowed to get a word in edgewise. "Mr. Cooper, we're not here to ask you to donate to any charity. I have some questions to ask you. My name's Kendall, Clay Kendall, and this is Amanda Mills."

"A pleasure, Miss Mills."

"It's nice to meet you," she answered, looking around with near openmouthed awe. The drawing room was incredibly luxurious, like a movie set, except that here everything seemed to be real. The antique furnishings had to be genuine. Watered silk draperies gowned the window, and settees and chairs were covered with fabulous brocades. Even the famous paintings adorning the walls were probably originals. Admiring a collection of Fabergé enamels, she sat down with Clay on a beautifully crafted blue and gold divan.

"Kendall . . . Kendall," Cooper repeated, tugging at his lip as he took the chair opposite. "The name does sound rather familiar. Ah, yes, now I recall." His countenance altered. He pulled at a lock of his steel-gray hair and a crafty look came into his pale blue eyes. "Clay Kendall, of course. You're the chap who recovered the stolen Egyptian artifacts a year or so ago. Practically priceless pieces, weren't they? Good show."

"Thanks. I was happy to find them," Clay said, sitting

back, draping an arm over the back of the divan above Amanda's shoulders, completely at ease. "And now that you know who I am, you must know why I'm here and what questions I want to ask."

"Sherry?" Bernard Cooper offered out of the blue, showing no reaction to Clay's words. When they declined, he took a fragile glass and a cut glass decanter from the ivory-inlaid table beside him, poured a sherry for himself, and sipped unhurriedly before raising questioning eyebrows. "You have me at a disadvantage. I must admit I have no idea why you're here, Mr. Kendall. Should I?"

"I think so," Clay responded, a knowing half smile curving his carved lips. "The Shalimar rubies, Mr. Cooper, they're what I want to talk about. Surely you aren't going to tell me you've never heard of them?"

"Dear me no, wouldn't think of it. Nearly everyone's heard of the Shalimar collection. Stolen recently, wasn't it?"

"Yes."

"Of course, I understand a bit of it now! *You're* trying to recover the collection."

"Right again."

"But why come see me?"

"Because I learned from a reliable source that the rubies were brought here to Bermuda."

"How extraordinary! I wonder if it could be true."

Amanda listened to this exchange with growing bemusement. Bernard Cooper was a pleasant man, but there was something mysterious about him she couldn't quite grasp—although Clay didn't seem to be having that problem.

But Clay knew what he was dealing with. This was no jolly country squire sitting in front of him, smiling broadly. Cooper was much more complicated, a man of rare cunning and sharp instincts. Self-protection was a way of life for him, but Clay had a hunch he could get him to open up a little.

"Let's not play games," he said matter-of-factly. "You're a legend, Mr. Cooper. So I know that if the rubies were brought here, you've at least seen them."

Cooper chortled, polished off his sherry in one swallow, and winked at Amanda. "A sly fox, this one," he said, referring to Clay, allowing his very proper accent to lose some of its crispness. He poured himself a refill, chortled again. "Since you seem to know a good deal about me, dear boy, perhaps you should call me Bernie."

"All right, Bernie. Was my source right? Were the rubies brought here? Have you seen them?"

"I saw them. Couldn't resist. I saw the collection at the British Museum in London years ago, but seeing isn't like touching so I couldn't resist actually holding them in my hands when I was given the chance. Fabulous jewels, quite exquisite."

"Then they were offered to you?"

"Offered at an incredible price, yes indeed."

"Did you buy them?"

Bernie grinned slyly. "What a question. If I did buy them, do you think I'd admit it?"

"You might, if you've already resold them. That way, there'd be no proof you ever really had them and you could just deny that you'd told me you did."

"You've a point there," Cooper conceded, chuckling. "But if you must know, I didn't buy the rubies. Oh, I'm not saying I wasn't tempted—I was. But the deal seemed too risky. I'm sure you already know I retired from the business. Me and the missus are golden oldsters now, living the good life."

"Even retirees like to dabble in their old professions once in a while."

"Yes. But the Shalimar rubies are too hot to handle right now."

Clay believed that, but he wasn't finished asking questions yet. "The man who offered you the collection—did he give you his name?"

"Called himself Adam Smith. Not a very original alias, is it? But I learned years ago not to be too inquisitive. Smith was good enough for me."

"How did he act?"

"Cool. Detached. Professional. Lifting the Shalimars wasn't his first caper, I'd wager."

"Describe him."

"About your age. Average height. Curly dark brown hair."

"Eyes?"

"I don't remember the color. Maybe brown."

"Could this be him?" Clay persisted, producing the photograph from Brad Charles's personnel file. "If the blond hair was darker and there was no mustache?"

"Possibly. My eyesight's not as tip-top as it once was, but this could be Adam Smith. The most striking thing about the man was his impressive self-confidence."

Amanda felt almost physically sick. Bernard Cooper's description was horrifically similar to the way she herself would have described Brad.

"This man," she blurted out, ignoring Clay's quick withering glance. He had told her to let him do all the talking, but now she had to ask. "This Adam Smith. W-was there a woman with him when he came to see you? About my age, my size? Hair a little lighter blond than mine?"

"Smith came alone," Cooper answered, grinning. "I certainly would remember if he had brought a lovely young thing with him."

She heaved a sigh of relief. At least there was still hope.

125

"Okay, after you refused to buy the rubies, what happened next?" Clay questioned, adroitly taking control of the inquiry once again. "Did he mention where he was going from here?"

"He said something about a few potential buyers, but I knew he was daydreaming. No one he mentioned would get involved with that collection. Too dangerous."

"Did you tell him that?"

"I did."

"And what else?" Clay persisted perceptively. "Maybe you gave him the name of somebody in the big leagues, somebody who'd take the chance of buying the rubies? Did you give him a name, Bernie?"

"Ah, that would be telling," the older man shot back, eyes twinkling merrily as he sipped his second sherry. "I learned in my youth never to give any information I didn't absolutely have to. And of course, there is a certain honor of tradition I must uphold. I'm sure you understand."

Honor among thieves—Clay understood perfectly. It was a credo passed down through millennia to the present but it wasn't one he was willing to accept as an excuse from Bernie Cooper.

He smiled at the man, shook his head. "Not good enough, Bernie." He stared deliberately at a trophy case at the end of the room, a case filled with engraved gold-plated plaques and larger, more grandiose prizes. A semblance of a smile crossed his lips as he inclined his head toward the accumulation of awards. "Obviously, you enjoy yachting and you must be very good at racing. But what would your fellow yacht club members think if they found out exactly how you made your fortune in London before coming to live here?"

Bernard Cooper's nostrils suddenly flared as his good humor failed him. "Threatening blackmail, Mr. Kendall?"

"Call me Clay. And call it whatever you like. I don't want

to consider it blackmail, but if that's what it seems to you, so be it. I still don't think you want your friends on this island to know the truth about your past."

"Quite right, I'd much rather they didn't," Cooper finally agreed, regaining some of his equilibrium, enough of it to produce a cocky smile. "You're a tough investigator, Clay. I'd heard you were, but now I know firsthand. So I'm willing to cooperate. What was your question again?"

"You know the question."

"Indeed. All right, I gave Smith the name of an associate of mine who might be willing to buy the rubies."

"And the name is?"

"Juan Alvedero."

"Where can I find Alvedero?"

"Granada."

"Spain?"

"Yes. Not Grenada, the Caribbean island."

"How can I contact him?"

Bernie Cooper chortled again. "When you squeeze people for information, you intend to get every last drop, don't you my boy? Well, to be honest, I haven't been in touch with Juan in quite some time. I used to be able to reach him by leaving a message for him at the Palace Hotel. You might try that approach."

"Is that the same advice you gave this 'Adam Smith'?"

"Precisely. I assure you I'm not keeping mum about anything. I do believe you'd expose my past—er, indiscretions—to my friends here, and I enjoy my life here too much to play risky games. My days of derring-do are long over."

"I'm glad to hear it," Clay said, rising to his feet and nodding at Bernie as Amanda also rose. "I appreciate the information."

"Happy hunting, Clay. You too, Miss Mills," their jolly

host said, escorting them to the front door. He gave Amanda an especially warm smile as they started out. "I assume you're Clay's associate?"

"Uh, yes, in a way, at least on this particular case," she answered, looking steadily at Clay, who stared back at her, stone-faced.

"Come on, Mandy. Our taxi's waiting" was all he said, before they both told Cooper good-bye.

"Judson, blast it all, man, where have you hidden my golf bag?" Bernie boomed out while closing the door behind them.

"So you've started calling yourself my associate now," Clay said tonelessly as they walked across the courtyard past the splashing fountain. "Going a bit far, don't you think?"

She gave him a somewhat sheepish smile. "Well, what was I supposed to say—that I'm an unwanted tagalong? Maybe you *could* just think of me as your associate."

"I don't think so," he murmured, his gaze roaming freely over her, conveying an obviously sensuous message. "Our relationship's personal."

"Well, yes, in a way but—"

"What did you think of Cooper?" Clay interrupted softly. "Quite a character, isn't he?"

"You'd better believe it. He was a fence in London, wasn't he?"

"So you figured that out?"

"I doubt I would have if you hadn't threatened to tell his friends about his past. Up until then I assumed he was a private collector. I mean, he's such a bubbly old gentleman. He just doesn't fit the image I have in my head of a fence."

"Oh, but he was no run-of-the-mill, two-bit fence. He never handled stolen property worth less than a hundred thousand pounds. Fine paintings, fabulous jewels. Legend has it he even found a buyer for a statue of Napoleon stolen from the gardens at Versailles."

"But if you know about him, surely the authorities in London did too. So why isn't he in prison?"

"He did serve some time, but he hired a clever, expensive barrister who got him an early release. That's when he decided to retire to Bermuda. He'd certainly accumulated enough money over the years to keep him and the wife in fine style."

"It's still hard to believe he was a criminal. He's so—so innocent-looking."

"Don't judge a book by its cover," Clay advised. "You're going to be in for a lot of surprises if you do."

Amanda stiffened. "Is that your way of saying that just because Becky seems shy, even a little helpless, that doesn't mean there isn't another side to her—one not so innocent?"

"Maybe that is what I'm trying to make you understand," he answered flatly, opening the back door of the waiting taxi. "But she's your sister, not mine. You know her better than I do. I'm simply following up on clues."

"Clues can be misleading."

"But I don't think they are this time."

Amanda got into the car and slid across the seat, giving him plenty of room. As they rode away from Bernie Cooper's mansion, she stared glumly out the window for a few minutes, striving to shore up her sagging confidence in Becky's common sense. Squaring her shoulders, she turned to Clay. "All right, what next? I suppose we should just go on to Granada?"

His clear black eyes narrowed. "We?"

"Of course. I'm going with you."

"Isn't there anything I can say to convince you to go back to Richmond, where you belong?"

She stubbornly shook her head. "Don't even waste your time trying."

He groaned. "I was afraid of that."

"I won't get in the way, I promise."

"We'll see about that," he retorted, none too convinced by her vow. But he couldn't afford to waste time getting to Spain, and since she was determined to stick to him like glue, he might as well give in—or pretend to. If she wouldn't let him out of her sight, at least he could keep a close eye on her, too. He gestured exasperatedly. "Okay, maybe you can be of some help. When I find Brad and Becky, she'll be more willing to talk to you than to me. And if they've already sold the rubies, I have to find out who they sold them to. So we'll fly to Europe tomorrow. We're closer to Spain here than we would be in the States. But I'm warning you, Mandy, no more Mr. Nice Guy. I won't come to the rescue and share my room with you again because I still think you should *go home.*"

She didn't know whether to believe him or not. But it didn't matter. "I'll be able to reserve a room in advance this time, as you did before we got here," she told him, her voice lilting. "Naturally, I have to stay in the same hotel you do."

"Naturally," he repeated, shaking his head and rubbing his brow. Was he crazy to allow her to keep following him? A worthless question, since she was determined to go wherever he went in pursuit of her sister. He didn't think it was at all likely he could give Mandy the slip now. In fact, he had a feeling she was going to stay as close to him as his shadow.

Amanda got out of bed before Clay the next morning. It was early, too early in fact, and she wished she hadn't awakened quite so soon. But she hadn't slept well at all. Tossing and turning, she had dreamed too much, and the dreams involving Becky and Brad had bordered on nightmares. Brad had been transformed into a caricature of a sneering gangster holding a gun on her sister. She awoke trembling, only to drift off again and dream about her parents. Her mother was crying, her sobs loud and agonized; her father looked pastily pale, quite ill. No, it definitely wasn't a good night. She was glad it was over. Her eyes felt gritty and she couldn't suppress a weary yawn.

Throwing back the sheet, she got out of bed, stood and stretched, and tiptoed into the bathroom, where she splashed water on her face and brushed her teeth. Feeling a little better, she walked back across the room to the French doors, which opened onto the balcony. Below her, on the silvery surface of the ocean, a black-and-white steamer plowed smoothly through the water, heading out to sea. She wondered where it would reach port, what it was carrying. Were there passengers aboard? Letting her imagination take over, she decided there were only two—one man, one woman, setting off on a magically romantic cruise and so obviously in love that the crusty old captain mellowed enough to offer them his cabin, which was more elaborate than their own.

"What nonsense," she whispered to herself after indulging in the fantasy for several minutes. Shaking her head, trying to clear away the cobwebs, she moved away from the door to prowl restlessly around the room. The pale gray light of dawn filtered through the loosely woven drapes, and the early morning air was cool. Hugging her arms to her chest, she briskly rubbed them, then slipped into her cotton duster. As she turned down the thermostat dial on the air conditioner, she noticed Clay had thrown all the covers off during the night. She tiptoed over to the side of his bed. Pajama pants clung low on his lean hips. His naked torso was so brown and firm, his finely chiseled face relaxed. Lying on his back, he had flung one muscular arm back on the pillow. His lean long fingers curved upward. A sudden need to touch him burned hotly in her veins, but she fought it and started to pull the sheet up over him.

Clay opened his eyes. They fastened on hers with incredible alertness. "You shouldn't look at me like that, Mandy," he said hoarsely. "How can I leave you alone when you do?"

His powerful hands caught hold of hers. With a little gasp she tried to pull away, but he wouldn't release her. "I . . . I'm sorry. I guess I was staring but I didn't mean—"

"Come here," he whispered, hauling her down onto the mattress beside him, enfolding her in his arms. Her fresh lovely face filled his vision. He brushed his lips across her cheek. "My sweet Mandy."

"Clay, I—"

"I want you. *Need* you."

"Clay, don't." She tried to struggle against him despite the warm weakness invading her limbs. "Stop."

"I don't think I can, honey, not now. And you don't want me to."

"Y-yes, I do. Stop," she repeated, though with less conviction as his teeth nibbled at her chin, shocking her system, inducing waves of delight that rushed through her. His warm mouth inched toward her own and she moaned softly, "Clay no, this is crazy."

"No it isn't."

"Yes, it—"

He kissed her.

She trembled. "It's—"

He kissed her again, firm lips lingering longer upon hers.

"Crazy. Oh, I—"

"It'll be even crazier if we don't make love. That's what we both want."

"Crazy, crazy, crazy," she chanted, emotions in a turmoil

as his large hands molded her back and pressed her hard against him. "I . . ."

"Relax," he coaxed huskily. "Open your mouth a little, Mandy. Kiss me back."

And she did, unable to stop herself when his demanding lips covered hers. She eased her arms around him, tightening them convulsively as the arousingly rough surface of his tongue flicked over hers. He tasted her sensitized inner cheeks. Wildfire rampaged over her, searing through her flesh to the marrow of her bones, exploding in the very center of her being. She melted against him, all warmth and acquiescence, dizzy with pleasure as he moved his hands over her.

"Warm, you're so warm," he murmured, lacing nibbling kisses along her neck while removing the thin robe she wore. The fine cotton gown beneath was also thin, but not sheer enough to satisfy him. He needed to see her lovely body and to feel her naked against him. Yet he held a tight rein on his desire, unwilling to rush her. Sliding his fingers slowly under the spaghetti straps of her gown he pushed them off her shoulders. They fell down loosely around her upper arms. He feathered his lips over her skin, inscribing erotic patterns that made her tremble and arch closer.

"Oh, Clay, that feels so good," she breathed, and felt the small smile of triumph that curved his mouth. Stepping her fingers down over his hard muscled chest, she sought the flat nipples encircled by fine dark hair and toyed with the taut knobs that rose erect beneath her caresses. His long, powerful body fascinated her. She loved to touch him. She loved . . . Did she love him? In that moment, it was easy to believe that if she wasn't already in love with him, she was very close to it. Never before had she felt so close to anyone. With a surge of emotion, she urged his mouth back to hers.

Exerting a gentle twisting pressure on her soft clinging lips,

133

he curved one hand over her left hipbone, impelling her down onto the mattress, moving above her, one leg covering both of hers. The tip of her tongue stroked the edge of his, parrying his tender invasion thrusts, and her fresh sweet mouth was irresistible. He felt he could never get enough of her or be close enough.

Clay's hands, searching and conquering, coursed over her, exploring every enticing contour, his touch hot and possessive through her thin gown. When his warm breath drifted into first one ear, then the other, and he nipped her earlobes again and again each in its turn, keen shivers of delight careened through her. She twined her fingers in his hair, enamored of its vital texture and clean crispness. He caught hold of one slender wrist, turned his head, and teased her palm with sweet tender lashes of his tongue. Superheated flames of passion erupted in her as the tingling sensations he induced became more and more exquisite. She curved her fingers along his jaw. Almost of their own volition, they feathered over his face, following the bridge of his nose, outlining the sensuous shape of his lips, brushing his eyebrows.

"You have such a light touch," he whispered. "Don't stop touching."

As if she could. In the cool of the morning, she threw caution to the winds for a time, lost in the magic they created together, glorying in her own femininity. His raw virility excited her. The glint of passionate intent in his warm black eyes quickened her breathing. She drew caressing fingers along the strong ridge of his spine before her hands came around his sides to his taut midriff and she played the heel of one over the slight hollow of his navel.

A swift tremor ran through Clay. "Mandy," he said gruffly, tilting her head back on the pillow and lowering his face to

134

her once more, his even teeth gently biting the fragrant skin at the base of her throat . . . and lower.

The top of her gown was slowly eased down farther and farther and she felt hot all over when he finally exposed the swells of her breasts. With one fingertip, he traced the twin rounded curves, his gaze imprisoning hers.

He smiled lazily. "Does this feel good too, Mandy?"

"Yes," she breathed. *"Yes."*

"And . . ."—he cupped the weight of her breasts in his hands, lean fingers lightly kneading her cushioned flesh—". . . this?"

"Oh, Clay, yes," she gasped, fever running through her bloodstream. "D-do you know what you're doing to me?"

"I know what *you're* doing to *me*," he answered in a strained voice as she fleetingly skimmed her hands along his thighs. And he could wait no longer to see her. He pulled down the gown, allowing it to drape around her waist while his eyes hungrily roved over her. In the pale light, her satin-esque skin glowed, creamy smooth and alluring. Her firm full breasts rose up to tempting rosy peaks. "God, I love to look at you."

"Clay . . . touch too," she said before she could stop herself. "Touch me."

"Oh, I'm going to. And taste too," he promised, toying with one ruched nipple, then the other. "Here. And here."

Which was what she wanted. His initial caresses were deliberately teasing and quite effectively inflamed her senses. Pleasures of the flesh enslaved her, and she stroked his shoulders and broad back eagerly as he did things to her, wonderful things, his fingers exploring every inch of her breasts.

When he lowered his dark head, she stopped breathing for a second, filled with glorious anticipation. He ringed kisses round and round her resilient flesh, drawing concentric circles upward, forsaking her left breast only to tantalize the right. After he slowly reached its summit, he took it tenderly into his mouth, sampling its sweetness.

Amanda quivered, and cradled the back of his neck in her hands. Under his tongue's light probing, her nipples throbbed. As he went from one to the other repeatedly, a clamoring need for completion bloomed open in her, creating a natural emptiness she longed for Clay to fill. Only Clay. He was special. No other man could affect her like this. Deep in her heart, she was sure of it.

With light pulling pressure, he drew the tip of her ivory breast deeper inside his mouth and heard her moan softly in response. Hands spanning her waist, supporting her lower back with his fingers, he arched her upward, savoring the taste of her, delighting in her warm, firm flesh. Arousing her aroused him; pleasing her gave him pleasure. She moved her fingertips in slow circles on his nape. His scalp tingled when she playfully tugged at his hair. Passion pulsated hotly in him, but he held it in check as he sought to make her need as consuming as his. The plump nubbles topping her nipples invited forays of teasing kisses, and with lips, teeth, and tongue, he leisurely seduced her.

"Never stop," she implored, on fire as wild currents coursed like electricity through her body, leaving no nerve ending untouched by lightning-swift power. When his mouth left her momentarily, she felt bereft.

"Does that feel good too, Mandy?"

"Yes."

"Yes," he repeated, his answering smile tender and knowing.

Anxious to be closer to him again, she came up into his arms, winding her own around his neck. Turning onto his side, he pulled her down facing him, and as their legs entangled, the feel of her supple body yielding to the firmer line of his made him realize fully that he'd never wanted any woman as much as he wanted her. Her rounded flesh surged against his chest. He felt the rapid thudding of her heart.

The light covering of his hair tickled her breasts. She moved sinuously against him.

Holding her face in his hands, he kissed the delicate line of her jaw, her temples, her forehead.

Shifting in his subsequent embrace, she fluttered her tongue in his left ear.

He groaned softly, a shudder washing over him.

She smiled a woman's secret smile, joyous in her ability to arouse him.

Slowly, ever so slowly, he lowered her gown down over her hips, then took it off completely and tossed it carelessly away.

Lost in deepening affection for him and the drugging effects of sheer physical ecstasy, she made no move to stop him.

Even when he glided his fingers over her midriff and carefully pushed them beneath the waistband of her panties, she reacted with a soft sound of delight.

Yet, as his hand moved down, down, down, she tensed instinctively, the muscles in her abdomen atremble.

"You must know I'd never do anything to hurt you," he whispered, sensing her sudden tension. "I only want us to do the most wonderful things together. Try to relax, Mandy."

But she couldn't. Much as she wanted to, she found it impossible. Despite her bodily receptiveness, she held back without meaning to. It certainly wasn't a conscious decision. Somewhere deep in her psyche, other more mysterious forces took control. She felt as if she were being ripped apart, but in the end it was doubt generated by her subconscious that rose up the victor and began to cool desire by degrees.

"Mandy," he coaxed, kissing her lips. "Relax, honey." She

kissed him back, but not with the fervent abandon she'd been displaying. Deciding patience and consideration might be the key to releasing her from her obvious uncertainties, he whispered, "We have all the time in the world, honey. If you aren't ready yet, I can wait for you. You're worth waiting for, but you can't go all tense on me. If you relax, I'll—"

"I can't!" she whispered back, confusion aswirl in her. Yet in a far recess of her mind, she knew the time wasn't right. Maybe it never would be right for them. She shook her head. "We can't, Clay. I can't—"

Her words broke off but the message was clear. And he felt cheated. Anger was his initial reaction. His teeth were clenched as he raised himself up to stare down at her. "I never would've thought you'd turn out to be a tease."

"I am not a tease!" she shot back, hating the accusation, angry because she knew that was something she had never been and never could be. Yet she realized she had given him some reason to doubt her sincerity and felt compelled to try to explain, "I just . . . You . . ."

"It's not a lot of fun for me when you call a screeching halt, if you know what I mean."

Her blue eyes flashed defiantly. "Don't try giving me that high school line about rejection being excruciating."

"I wouldn't think of it. Physically, it's endurable," he admitted, simmering down. "But good God, woman, do you know what you're doing to my ego?"

His expression grew gentle. She caught her lower lip between her teeth, again feeling as if she were being pulled apart inside. He was such a charismatic man and wondrously tender. She did want him, did want to give herself completely to him, yet innate caution held her prisoner. She shook her head. "I'm sorry, Clay. It's just that I don't know if I . . ."

"You *are* afraid of me, aren't you?" he asked as she scrambled off his bed, found her robe, and hastily wrapped it around her. "Why, Mandy?"

"I'm not . . . afraid," she told him for the second time since she'd known him, but still she wasn't sure her words were true. They sounded good. Forcing what she hoped was a nonchalant shrug, she smiled weakly at him, then swept up the clothes she had laid out to wear. "Well, I'd better get dressed."

"You're running away from me."

"No. I, uh . . . we can't dawdle around here, you know. Wouldn't want to miss our flight to London."

"But our plane doesn't take off until one forty-five this afternoon."

"Still, we don't want to take a chance on missing it."

"Little coward," he called after her as she slipped into the bathroom.

And maybe that's what she was. Maybe she was afraid she was falling in love with him but wasn't all that important to him, and might never be. That *was* scary. She didn't want to get hurt. She gazed into the vanity mirror, all too aware of her flushed cheeks, beckoning eyes, sensually parted lips. This was the woman Clay saw when he looked at her. Why did he have to be so damn sexy? Why did she have to like him so much? Why? Why? *Why?*

It was a good thing they'd been able to reserve separate rooms in the same hotel in Granada. If she'd had to share another one with him, she had a feeling even her subconscious would have fought a losing battle against ultimate surrender.

CHAPTER EIGHT

Amanda and Clay arrived at Heathrow Airport about midnight, London time. After a long layover they caught a connecting flight to Granada, and by the time they reached their hotel, day was breaking. The little bit of sleep they'd gotten on the plane wasn't enough, so Clay suggested they spend the morning in bed.

"Separate beds, of course," he added as the bellman unlocked the door of her room while Clay waited in the hall to be escorted to his.

But even after a few hours rest, Amanda still felt dreadful. "Jet lag's not much fun, is it?" she remarked as they went out for lunch at twelve thirty. "How do you feel?"

"Lousy," Clay admitted, and shrugged. "But we'll get adjusted to the time change in a day or two."

"If I live that long," she mumbled, yawning.

A good meal did help. At the charming restaurant, Sirocco, they sampled specially prepared prawns, which were delicious. After swallowing the last of her wine, Amanda was beginning to feel human again, though she wouldn't have minded another nap.

But Clay was ready to get down to business. When they left the restaurant, he hailed a taxi, directing the driver to the Palace Hotel. As they traveled through the streets she slipped on sunglasses to protect her tired eyes, and looked out the window.

Nestled in a valley fringed with forests of chestnuts and regal pines, Granada sparkled in the bright sunlight, its white buildings and agate-colored roof tiles aglimmer. On a plateau of solid rock rising above the town stood the ancient Moorish castle, Alhambra, its dusky red walls set against the austere splendor of the Sierra Nevada mountains. Encircled by pines and emerald cypresses, the palace was immense. Amanda glimpsed it from several different angles as they moved through the city.

"Beautiful," she murmured. "I bet that place has seen a lot of intrigue. It even looks mysterious."

"Yes," Clay agreed. "It had quite a past, according to the history books."

"Do you know how old it is?"

"Six or seven centuries, I think."

"Mmm, about the same age as the springs in this seat," she quipped as the taxi hit a violently jarring bump. But she immediately forgot her discomfort as they passed a lush green park filled with brightly colored flowers. "This is a pretty town. Ever been here before?"

"Nope, this is the first time."

Conversation ceased as the taxi stopped in front of a hotel that surprised Amanda by its elegance. Because they were told they could contact a fence there, she had expected to be taken to some seedy establishment on a back street.

Clay took out his wallet to pay the cab fare, and she opened her purse, intending to pay her half. But when she tried to hand him the money he gently brushed her hand away. "We don't have time to complicate matters right now. You can just owe me."

141

"How much?" She pulled out a small notebook. "I'll keep a record."

"Forget it."

"But I want—"

"Mandy, we don't have to go to that extreme. I would've had to get a taxi even if you weren't tagging along, so I'll pay for it. All you have to worry about is your hotel bill."

"And my meals."

Shaking his head, bored by the subject, he escorted her across the sidewalk and through a small arcade. They walked into a sumptuously appointed lobby, where members of the beautiful set idled time away amongst the marble columns. At the front desk, they awaited the attention of the clerk. Clay propped one elbow on the counter. "Time to try my Spanish."

"Oh, you speak the language?"

"I mangle it mostly. But I know a few words and phrases. I hope it's enough to get us the information we want."

When the dapper young clerk greeted them at last with a flashy white smile, Clay did his best to communicate intelligently. Obviously he succeeded to some extent. The clerk's expression grew wary at the mere mention of the name Juan Alvedero.

"Juan. *Sí,*" he responded, lowering his voice while switching to fractured English. "What you want him?"

"Business."

"Ah."

"Well, can you help me get in touch with him?"

"*Sí.*"

"Would you tell me how?" Clay patiently persisted. "I need to see him as soon as possible. *Lo más pronto posible. Entiende?*"

The clerk understood. Nodding, he thrust a pad of paper

and pencil across the desk at Clay. *"Nombre,* please? Your name? *Teléfono?"*

Complying quickly, Clay wrote down his name, the phone number of his hotel, and the number of his room. He handed the pad back.

The man nodded again. *"Bueno.* Juan, he will call."

"Today?"

"Sí, hoy."

"Gracias."

"Señor." Ducking his head, the clerk glided into the office behind the desk, closing the door after him.

"Well, it's back to our hotel to wait," Clay said, his hand curving lightly against the small of Amanda's back as they left the lobby and went out into the golden sunshine again.

Fifteen minutes later, she opened the door to her room, tossed her purse onto her bed, and walked across the room to the doors that adjoined her lodgings and Clay's. She opened her door and rapped her knuckles against his. Within seconds, he had it unlocked and open, his dark eyebrows raised inquiringly.

"I want to keep the doors open," she informed him. "So when Alvedero does call you, I'll hear the phone ring. I don't want you sneaking out of here to meet him without me."

He pulled back, acting injured by the very suggestion. "You really think I'd do that?"

"In a minute, if you had half a chance."

"You don't miss a thing do you, Mandy?"

"Not if I can help it."

"All right, we'll leave the doors open, then. I'd hate to think of you having to press your ear against the wall, waiting for my phone to ring."

She smiled victoriously, and asked, "How long do you think it will take for him to call?"

Clay spread his hands open. "I have no idea. All we can do is wait."

"I guess I might as well read for a while, then."

As Mandy turned away Clay reached for her hand. "Instead of reading, how about a few games of cards? I always carry a deck with me. In this business, I have to do a lot of waiting sometimes, and even solitaire breaks the monotony."

Looking up at him, she tucked a wayward strand of hair behind her left ear. "Solitaire? Sounds awfully lonely to me."

"Can be. So give me a break and play with me. Okay?"

"Okay. What'll we play?"

He flashed a wicked grin. "I was thinking about strip poker."

"Think again, señor," she retorted, grinning back. "I'm no fool."

"I know, but I had to give it the old college try, didn't I? All right, if strip poker's out, how about five card stud?"

"Why not?" she said, but added, "I have to warn you though. It's been a while since I've played poker. I'm probably a little rusty."

Ushering her into his room, he chuckled. "We definitely have to play for money, then."

They sat down at the small round table across from his bed. Deftly he shuffled the deck. She cut it and he dealt. She picked up her hand, examined it with supreme concentration, then discarded the four of clubs and the seven of diamonds. After Clay dealt her two new cards, she wound up with two pairs and displayed them with a smile.

"Sorry," he blithely said, showing three nines. "I win."

"You mean three of a kind beats two pairs?" she asked, feigning ignorance. "Are you sure about that?"

" 'Fraid so," he answered, reshuffling the deck and dealing again.

144

He won the next three hands, but after that, she turned the tables on him and began to win time and again. When she took her turn dealing and dealt herself a straight flush, she laid it down, stared at the four of a kind he presented and tried to inquire solemnly, "What's better—your hand or mine? I can't seem to remember." But then she had to laugh out loud as realization flared in his eyes.

"You flimflammed me," he accused, shaking his head. "You pretended you didn't play much poker. Little hustler."

Merry laughter bubbled forth from her. "I hope you don't mean you think I'm a 'lady of the evening'?"

"No. I think you're a card shark."

"Well, I have to admit I deceived you a little. I play poker with friends at least once a month."

"You . . ." he began, but the shrill pealing of the phone on the stand beside his bed interrupted him. Leaping to his feet, he went to answer it, spoke once, then replaced the receiver. He turned around to look at Mandy, his expression somber. "Alvedero. He'll meet us in an hour. Ready to go?"

Amanda nodded automatically, though she wasn't all that sure she was ready for anything of the sort. Juan Alvedero might be able to implicate Becky in the theft of the Shalimar rubies—her own little sister. If the news turned out to be bad, Amanda didn't really want to hear it. Yet denying the truth would solve nothing. Simply saying Becky was innocent didn't make it so. Amanda had to go on to the end of this case, although the ending might prove bitter and painful.

After she fetched her purse, they left the hotel and caught a taxi. "Let me handle Alvedero," Clay told her as their driver started the meter running. "I want him to believe we're only interested in the rubies, so don't ask him any questions about Brad or Becky. We'll get around to that later. Understand?"

"Yes, *sir.*" She saluted.

145

"I'm serious, Mandy," he said sternly. "Don't cause trouble."

"All right, all right, I get the message."

Twenty minutes later they joined a guided group touring the palace-fortress, Alhambra, because visitors weren't allowed to wander around on their own. As they passed through a courtyard to enter a cool, quiet gallery, Amanda discreetly eyed the men in their party, wondering which one was Juan Alvedero. There was a short man with a pencil-thin mustache and beady eyes who looked suspicious, but he made no move to approach them.

"Where is he?" she whispered to Clay. "Think he might've changed his mind about meeting us?"

"I doubt it. I told him what we look like, what we'd be wearing, so he knows who we are. He's probably being cautious, looking us over."

"Wonder why he wants to meet here?"

"Who knows? Maybe because it's the perfect place for intrigue, like you said earlier."

"Well, I wish he'd let us know who he is."

"Relax. He will when he's ready. Until then, just act like a regular tourist."

Their guide, an attractive middle-aged woman, droned on in Spanish, French, and English. Touring the palace was like walking back into a bedazzling past. Graceful columns supported filigreed arches; tiles of green and red and white geometrically covered the lower walls. Plasterwork moldings of floral motifs painted gold or blue or red decorated the upper walls and high domed ceilings. The delicate beauty of the Moorish architecture was fascinating. They passed through a chamber with a carved wood ceiling inlaid with silver and ivory, then through a grand hall, their footsteps clattering on the marble floor. They moved into a veranda-enclosed courtyard with fluted columns and four white walkways that led to a sculpted fountain supported by stylized stone lions spouting streams of water from their round mouths. The single column of water that bubbled up from the fountain's center tumbled into the basin, and bright sunlight created rainbow colors in the splashing drops.

Amanda smiled at Clay. "Magnificent, isn't it?"

"We are now in the Court of the Lions," the guide informed them. "Once the fountain flowed with the blood of thirty-six beheaded princes who displeased the caliph."

"Terrific," murmured Amanda, grimacing. "The place just lost some of its appeal."

"More than some," Clay emended.

Everyone in the group seemed somewhat relieved when the guide led them away. While they were examining the intricate scrollwork in the next chamber, Clay felt a light tap on his shoulder. He turned around, casually inclining his head at a tall dark-haired man.

"Señor Kendall?" the man quietly inquired.

"Yes. Señor Alvedero?"

"Sí. If you and the señorita would come with me," Alvedero added in flawless though stilted English, "we will find a place more private to discuss business."

Tensely clutching her purse, Amanda stayed close to Clay as they discreetly glided away from the group, left the chamber, and followed Alvedero into a terraced inner garden bordered by myrtle and cypress trees. He led them past the fountain and up the mosaic tiled terraces to a bench secluded under an overhanging myrtle bough. With a gentlemanly sweeping gesture, he indicated she should be seated.

Smoothing her skirt, she sat down, her gaze never leaving Clay and the man.

"So, Señor Kendall," Alvedero began. "How may I help you?"

"I understand the Shalimar collection was offered to you," Clay announced, the expression overlying his sculpted features impassive. "I hope you bought them."

"What is your interest in the rubies?"

"My employer, an American, might like to buy them if we can agree on a price."

"What is your employer's name?"

"Sorry. That's confidential. But I assure you he is genuinely interested in acquiring the entire collection."

Juan Alvedero stroked his patrician nose. "I cannot offer the entire collection. It was offered to me intact, but I did not think I would be able to find a buyer for such expensive merchandise. Therefore I bought only the bracelet. Would your employer be interested in it?"

"By all means. He wants the entire collection. We can buy the bracelet first, then try to track the other pieces down," Clay said, lying with great aplomb. "May we see the bracelet?"

"That can be arranged."

"Fine." Clay placed his hand on Mandy's shoulder, squeezing lightly. "This is Miss Mills. She's a gemologist, and she'll have to examine the bracelet to make sure it's authentic."

She bit back a shocked gasp, managing to look steadily at Alvedero and ask, "Any objections?"

"None."

"Then we'd like to see the bracelet as soon as possible," Clay persisted. "How about tonight?"

"I will bring to your hotel."

"About eight o'clock, then. You know the room number."

"*Sí,* I have it," the Spaniard said, patting the breast pocket of his jacket. Then he gave a curt nod and walked away from them.

"Why did you tell him I was a gemologist?" Amanda softly exclaimed the moment he left the garden. "I won't know if those stones are real rubies or pieces of glass!"

"Don't worry. They'll be the real stones. Alvedero can't afford to cheat his customers. Word would get around fast and he'd be out of business," Clay explained, taking her elbow as they stepped down the terraces. "And I wanted this to look right tonight. He expects someone to examine the bracelet. All you'll have to do is look it over carefully with a jeweler's loupe and then say you're satisfied."

"But what happens after that? We can't *buy* the bracelet."

"No. We'll talk about price and I'll tell him I have to speak to my employer before closing the deal. Then I want to find out if he knows where Becky and Brad are now. We still have the rest of the collection to find. Let's hope he knows something about their plans. And after he leaves the hotel, expecting to hear from me tomorrow, I'll alert the police. He'll be arrested and at least one of the pieces will be recovered."

"Or maybe we'll find out it *wasn't* Becky and Brad he bought the bracelet from," she had to suggest, although the hope of that was dimmer than it had ever been. And the sympathy she detected in Clay's eyes didn't offer any encouragement. She sighed. "Well, Alvedero certainly isn't a talker like Bernie Cooper but he's no less a surprise. It's hard to believe he's a fence. He looks like he should own a vast estate with olive groves."

"Cooper and Alvedero are just high-echelon criminals, although men like that prefer to call themselves art dealers."

"Uh-oh, here comes trouble," Amanda murmured, looking across the King's Salon, which they had just entered. "A guard, coming right for us. We're not supposed to be walking around alone."

The uniformed man marched up to them, scowling, gesturing dramatically. He chastised them in rapid-fire Spanish, and asked, *"Americano?"*

Clay nodded. *"Sí."*

"You must not be here, señor. The guide—"

"Sí, sí, I know. *Lo siento mucho,"* Clay apologized, chuckling and shaking his head as if he were a flustered tourist. "We strayed away from our group for a minute. Now we can't find our guide. We're lost."

"Nice story," Amanda whispered as the guard ushered them through a great marble hall. "You're a very convincing liar."

"In this business, you have to develop a knack for making excuses for being somewhere you're not supposed to be."

"Are you as devious in your personal relationships?"

His eyes captured hers. "I consider myself honest. I've never lied to you, have I?"

"Not that I know of."

"Have a little faith, Mandy, and stop thinking of us as enemies."

"What are we, then?"

"Reluctant partners," he answered, taking her hand, linking his fingers with hers. "Believe me, I wish we'd met in some other way. Socially. It would have made things much simpler."

"Yes. But we didn't meet socially. We met because you're after Becky."

"I'm after the rubies," he corrected. "And we aren't enemies."

She didn't answer as they were escorted to the gate where they had originally entered the Alhambra. Deep inside, she didn't really feel he *was* the enemy. But her trust created confusion. Maybe it made her disloyal to her own sister.

Juan Alvedero arrived at Clay's hotel room promptly at eight that evening. Aristocratically spiffy in a black tuxedo, he shook Clay's hand and gave Amanda a stiff half bow. "I am sorry. I cannot remain here long," he told them both. "My wife wishes to go to the opera tonight."

"This won't take more than a few minutes," Clay calmly assured him, glancing suggestively at Amanda. "Miss Mills."

Miss Mills felt like a perfect ninny when Alvedero produced a velvet pouch from his pocket and handed it to her. She was no actress, but Clay's little ploy demanded at least an adequate performance from her. Sitting down at the round table, she opened the pouch, spilled out the bracelet and pretended she was accustomed to handling priceless jewels. Lifting the loupe to her right eye, feeling even more like a ninny, she proceeded to "examine" the stones. The gold filigree setting was exquisitely delicate for such a heavy piece. The pavé diamonds dazzled. And the bloodred square-cut rubies glowed richly in the light. She had never held in her hands anything so valuable, yet she forced herself to handle the bracelet in what she hoped appeared an expert, almost blasé manner. After nodding occasionally, she at last lifted her head with a smile.

"Absolutely divine," she pronounced. "This is the bracelet from the Shalimar collection."

"You're sure?" Clay questioned, exactly as they had rehearsed. "How can you tell?"

"I can tell because I'm familiar with the last appraiser's report," she replied with just the right touch of smug superiority. "He described each of the stones in great detail, and these match his description. For instance, there is a tiny flaw in—"

"Fine, I'll take your word for it," Clay cut in, looking at Alvedero. "How much?"

The man adjusted his bow tie. "One and a half million dollars, señor."

Clay whistled. "Isn't that a bit high for just the one piece?"

"Perhaps. But that is the price."

"All right. But I have the authority to pay only ten million for the entire collection, so I'll have to check with my employer to see if he's willing to pay what you're asking for the bracelet."

"*Bueno.* When may I expect to hear from you, Señor Kendall?"

"Tomorrow."

"Until tomorrow, then." After retrieving the bracelet from Amanda and returning it to the pouch, Alvedero started toward the door.

"Señor, just one more thing," Clay said, intercepting him. "My employer is very interested in buying the entire collection. What can you tell me about the people who sold you the bracelet? I'd like to find them if I can."

"The man called himself Brian Walters."

"The man? You mean he was alone?"

"I dealt only with him, but when I went to his hotel to pay him, a young lady left the room as I was going in."

"Can you describe her?"

"Pretty. Blond."

"About how old?"

"Hmm, twenty perhaps."

Amanda had to slap a hand to her mouth to stifle a tortured moan. The description fit Becky. Blond. Pretty. And she looked younger than she was. This was precisely what she had dreaded hearing, and her stomach suddenly felt as if it were

152

tied up in hard tight knots. Fighting tears, she sank the edge of her teeth into her lower lip.

"So you saw this Brian Walters in his hotel," Clay persisted. "What hotel was that?"

"The Ferdinand in Jaén, a small town approximately seventy kilometers north of Granada."

"I see. And when did you last see him there?"

"Two days ago."

"Did he mention where he planned to go next?"

"No. I must go. My wife—she becomes impatient, I am certain."

As Juan Alvedero stepped out into the corridor and closed the door behind him, Amanda buried her face in her hands. "I still don't want to believe Becky's mixed up in this but . . ."

"I'm sorry, Mandy," Clay muttered compassionately. He went to her, feathered one hand over her shining hair. "I wish it didn't have to be like this."

"So do I! Oh hell," she sobbed. With an effort, she mustered enough self-control to regain a semblance of composure, impatiently brushing away a tear. "Okay. What happens now?"

"I contact the police. I'm afraid Señor Alvedero probably isn't going to get to stay for the whole opera."

Her eyes widened, focused on him. "But isn't it dangerous to turn him in? If he's arrested for possessing the bracelet, he'll know you called the police. What if he wants revenge? What if he sends somebody here to—"

"I doubt he will do that, because if I'm attacked after reporting him he'd be the prime suspect. Why risk that? After all, he's not going to be in that much trouble. With a good lawyer, which he can easily afford, he'll probably get a very light sentence for possession of stolen property."

Despite Clay's logical argument, Amanda nervously paced the floor while he called the police and told them his story.

Twenty minutes later, after talking to an officer and then to his superior, doing his best to overcome the language barrier with each of them, he hung up the receiver with a sigh of relief.

"Well, they were interested. All I had to do was mention Alvedero's name to grab their attention. Apparently the authorities have been trying to get something on him for years. They appreciated the tip."

"Maybe they did, but—"

They heard the phone in her adjoining room ring faintly. She ran toward the separating doors, calling back over her shoulder, "Must be Mom or Dad." She dashed across her room to the telephone atop the nightstand. "Maybe they've heard from Becky."

Clay stood on the threshold as she eagerly picked up the receiver.

"Mom?" she called out, undaunted by the crackling noises of a bad connection. "Is that you?"

The line miraculously cleared. The first thing she heard distinctly was the sound of her mother crying, and her heart sank, seemingly into a bottomless pit. "What's the matter?" she breathed. "What's wrong, Mom?"

"Oh, just everything," the older woman answered, hiccuping. "There was an article in this morning's paper, saying that Becky and Brad are the prime suspects in th-that robbery. I had to call you. Have you found her yet?"

"No, Mom, I—"

"You should've seen the way my friends looked at me today after reading that nonsense! I know some of them were whispering behind my back. When's this going to end, Amanda? You have to find her so she can explain she's not guilty of anything."

"I'm trying to find her," Amanda said softly, hesitating.

But only for an instant. She had to warn her parents that things could get much worse for all of them, especially Becky. "Mom, I have to tell you something. It's beginning to look like Becky did have something to do with stealing the rubies from the museum."

She heard only silence for a long while. "I can't believe you're saying that about your own sister!" her mother gasped at last. "That man, Clay Kendall—he's brainwashed you!"

"No, Mom. It's just that I know more of the facts now, and it looks like Becky—"

"I won't listen to this!" Mrs. Mills cried, slamming the phone down with a noise that was painful.

Dully, Amanda dropped the receiver into its cradle. Her shoulders slumped. She chewed her fingernails.

Clay could feel the hurt raging through her. He stepped toward her. "Mandy, I . . ."

"Now Mom's mad at me for doubting Becky," she mumbled. "Oh, what a hell of a mess this all is."

"I know, Mandy."

"I want to be alone for a while," she said, her voice breaking revealingly. "I th-think I'll just go to bed."

"Okay. If that's what you want," he answered gently, stepping back into his own room, closing her door after him.

CHAPTER NINE

Clay couldn't sleep. He was worried about Mandy. In the darkness of his room he could see light under her door, and he wondered how she was faring after that distressing talk with her mother. Not very well, he suspected. Getting out of bed, he went to her door and listened, not surprised to hear muffled sobbing. He entered quietly and saw that she had her face buried in the pillow.

"Mandy," he softly said, drawn to the bedside. "I know you're upset, but . . ."

"Oh, I'm all right," she mumbled, flopping over onto her side to look up at him blearily. She sniffled. "I'm sorry. Didn't mean to bother you."

"You didn't. I wasn't asleep."

She pushed back a strand of hair trying to cling to her damp cheek. "I must be a pretty sight. I always look awful when I cry. Red spots all around my eyes and my nose turns pink."

A small smile of sympathy touched his lips. "I have to admit you look a little frazzled."

"I *feel* frazzled."

"Here." Taking a tissue from the dispenser on the night-stand, he gave it to her to replace the one balled up in her fist. "Try a new one. That one must be soggy."

"It is." Accepting the tissue, she dried her eyes. "Oh hell, I hate to cry."

"Your mother didn't mean what she said, Mandy."

"Maybe not, but what was I supposed to do? I had to warn her. Having false hope now will just make it worse for her and Dad if it turns out bad."

Another stream of tears spilled down her face. Clay sat down beside her to rub her shoulder. "It'll all work out somehow. You just did what you had to do. Your mother will understand that when she settles down."

"*If* sh-she settles down. Damn that Becky! First she wouldn't grow up and now it looks like she's decided on a life of crime. And for what? *Brad*—or whatever his name is. How could she let him sweet-talk her into doing something illegal? If only she'd confided in me. If only I'd asked her more questions about him."

"Enough," Clay gently commanded. "You can't feel guilty for not trying to live her life for her."

Amanda's chin trembled. "I know that. I just wish I could go to sleep and get away from reality for a few hours. I tried, but all I did was toss and turn."

"Can I do anything?" he asked. "Maybe a back rub would help."

"Just hold me," she whispered thickly, reaching for him. "Hold me for a little while."

Lying with her, he enfolded her in his arms, stroking her hair. Saying nothing, he allowed her to cry it all out. Although he kept her supplied with tissues, her tears wet his chest. He didn't mind, knowing this outpouring of emotion would relieve some of her tension. Muffled sobs shook her. Holding her tight, he massaged her back, hoping to loosen taut muscles. He made progress. Slowly she began relaxing in his embrace.

"Oh, I wish she hadn't done it," she said, then repeated it like a chant. "I wish she hadn't. I wish she hadn't."

"I know," he murmured, his deep voice consoling. "But all we can do now is try to help her."

"We? *You* want to help her?"

"If I can. She made a mistake, but we all make mistakes. I'd hate to see hers ruin her life."

"But h-how can you help Becky? You said you probably wouldn't be able to let her go if we found her."

"There are other ways to help. Maybe I could look into her relationship with Brad and supply her lawyer with information—maybe Brad is a Svengali who's practically able to mesmerize her. Get her to do things she'd never normally do."

"But that's a real long shot, isn't it? I mean, as a defense?"

"It's something to consider."

"I don't want to have to grasp at straws," she uttered, another sob punctuating her words.

Clay stroked her hair. In time her crying subsided and she went limp against him, heat radiating from her into him. Trailing the edge of one thumb across her tear-streaked cheeks, he inquired softly, "Feeling better?"

"A little." She nuzzled her face in the hollow of his right shoulder. "Thanks for being so nice."

"Mmm, I'm a regular saint."

His wry tone made her smile weakly. "But you could've stayed in your room and let me cry by myself."

"No. I couldn't do that."

"Maybe you should have. You could've avoided getting all wet."

"Tears can't hurt me. I'm tough."

He *was* tough, yet incredibly tender. In that moment, she knew she wasn't *almost* in love. She did love him. Wild exultation rushed through her as she realized exactly how important he had become to her. Swept away in a tide of raw emotion, she raised her head.

She kissed him.

"Oh God," he growled, tightening his arms fiercely around her, his hard mouth taking sure swift possession of hers. The touch of her lips upon his had caught him off guard, and desire, never far beneath the surface, erupted white-hot and pulsating. Aching need surged through him, demanding release. And her sweet taste demanded all the self-control he possessed to allow him to pull away from her at last. "I . . . thought you wanted to sleep."

"I want you more," she confessed, overflowing with loving passion. "Love me, Clay. Love me now."

His lips hungrily covered hers. "My sweet Mandy," he gruffly whispered, "that's an invitation I can't refuse."

"Don't want you to," she whispered back, holding his face between her hands. She ran her fingers through his hair and lightly drew the tips of her nails down his back. Her heart thundered as he impelled her down into the softness of the mattress, his hard body evocatively heavy upon hers. With the gentle pressure of one knee he parted her legs, hitching the hem of her nightgown up. Her pulse pounded with the contact between his skin and the smoother surface of her own. She wrapped her arms around his waist, pulling him closer. When he pushed the tip of his tongue into her mouth, she trembled.

"Are you sure this is what you want, honey?" he groaned, nibbling her soft succulent lips. "Are you?"

"Oh yes, Clay, yes."

"You'd better be. I'm not sure I could let you go now if you changed your mind."

"Don't talk, kiss me," she breathlessly implored. "Kiss me, kiss me, *kiss me.*"

He did. He had to. Her nectar drew him as a bee is drawn

to flowers, and his lips hardened against the shapely fullness of hers, exerting a swift, graduating pressure as he yearned to drain all the sweet, faintly clove-scented moistness from her mouth. She opened eagerly to him, her tongue tangling daringly with his, her breath mingling.

Loving Clay with an irreversible madness that swept through her bloodstream. Amanda arched closer and closer to him, small hands glancing down along his broad back to squeeze his lean buttocks, adoring the heat of male flesh emanating through the thin fabric of his pajama pants.

On fire for her, he pulled her gown up around her waist and curved his hands over her full breasts, feeling her responsive throbbing. He pressed his fingers downward into her resilient flesh, caressing the feminine mounds of delight. Passion was a roaring river in him, swamping his senses, building like a massive tidal wave.

Amanda was lost in love and the searing need to give and to take anything he could give in return. She was making herself totally vulnerable to him. She knew it. Yet that was what she wanted, *needed* to do. The powerful demand of his lips upon hers torched firestorms over every inch of her skin. She felt gloriously alive, hopelessly in love.

"Clay," she said his name with a sigh, rubbing her tongue over his, adoring the velvety abrasive surface she encountered. His warm breath caressed her mouth. Her hands floated around his sides, edging in to knead his flexed pectoral muscles.

As her light slender fingers moved over and around his nipples, toying with their centers and quickly arousing them to firmness, he pushed his hands up under her gown, needing to feel again the heat of her flesh. Sweeping his palms over her breasts, he felt the peaks surge up hard against his skin. She breathed faster and covered his hands with her own, pressing them down, silently urging him to continue touching her. And touch he did, fingertips circling upward, scaling the lush mounds of her flesh.

"You're soft as silk," he told her as she caressed his shoulders and neck. Their gazes met, locked. A special glow shone in her blue eyes and lighted her features. When she lifted her head to brush her lips over his, he gruffly repeated, "Soft as silk. Have I told you lately how lovely you are?"

"Tell me again. I like to hear it."

"You're beautiful, Mandy."

"You make me feel beautiful."

"And you're so sexy."

"You make me feel that way too."

The slight pressure of his thumb on her chin tugged her mouth open a little as his lips descended to possess hers. Deep plunging thrills raced through her. No other man's kisses had ever delighted her the way Clay's did. Her love for him made all the difference. Confident, she made bold little advances into his mouth with her tongue.

"God, woman, you drive me crazy," he groaned, stripping off her gown. Winding her thick, shining hair round one hand, he tilted her head back on the pillow, his lips grazing the curve of her neck. He kissed her taut, opalescent breasts and nibbled the passion-tipped nubbles, drawing first one then the other deeply inside his mouth with a wondrous pulling pressure that made her tremble.

He released her briefly to shed his pajamas, allowing her to gaze upon his virile body. Love and heightening desire merged inseparably as he leaned over her once more and she ran her hands up and down his sides.

Patiently, tenderly, he kissed her many times. She responded with ardent abandon, her soft lips inviting the demanding possession of his, and he slipped her panties down over her hips and off completely. "Please don't say no now. I think it's too late for me to stop."

"I don't want you to stop."

His jet black eyes glinted. "I've been waiting for this night."

"Me too," she admitted. And she had been. Even when she had fought her growing feelings for him, anticipation had resided deep inside. Now that the night had arrived, she gloried in every moment of it. His hands wandered over her, caressing her with fire. She rubbed a silken thigh up and down between his, joy leaping in her at the depth of his response. Poised over her, his taut body dangerous with the sexual tension coiled tightly in him, he transported her from plateau to plateau of mounting pleasure as they whispered to each other. Her eyes fluttered open; she touched his face. Passionate intent sharpened his finely honed features, yet the unfilled needs raging in him were tempered by the tenderness in his eyes and the set of his lips, causing happiness to well over in her. He claimed her mouth with an evocative insistence that made her ache for more and more of his kisses, and she returned them with undeniable eagerness.

It was the time to explore, to learn what responses meant, to begin to discover how to please each other. Not one to hurry through the preliminaries, Clay plied her with his mouth, tongue, lips, and hands, toying with her lovely full breasts, teasing the rosy crests, tasting her skin. The faint garden-fresh fragrance of her perfume clung to her. In the gilded glow of lamplight, the fair hair framing her face shimmered like a skein of spun gold. Her tears had disappeared, apparently forgotten.

They *were* forgotten. So was Becky, even her parents, the whole rest of the world. For the time being, nothing mattered except that room, that bed, and Clay beside her. She wanted to go on holding him forever, loving the hard muscle that shaped his flesh and lay so close under the surface of his heated skin. She was fascinated by his body, its textures, angles, and degrees of resiliency. Winding a lock of his dark hair around one finger, she tugged it lightly. She scampered her fingertips along his powerful arms. She surrendered conscious deliberation to near primitive feminine instinct in order to entice him, and succeeded in that quest, smiling sensuously when she played with the whorls of his ears and a responsive shudder coursed through him. And when he swiftly turned her onto her stomach, straddling her, excitement hammered the pulses in her temples.

The very flesh and bone structure of her smooth back intrigued him. He followed the contours of her shoulder blades with his stroking fingers. Feathering the tip of his tongue down her spine, feeling shivers prance over her, he explored the sparse, scarcely visible peach fuzz hair along the arch of her back. Then he turned around, his hands shaping her long legs, squeezing her shapely thighs, the gorgeous curve of her calves, the delicate trimness of her ankles. Bending down, he kissed the soles of her slender feet and even the ends of her toes, nibbling the rounded mound on the bottom of each.

"Tickles," she protested, a small giggle escaping her. "Not fair."

"Ah, but you have such pretty toes," he murmured, chuckling as he turned back around. "And delectable too. I couldn't resist a couple bites."

Laughing softly with him, she rolled over between his legs, then pulled him off balance without any warning whatsoever, making him fall down beside her upon the mattress. Quickly astride him, she gave him a wicked, purposeful grin. "You made me wild. Now it's my turn," she intoned, meaning to sound ominous but sounding provocative instead. "Watch out, Mr. Kendall, I'm about to drive you crazy."

"You won't have to go far," he conceded, his deep voice appealingly husky when her hair fell forward over his chest and midriff. As she showered flurries of kisses over him, he clasped her head in his hands while she guided her parted lips over his flat nipples, his midriff, his sides, and the inner surfaces of his arms, to the rapid pulse in his wrists. Through half closed eyes, he watched what she was doing to him. The sweet round hills of her capped breasts grazed him, generously full and cushiony and hot. He cupped the arousing weight of them in his hands, massaging, caressing, ardently probing the sweet mystery of her very own individual womanhood. He had known intimacy with other women but had never so fiercely needed any of those women as he needed Mandy now. She sent a fever raging through his veins, and when the end of her tongue flickered across his abdomen, he could stand the arousing torment no longer. Turning swiftly, he swept her back beneath him and looked down at her glorious nakedness, his smoldering eyes lingering here and there, his heart drumming hard in his chest. So satin-smooth and silky her skin was. So amazingly receptive its hot surface. Those other women in his past, those he had desired and ultimately spent a night or two with, suddenly paled to insignificance in comparison with Mandy. Intelligent and quick-witted, loyal, warm, and giving, she was a rare delight. His seeking lips urgently laid claim to her throbbing breasts, her straight shoulders, the slim column of her creamy neck. When he gently eased the edge of his right hand between her thighs, he captured her sibilant sigh of encouragement in his mouth.

Every nerve ending vibrantly alive, she parted her legs as he touched her there, and fiery wanting exploded in her center, more hot and consuming than it had ever been. Then his fingers drifted down around her knees, and she felt empty, oh so empty.

"Clay, don't stop now," she implored. "Never stop."

"Touch me too," he gently commanded, pulling one small hand downward between them. "That's what I need so much —for you to touch me too."

And she did, intimately, her fingers curving around him, stroking the iron hardness that pulsated against her brushing palm. The raw power she encountered made her almost dizzy, but not dizzy enough to come near to swooning in the old-fashioned way. She longed to participate fully in their love-making and knew Clay expected and wanted her to. She caressed him, rounded her hand over him, and opened her legs wider as he touched her again and again, his fluttering finger-tips charting every rising hill and warm valley of her feminin-ity. Gently, he opened ultimate warmth, entered tactically shallowly with one tenderly exploring caress and another, then another.

"Oh, yes," she breathed, arching upward, winding her limbs around his long, muscular body. But when he grasped her ankles, raised her parted knees, and she felt him throb demandingly against her, she tensed a little.

"Let yourself go," he coaxed, nibbling the corners of her mouth again and again until she relaxed once more. "Yes, you can relax. I'd never do anything to hurt you, Mandy. Trust me."

"I do," she murmured, gazing up at his beloved face, lost in the fathomless depths of his eyes. "I do trust you."

"Then tell me what you want."

"You."

"Sure?"

"Clay!"

"Mmm, I think you finally *do* want me as much as I've been wanting you," he whispered, blowing into her left ear, feeling her quiver. "And that's what I need."

165

Tightening her arms around him, she pressed him closer. "Take me."

"Soon."

"Now."

"Yes," he growled, the remnants of his self-control dissolving. With a gentle invasive thrust, he merged his body with hers, making her his. He stroked upward until her luscious warmth enclosed him completely.

"Oh, *Clay,*" she softly gasped, filled with his potent throbbing. Some of her inner emptiness was immediately appeased, although the deeper aching quickened. But in her soul, she experienced a certain completion. Lost in love and love's intrinsic need to give, she wrapped her arms and legs tighter around him, her parted lips finding his. "Love me, Clay. Love me now."

"My sweet Mandy," he said almost reverently as they began to move in a slow rhythm together. Like a flower opening, she received and welcomed him each time he immersed himself in her.

His lips caressed the soft shape of hers. His tongue licked the sweetness within her mouth. Their kisses deepened and lingered. The unbridled joy that came with even partial fulfillment brought happy tears to her eyes, and adoring him, she breathed a throaty sigh and eagerly met his slow, rousing thrusts. When he kissed the side of her neck, then the hollow beneath her left ear, she nuzzled her cheek against his.

"Mandy, honey," he said, his tone hushed as his hands drifted all over her, leaving trails of warmth wherever they went and burning away any lingering inhibitions she might have had. Love made her utterly receptive. He could have asked anything of her and she would gladly have given it. He was an aggressive lover, yet capable of inexpressible gentleness. Demanding yet patient, he evoked ardent responses.

When their eyes met and they exchanged sensual smiles of intimate understanding, the sheer emotional power of those moments took her breath away.

He felt as if he were melting into her, that they were becoming one spiritual being. Excited by her body, overcome by her warmth, fascinated by the very way she moved and the words she softly spoke, he found a profound sweetness with her he had never experienced before.

They were carried along together, rising, sensation spiraling and building, and once begun, there was no stopping it—none —until delight soared up to the most exquisite spire. Braced above her on fully extended arms, he looked into her expressive eyes, possessing her emotionally as well as physically.

He moved harder, faster, and she moved with him as the delicious friction of flesh against flesh became more and more keenly piercing.

"Clay!" she cried out, pressing her nails into the corded muscles of his shoulders as pleasure doubled, redoubled, then exploded in a crashing tidal wave that ebbed, then crested again, suspending them together on the sharply honed edge of ultimate completion.

As the shuddering waves of pleasure slowly subsided, they held each other, closely entangled. Beneath her hand against his chest, she felt his steadily pounding heartbeat begin to slow. Her body still tingled from his touch, and she drifted contentedly in the magic of fulfillment. In the warm afterglow, she snuggled nearer and brushed her lips over his collarbone.

Cradling her in one arm, Clay tenderly swept her hair back from her cheeks. "Mandy," he murmured, rubbing a silken tendril between thumb and forefinger. "Maybe I should apologize for what just happened."

"But why?" she exclaimed, fear pouncing on her heart and

gripping her throat as she tilted her head back to look up at him. "Are you sorry it happened?"

"Maybe I should be. Guess I ought to feel like a real cad. After all, when I came in here you were crying, upset about your family. Vulnerable. Maybe I took advantage of the way you were feeling."

Breathing a silent sigh of relief, she smiled. "You should know me better than that. I don't let people take advantage of me even when I'm in a blue mood. We made love because we both wanted to."

He pretended to wipe imaginary sweat from his brow. "Phew. I'm glad you said that, because I don't think I could've apologized anyhow. I'm not at all sorry about tonight."

"Neither am I."

"No regrets whatsoever?"

"No. None."

"You're positive?"

"Stop that, you nut." She prodded his side with an elbow. "I know you don't need that much reassurance."

Chuckling softly, he kissed her forehead.

"Still," she added musingly, "one thing does surprise me."

"Hmm, what's that?"

"I never imagined we'd make love in Granada."

"What's wrong? Don't you like it here?"

"Sure, it's a beautiful city, romantic. Too perfect."

Clay cocked one eyebrow. "Run that past me one more time. Your logic's baffling."

"It's really simple. Sort of a variation of Murphy's Law: events rarely occur where they should. You see—"

"Never mind," he cut in wryly, silencing her with a finger against her lips. "I had a bottle of sherry brought up to my room after dinner. Would you like a glass?"

168

Stretching lazily, like a kitten, she nodded. "Sounds delicious. Want me to get it?"

"Indeed not. I'll serve, madam," he mimicked the precise accent of Bernard Cooper's uppity British butler.

She watched him, a loving smile on her lips, as he got out of bed and strode across her room into his, unabashed by his nudity. After another little stretch, she snuggled down into the mattress. Warmth had spread from the tips of her toes to her scalp. She felt more relaxed than she had in weeks—since Becky's trouble began, as a matter of fact. And her love for Clay was growing stronger every minute. She even missed him during the brief time he was out of sight in his room. He returned soon, though, and propping pillows against the headboard, she sat up in bed with the sheet draping her bare breasts. She took the two glasses he handed her and held them as he got under the light cover beside her. Her fingers brushed against his as she gave him one of the drinks.

Capturing her gaze, Clay touched the rim of her fragile stemmed glass with his. "To Granada. The perfect place."

"Granada," she agreed rather huskily before she took the first small sip and liquid warmth glided smoothly down her throat. The taste was wonderful but stronger than she had expected. Her eyes practically watered. "I've never tasted sherry like this."

"It's Manzanilla, very popular in this country but not technically a sherry. It has more kick."

"I'll say."

"If you don't like it . . ."

"I didn't say *that*." Her eyes sparkled merrily as she took another tiny sip and slowly swallowed. "In fact, I like it better than sherry. But I didn't know you were such a connoisseur. When did you acquire a taste for this?"

"I'm just acquiring it. I've never had it before tonight either," he easily admitted. "But I'd heard about it and decided I might as well try it while I'm here."

"My compliments to the wine steward," she said jokingly.

Then a silence fell over the room, but a silence cozy and warming. But this night would have to come to an end. And after several minutes, Clay quietly cleared his throat, then announced, "In the morning, we'll rent a car and drive to Jaén."

"Okay," she murmured, wishing she didn't have to return to painful reality. "But don't you think we'll probably be wasting a trip? Do you really believe Becky and Brad might still be there?"

"I believe they could be. I have to check it out."

Another silence followed and Amanda soon drifted back into a gloriously happy frame of mind. Perhaps the drink helped a bit. She looked around, memorizing the fine detail of the carved Moorish-style furniture and the bright reds, blues, and yellows that enhanced the decor. She knew she could never forget this room in Granada, Spain.

"More Manzanilla?" Clay asked, interrupting her reverie. "How about a refill?"

"No, thanks. But don't let me stop you."

"I'm fine," he assured her, taking her empty glass and placing it with his on the nightstand. He turned back and swiftly slipped his fingers beneath the edge of the sheet she had covered herself with. Relentlessly, he tugged it from her grasp and exposed her lovely breasts.

"*Clay,*" she whispered, her next breath catching somewhere deep in her throat when he reached out to trace circles around her roseate nipples, the balls of his thumbs bringing forth the firm, aroused tips. Amazing how his every caress created a turmoil in her senses. She smiled teasingly at him. "Hey, what's the big idea?"

"The idea is making love. I want you again."

"You sex maniac."

"Where you're concerned, I am. And I want to make our first night together one you'll never forget."

"Oh, Clay. You've already done that."

"Mmm, but just to be sure," he whispered, pulling her over astride him, the gentle outward pressure of his thighs parting hers wider. Cupping her smooth, firmly curved bottom in his hands, he eased her closer, entered her sleek warmth, felt her settle down upon him. He searched her face. Although she had closed her eyes as they joined together, he recognized the bliss illuminating her features.

They drove from Granada to Jaén the next morning, found the Hotel Ferdinand and a parking space for the car, and went into the lobby. Amanda paid no attention to her surroundings, hanging back a few feet when Clay approached the desk. Clasping her clutch purse tightly against her side with her upper arm, she squeezed her hands together, her nails digging into her palms. This might prove to be Becky's last stand. She might be caught here and quickly extradited to the States for trial. The knowledge tore Amanda apart inside. Much as she needed to find and talk to her little sister, she couldn't bear the thought of her being returned to Richmond in handcuffs and going straight to jail.

Amanda's eyes bored into Clay's broad back as he spoke to the desk clerk. But as they conversed in Spanish, Clay struggling over certain words, she understood nothing being said. The suspense was horrendous. After all this time, she had to know if Becky's days of freedom were numbered. How much longer could she stand to wait to hear the truth from Becky's own mouth? Did she ever want to hear it? She didn't know. Confusion scrambled her brain, and the stony expression on

171

Clay's face when he turned away from the clerk toward her did nothing whatsoever to alleviate her bewilderment.

As he none-too-gently curved one large hand around her arm she glanced sideways at him, letting him impel her across the tiled lobby floor. "So. They're not here."

"How did you guess?" he drawled, his low voice sarcastic. "Such a coincidence that they checked out about two this morning, heading for parts unknown."

"A coincidence? I don't understand what—"

"Don't you? I'm not so sure of that." Out on the sidewalk, he spun her around to face him, his eyes piercing the depths of hers. "What exactly did your mother tell you when she called last night?"

"Mom? But I told you what she said. She talked about Becky being named as a suspect in the robbery in the newspaper and—"

"And what?"

"And nothing. Clay, what are you getting at?"

"Just this. Maybe your mother told you she'd heard from Becky and you discovered she was really here, in this hotel with Brad," he said curtly. "And maybe you warned your sister I was close on her trail and that's why she and her lover conveniently checked out just in time. Makes sense."

"It doesn't make any sense at all," she retorted, her own anger flaring up to a level matching his. She glared at him. "You're crazy. How could I have called Becky even if I had known for sure she was here. We spent the night together. Remember? I didn't have a chance to call anybody."

"Yes you did. I woke up once and saw you going into my room. Why?"

"Because I was going to the bathroom and I saw you'd left your lamp on. I went in to turn it off."

"You were in there too long just to do that."

172

"That's right, because I went to your bathroom instead while I was there so I wouldn't disturb you by closing the door to mine."

"Why should I believe that story?"

"Because it's the truth," she retorted, a sharp ache gathering in a knot in the center of her chest. Last night, she had felt so close to him. Now he seemed like a stranger again. The change hurt her badly but she held her head up high. "You'll just have to trust me."

"I don't think I can. You were in my room a long time."

"But if I'd used the phone, you would've heard me."

"Not if you whispered."

"But—"

"I told you before and I'm telling you again: I won't let you interfere in this case," he cut in harshly, tightening his grip on her arm, his fingertips pressing down near delicate bone. "You want to protect your sister and I want to protect my professional reputation. And the last time I called Langley, Virginia, to talk to my CIA contact, he told me the agency is concerned that I'm letting you come with me while I'm trying to find Becky and Brad. Maybe they're right to worry. If I knew you did warn Becky last night, I'd . . ."

"You'd what?" she challenged hotly, yanking her arm free from his powerful hand. "Go ahead. Say it!"

"If I knew you'd warned Becky, I'd be the one sorry about what we had together."

"My, my, my. Whatever happened to your gentlemanly manners? To say such a thing!" she shot back carelessly, masking the biting pain his words caused. "Your mother would be ashamed of you, Clay Kendall."

His jaw set, he didn't bother to answer as he ushered her down the sidewalk toward the rental car.

"What happens now?" she asked urgently. "Where do we go from here?"

"Home. I'll have to wait for another lead."

"Clay, I—"

"Get in," he commanded, yanking open the door on the passenger side of the white sedan.

She settled stiffly into the passenger seat. And after he walked around the car and got in, lowering himself beneath the steering wheel, she stared straight ahead, unwilling to give him even a quick corner-of-the-eye glance. For the moment, resentment outweighed the abiding love she felt for him. And she maintained a stony silence as they drove back to Granada.

CHAPTER TEN

Amanda stared glumly out the store window. She was tired of trying to stay frantically busy in order to keep her mind off her problems. The ploy wasn't working anyway. Becky's predicament wasn't easily dismissed, and of course she couldn't help fretting about Clay. In the four days since they'd returned from Europe, she had neither seen nor heard from him, and she wondered if he still believed she was helping her sister stay one step ahead of him. It was ironic. Despite the intimacy they had shared, barriers remained between them. Obviously he didn't quite trust her, and she wasn't at all sure she could trust him to try to help Becky in any way possible, as he had promised. Maybe he had said that simply to gain her complete cooperation.

It wasn't fair. She loved him and perhaps they could have had a lasting relationship, if only life were simpler. But maybe he didn't want that. Since he hadn't even bothered to phone her in four whole days, he was apparently finding it quite easy to do without her in his life. Or maybe . . . Countless depressing thoughts flitted through her brain as she stood at the counter, gazing blindly out at the street. Although she periodically glanced at her three browsing customers to see if any one of them wanted her assistance, she was more concerned with personal matters than business.

She sighed softly, propping her elbows on the countertop

and resting her chin in her hand. The composed expression on her face was at variance with her tumultuous emotional state, and she nearly jumped out of her skin when Betsy Ann suddenly appeared beside her.

"Earth calling Amanda. Earth calling Amanda," the clerk said in a teasing singsong. "Come in, please."

Amanda smiled apologetically. "Sorry, guess I did seem a little out of it. Just woolgathering."

"You were not. You're worrying again, I can tell."

"Gee, I didn't know I was so transparent."

"You're not, but we've known each other for a long time. I can tell when you're upset. Your eyes look different."

"Oh, my, I'd better try to control that."

"Listen, you haven't asked me for advice, but I'm going to give a little anyway," Betsy Ann announced somberly, her tone affectionately concerned. "You can't carry the weight of the whole world on your shoulders. You'll give yourself ulcers trying, not to mention a strained back. Know what I mean?"

"Yes, but—"

"You've been working like a slave since you got back and I know why. You're trying to escape from the problems Becky's caused. But you're not escaping. You're too quiet, you get that way when you're sad. And you're working too hard. Lighten up. Think of your health. You can't worry yourself sick."

"I know that," Amanda said quietly, appreciating her friend's concern. "But I want to be loyal to my family."

"Child, you're as loyal as the day is long. Everybody who knows you can see that. But you need to take a break once in a while, that's all I'm saying. You have to relax sometimes and think about yourself."

"You're right. I'll try."

"Good. Start now. I can take care of these customers, so you take yourself across the street to Rosalyn's, enjoy one of her scrumptious pecan tarts, and have a cup of coffee with her."

"Oh, well, I—I'm not really hungry so—"

"Scat," the older woman commanded, herding Amanda to the door and out. "Stay as long as you like."

Defeated, Amanda shrugged and smiled. She left the store and waited for a break in traffic before she could cross the street. When she opened the door of the bakery, the comforting scents of nutmeg, cinnamon, and poppy seeds wafted to her nose, inviting her in.

Rosalyn White looked up from serving a customer and flashed her a big smile. Amanda wandered over to the display cases filled with a mouth-watering, calorie-filled assortment of breads, pastries, and pies. She heard the soft whirr of the computerized cash register and looked up with a smile when Rosalyn walked over to her, half heartedly complaining, "Where've you been keeping yourself? I've been expecting you to drop by since you got back."

"I meant to every day, but I've been really busy."

"So Betsy Ann tells me."

Amanda's answering laugh was bubbly and merry. "She's something else, isn't she? I think she's adopted me, but I don't mind. She's a sweetheart. She just worries about me too much."

"There's a lot of the mother hen in her," Rosalyn agreed. She waved her hand over her tempting wares. "See anything you want?"

"Everything. But you know me. Your pecan tarts are my downfall. I have to have one."

Plucking a square waxed paper sheet from a dispenser, the bakery proprietress removed a tart from the tray, its glazed topping appetizing, its pastry shell so flaky that it looked as

177

though it would literally melt in the mouth. "How about this one?"

"Oh, lord, it looks delicious," Amanda murmured, pulling a dollar bill from the pocket of her dress. "Here you go."

"No charge. My treat."

"Now, Ros, I—"

"I insist."

"Okay, you talked me into it. Thanks."

"Want it to go?"

"I'd rather eat it here," Amanda answered, deciding to take Betsy Ann's unsolicited yet kind advice and try to relax a little, "if you have time to chat a few minutes and offer me coffee to go with it."

"I've always got time for woman talk," the other woman declared, smiling as she waved Amanda into the back room adjoining the kitchen. "And I'll even have a chocolate éclair, although it'll ruin my diet. But what the heck? Del says he loves having a pleasantly plump wife."

Out in the shop, the bell above the door jingled. When Rosalyn went to attend to the new customer Amanda poured coffee for both of them, adding sugar to both and cream to her friend's, remembering exactly how she liked it.

Two minutes later, Rosalyn came back, darting into the kitchen and calling over her shoulder, "Just one more thing. I've got a new baker's apprentice so I'd better remind him to put the last batch of dinner rolls into the oven."

"You have a new apprentice? What happened to the girl who was here? Peggy? Wasn't that her name?"

"Yes. She was very sweet but—how can I say this kindly? She was kind of spaced out."

"Drugs?"

"I think so."

"That's a shame."

178

"Yes. I hated to have to let her go but I had no choice. I asked her to go to a drug rehabilitation clinic, even gave her the phone number and address. I hope she went." After instructing her new helper, Rosalyn came back to drop into the chair across the small table from Amanda with a sigh. "Ah, now we can catch up on each other's news. You took a few days off. Have a good time?"

Amanda laughed mirthlessly. There was no simple answer to that question. Being with Clay had been heavenly, but the purpose of their journeys together hadn't been prompted by romance. She shrugged, flip-flopping one hand from side to side. "Actually, it wasn't a vacation."

"Mmm, I was afraid of that. You went away because of Becky, huh? I read what they put in the paper about her and I just can't believe it! I know there has to be some mistake. Becky, a thief? Never!"

Amanda nearly moaned.

"Did I say something wrong?"

"No, of course you didn't. But I have to tell you something very unpleasant," murmured Amanda, gnawing her lip. "It's beginning to look more and more like Becky was involved in stealing those damn rubies. That boyfriend of hers, Brad Charles, may have talked her into—"

"No, couldn't be! I mean, I know Becky's never been as mature as you, or as independent, but surely she'd never let herself be conned by a crook?"

"I'm not so sure. I'm not sure of anything anymore. I just know this is one hell of a mess. And I've made it even more complicated," Amanda declared, her voice raw-edged as the words tumbled out in her rush to confide in somebody. "You remember that man I thought was following me, the one you waylaid out on the sidewalk that day so I could get away? Well, he showed up at my house that very same night. He's been hired to recover the rubies and, well, to make a long story short, I've done something very dumb, I think. I've fallen in love with him."

Rosalyn simply stared at her, coffee cup suspended halfway between the tabletop and her lips. "You're kidding? You're not kidding. How on earth did that happen?"

"How should I know? Why do people fall in love? It just seems to happen, that's all."

"Well, what's his name, Amanda?"

"Clay Kendall."

"It's incredible. First you thought he was some kind of weirdo following you around, and now you're in love with the guy. Obviously you've gotten to know him—but how?"

"We both want to find Becky—for different reasons, but it's brought us together. And when he went to Bermuda and Spain looking for her I followed him, so we were together even more."

"You followed him?" Rosalyn exclaimed, her mouth falling open slightly. "I never would've had the nerve to do that."

"I didn't have much choice," Amanda explained. "I knew if he did find Becky, she'd need me. And besides, I had to do something. Mom and Dad are all torn up about this, and I hoped they'd feel a little better if I at least did something, anything. But it really didn't help because we didn't find her. Everything's the same as it was."

"Not quite. Now you're in love. So tell me about Clay Kendall. He sure must be something special."

"That's just it—he is." Sighing pensively, Amanda drummed her fingers on the tabletop. "He's a wonderful man, exciting, sexy, intelligent, witty."

"Oh-ho, you really are in love. You make him sound perfect."

"Not quite perfect, but close enough for me."

"You should be happy, then. I know Becky's situation makes it more difficult for you and him. But it's not every day you fall in love, so you should enjoy it."

"That's not as easy as it sounds. I know what he means to me but I don't know if I mean anything to him."

"Come on, Amanda, you must have some idea."

"All right. He does like me . . . most of the time. When we have disagreements, they're about Becky. But I still don't know how he *feels.*" The corners of Amanda's mouth drooped a bit. "Since I haven't heard from him in four days, I'm afraid he must not care very much. I mean, when a man doesn't even make an effort to see you . . ."

"Being in love *can* be the pits," Rosalyn commiserated. "I wish I knew what to tell you."

"I've been thinking I should make the next move. Since he won't call me, maybe I should just call him."

"Great idea! Do it!"

"I think I will," Amanda decided, her face brightening. "What have I got to lose?"

"Atta girl." The bell in the shop tinkled and Rosalyn hopped up, winking. "Call him right now while I wait on this customer. You'll have plenty of privacy back here."

Amanda hastily pushed the buttons on the phone before she could lose her nerve, and waited for the first ring, which was cut short when Clay's answering service picked up.

"I need to locate Mr. Kendall," she told the woman on the other end. "Where can he be reached?"

"Nowhere at the moment. I'm sorry, ma'am," the lilting voice came back. "Mr. Kendall's out of town."

Amanda's heart lurched. Had he gotten another lead? What if he found Becky this time and Amanda wasn't there? A horrible vision filled her head of Becky being cornered somewhere. Struggling to steady her voice, she inquired, "Would you tell me where Mr. Kendall is and how I can get in touch with him?"

"I'm not allowed to give out that information, ma'am, unless specifically instructed to do so."

"But Mr. Kendall is searching for my sister and it's important for me to talk to him as soon as possible."

"I wish I could help but I have to go by the rules. I can't afford to lose my job."

"I see," murmured Amanda bleakly. She did understand the woman's position, but understanding was cold comfort. "Then could you possibly tell me when Mr. Kendall's expected back?"

"Yes. He should be back by Thursday evening, unless he's delayed for some reason."

After expressing her thanks Amanda hung up, but her hand still maintained a tight nervous grip on the receiver. The words *unless he's delayed for some reason* echoed in her head. Delayed because Becky and Brad had miraculously moved on before he reached them once again? Delayed because he was having to chase them from one place to another? Balling one hand into a fist, she struck the table, feeling betrayed because he hadn't let her go with him, although that was a strictly illogical reaction. After all, he'd always made it quite clear he didn't want her with him during his investigation. Little wonder he hadn't let her know if he had gotten a new lead. It made sense, yet it still hurt. Love was playing havoc with logic and sheer common sense.

After one last sip of coffee, she got up and walked out into the shop, joining Ros behind the counter.

"Come back to see us," Rosalyn called to the departing customer before turning around, her eyes bright with excitement. "How did it go?"

"I didn't get him. His service answered. He's out of town,

182

probably hot on Becky's trail this very moment. Oh God, I must be crazy! How can I be in love with a man who's trying to prove my sister's a thief. Sometimes I feel so damn guilty!"

"Don't you dare feel that way!" Rosalyn admonished, waggling her right forefinger. "You fell in love with him. Like you said, love just seems to happen. And it's nothing to be ashamed of. Becky's in trouble. I know that's painful for you, but you didn't cause her problems. There's no reason for you to feel guilty about falling in love with a wonderful man. Oh, I agree it's a crazy mixed-up mess. But remember: Nothing worthwhile is ever easy."

"Thanks, Ros," murmured Amanda, her spirits lifting a little. "It's helped me to be able to talk to you. I sure can't tell my folks exactly what's going on. They already think I'm something of a traitor because I'm having doubts about Becky's innocence. If I told them I was in love with the man they consider her worst enemy, they'd probably disown me and never speak to me again. So thanks for lending a sympathetic ear."

"Any time. I know you'd do the same for me."

Amanda eyed the freshly baked chocolate éclairs on a tray behind the plate glass. She nodded decisively. "I'll take one of those. Betsy Ann loves them, and she deserves a treat."

And a few minutes later, when she scurried across the busy street toward her shop, she did feel more relaxed. Not great, but better. It did help to confide in a friend.

Clay's plane touched down in Richmond at six fourteen Thursday evening, three minutes ahead of schedule. He disembarked without delay, walked into the terminal, and found a bank of pay telephones, two of which weren't in use. Taking the nearest one, he inserted the proper amount of coins in the slot and called his service, then jotted down the messages he received in a pocket notebook, scribbling in his own particular personal shorthand, which was indecipherable for anyone except himself. That task accomplished, he walked outside to the long-term parking area where his ivory sedan waited. He never would have left his vintage Jaguar roadster in such a place, where it might have been scratched or dented, or even stolen. Generally, he didn't place excessive value on material possessions, but that roadster of his was an exception.

One palm curved over the steering wheel, he swung out onto the highway leading into the city. Traffic was heavy and he was heading west toward the glaring setting sun, which made his eyes ache. It had been a long, tiring day. He stroked his jaw with his free hand. He needed a shave and wanted a shower, but those things could wait. Before he headed home, he had something to do.

Amanda had called Clay several times during the afternoon, but to no avail. She always got his service instead of him. At home, she tried his number again about six fifteen but got the same old song and dance: "Mr. Kendall is out of town. Would you care to leave a message?"

She saw no point in doing that and always politely declined. Hanging up after the last call, she pressed her lips tightly together and began to pace back and forth across her living room. Why wasn't he back yet? Was he a few steps behind Becky and Brad, bound to catch up with them sooner or later? What exactly was happening? So many questions. No answers. And she felt almost like screaming; she was that tense.

As she stalked across the floor, Bossy stirred on the cold hearth where she lay, rested her black velvet nose on her big paws, and followed her mistress with mournful brown eyes. She made a soft sound, almost a whimper.

Amanda glanced over at her dog, recognized the woebegone

demeanor, and walked over to stroke the retriever's sleek golden head. "You always sense how I feel, don't you, you old sweetie?"

Bossy's ears pricked up at the endearment. Her tail thumped a joyous tattoo upon the hearthstones. She couldn't express her devotion in words but it was obvious as she nuzzled her warm nose against Amanda's wrist.

"No wonder pets make lives brighter in nursing homes, children's hospitals, even prisons," Amanda said to her furry friend. "You're a real comfort. You can be an old poop, Bossy, but I'd be lonely as hell without you."

The dog wagged her tail ecstatically again but abruptly stopped and sprang up like a released spring, paws spread wide, her long body a mass of flexed muscle, head hunched down as her initial growl erupted in a series of deep guttural barks, as someone knocked sharply on the front door.

"Hush, now. Let's see who's out there before you start acting vicious," Amanda called when Bossy pranced to the door, hackles raised. Following, she stretched up on tiptoe to peek through the peephole. When she saw Clay on the other side of the door, she didn't know whether to be relieved or even more upset. At least he wasn't a stranger. He presented no real danger to her—not physically. She spoke to Bossy in a calming tone as she unlocked and opened the door.

Recognizing Clay in an instant, evidently remembering he had kindly scratched her rump and was therefore a true friend, Bossy lunged toward him, nearly bowling him over in a frenzy of delight until her mistress commanded her to sit. Reluctantly, she sat.

Amanda's eyes darkened as they met Clay's and she sank her teeth into the fullness of her bottom lip before asking huskily, "Did you find her? Bring her back with you?"

A faint frown etched his brow. "Becky?"

"Of course Becky! Who else?"

"I had to go out of town, but it had nothing to do with your sister."

"Then where the devil *have* you been?"

"New Orleans."

"New Orleans? Why?"

"If you'll calm down and stop interrogating me, I'll tell you," Clay growled, black eyes glittering with anger at himself and her. He longed to grab her, haul her into his arms and hold her, but knew he shouldn't want to. And she was acting hostile but she shouldn't be. He clenched his jaw. "Want to hear what I have to say, or would you rather make up your own story, whether it's true or not?"

She glowered up at him. Yet she loved him completely and ached to fling herself against him. Right now she had far too much pride to show how much she cared while he used that sarcastic tone of voice. Jutting her chin out a fraction of an inch, she motioned him toward the sofa.

"I can't stay long. Have to meet someone for dinner," he said, taking the cushion next to her as they both sat down. "I went to New Orleans on another case. Nothing to do with the Shalimar rubies."

She folded her hands primly in her lap. "I see. I was afraid you'd gotten a new lead on Becky and Brad."

"Not yet. That's what I came to tell you."

"Thank you. I'm surprised you want to tell me anything, since you suspect I know where she is and I warn her whenever you get close."

"Do you know where she is?"

"No. If I did, I'd go get her and drag her home myself just to get this mess over with. For her sake and everybody else's."

Eyes narrowing, Clay surveyed her face intently. "You sound convincing, but I know family loyalty can be strong."

"Then you still don't believe me?"

"I'm not sure." After glancing at his wristwatch, he rose to his feet. "I have to go."

They were treating each other like strangers, and Amanda hated that. It seemed as if the closeness they had shared was forgotten; at least he didn't act like he remembered their night in Granada. Hurt twisted through her heart like a knife as she walked him to the door. Even Bossy seemed to sense their tension. Her ears drooped and she watched them with big forlorn brown eyes.

Pausing on the threshold, Clay raised his right hand as if he meant to touch her, but dropped it again. He stepped out onto the porch, saying only, "I'll be in touch."

"Will you really?" she muttered aloud after shutting the door behind him. Feeling terribly alone, she sank down on her knees beside Bossy to give the dog a hug. "Wonder who he's having dinner with? A woman? Could be. There might be lots of women in his life. I don't know." The very thought of him touching another woman made her moan softly as she stroked the dog's fur. Faithful Bossy tried to comfort her with a small lick on her jaw but it didn't help much.

Saturday, Amanda made a decision. The sitting and waiting was driving her straight up the wall. She could stand it no longer. If Clay did get another line on Becky and Brad, she wanted to know it, and since she doubted he'd share that information with her, there was only one thing left to do: she would have to spend time with him, be around in case he got a call. She had an excuse to visit him too. The water main for her street had broken, and she would be without water for at least a couple of days. The more she thought about it, the better the idea seemed. Her plan might not work but it was worth a chance.

As she drove to Clay's house around seven that evening with Bossy on the backseat, sheets of rain lashed the car, flooding the windshield between the rapid swishing of the wipers. Taking it slow and easy, she watched out for other drivers and finally turned safely onto Melrose Street. Pulling into the circle drive, she coasted between the maple trees, which dropped great plops of rainwater down on her car roof. The indoor lights of the rambling stone house shone out cheerfully into the wet, windswept night as she stopped the Mustang, cut the engine, and put on her hat, tucking wayward strands of hair under the brim. For a few seconds, she sat staring at the house. If her plan did work, she and Clay would be in close contact again, and she wasn't at all sure how that would work out, considering the recent tension between them. But there was only one way to find out what would happen.

"Well, here we go," she murmured, grabbing her bag before throwing open her door. She dashed across the slick flagstones beneath the roof of the veranda, but the rain was driving toward the house and hard droplets continued to pepper the backs of her legs as she rang the bell.

"Mandy!" Clay exclaimed when he opened the door and found her there, suitcase in hand, Bossy at her side. "What the devil . . ."

"I'm hoping you'll take us in." She plunged right in, going for broke. "It's an emergency. You see, my street's being repaved and somehow the water main got broken in the process, so I don't have water and it's going to take a few days for the repairs. I thought maybe you'd take pity on the homeless."

Before Clay could answer, Bossy forgot her manners, pushed past him into the foyer and shook herself violently, showering the floor as the wriggle ran from her head to the very tip of her tail.

"Come back here, you old poop," Amanda commanded, clicking her tongue at her. "It's not going to kill you to be a little wet. We haven't been invited yet."

"Oh, get in here," said Clay with some impatience, grasping her by the arm to pull her inside. "Can't let you stand out there and get drenched."

"I thought I could count on you. I hate to be a bother, but none of my friends really have room for me *and* Bossy, and some of them just don't care for animals. But you like them. I would've gone to stay with Mom and Dad but they're still a little miffed at me."

Clay frowned. "You mean they're still mad at you for telling them Becky might have been involved in the robbery?"

"Not mad, exactly. More disappointed, I guess," Amanda explained, spreading her hands resignedly. "They just can't seem to accept that possibility yet, so it wouldn't be all that comfortable for me to stay with them right now. You understand, don't you?"

"I understand more than that," Clay tonelessly replied, eyeing her with more than a little suspicion. "You have another motive for coming here. You want to be around in case I get another lead. Right?"

She grimaced almost comically. "I knew I couldn't fool you. Yes, that's the main reason I came here."

"You can be a very brazen woman."

"When I'm forced to be. I'm not usually this way."

"Couldn't prove it by me," was his dry retort. "What if I won't let you stay?"

"You couldn't be that coldhearted."

"Couldn't I?"

She wasn't sure. His expression told her nothing. But since she had gone this far, it was crazy to stop. Taking off her hat, she allowed her damp hair to tumble down around her shoulders. "You wouldn't send me back out into that terrible rain-storm. The trees are bending over the streets in the wind and you can hardly see to drive. And look at me, I'm already drenched. But if you can't have pity on me, think about poor old Bossy. She's such a sissy. Getting rained on scares her. Surely you can't just toss her out into the cold cruel night."

Clay nearly smiled at the melodramatic performance but caught himself in time. Instead he shook his head while muttering, "I must be out of my mind, but okay, you can stay until they repair the water line. I never want to be accused of being cruel to animals and if Bossy's that sensitive . . ."

"Oh, she is. Aren't you, girl?"

Swishing her wet tail back and forth, the dog managed to look desolate enough to be convincing.

"It's a conspiracy," Clay drawled. "You must have trained her to give that performance on cue."

"Oh, no, she learned that hangdog look all on her own. I guess I've spoiled her too much, because she always acts like a few raindrops falling on her are the worst kind of torture."

"She's not only spoiled, she's very bright. Nobody's fool. She knows how to get precisely what she wants from you."

"And from you too."

He threw up his hands. "Looks that way. You might as well take your coat off, Mandy. Are you wet clear through?"

"Luckily my clothes are still dry. It's just my coat that's dripping."

"You can hang it up over there," he directed, motioning at a wooden coat tree in the corner. "While you do that, I'll pour you a brandy."

When he left her alone in the foyer and Bossy trailed after him, Amanda heaved a deep sigh of relief. She had hoped to convince him to let her stay, but she wouldn't have been all that surprised if he'd tossed her out instead. Glad the worst of the confrontation was over, she stilled her shaky hands and followed him into his study, where he was turning away from the liquor cabinet, two small glasses containing clear ruby red liquid in his hands.

Settling down on the sofa, smoothing the skirt of her midnight-blue dress, she accepted the drink he handed her with murmured thanks and raised her glass as he dropped into the opposite chair. "A toast," she announced with a big smile. "To friends who come to the rescue when needed."

"You can drop the Pollyanna act, Mandy," he said quietly, sitting back to stretch his long legs out in front of him, ankles crossed. "Your eyes never lie. I can tell you really wish you didn't have to do this."

She took a short breath and released it in a sigh. "You're right, I wish I didn't have to. You're very perceptive."

"And you're obviously getting desperate."

"That may be an understatement."

"How are you going to explain staying at my house with me to your parents?"

"I've already told them I might be here a few days."

Clay's eyebrows shot up. "They approve of this?"

"They're desperate too."

"Desperate enough to encourage you to move in with a man? I only met them once, but they seemed fairly old-fashioned, especially where their daughters are concerned."

"They are. But they know they can trust me."

"Fine. But how can they be sure they can trust me?"

Amanda smiled. "I told them they could."

Smoldering coals glinted in the depths of his eyes. "Are you sure of that?"

"Yes," she answered, sipping her brandy. Him, she *could* trust. It was herself she worried about.

Dropping that particular subject for the moment, he

stroked his strong jaw. "This little plot of yours might not work, despite all the trouble you're going to. You have to work during the day, so if I get a lead on Brad and Becky you won't know about it. I could be on a plane and out of the country before you got back here in the evening."

"I know, but I'm hoping you'll get the next lead at night while I am here."

"I might not tell you if I did. I could just wait until the next day, when you're gone, before I take off."

"Don't do that, Clay," she implored, honest anxiety mantling her features. "I have to go with you. And you don't have to worry; I don't know where Becky is, so I can't warn her you're hot on her trail. Really."

"Even if that's true, you shouldn't go with me wherever I do finally go to recover the rubies." He leaned forward to rest his elbows on his knees as he regarded her somberly. "I never should've let you tag along to Bermuda and Spain."

"You didn't have much choice."

"If I had tried hard enough, I could have given you the slip. And I should have. You can't possibly understand the danger involved in a case like this, but I do."

Her clear blue eyes met his. "Bernie Cooper and Juan Alvedero didn't seem like such dangerous characters."

"That's where you're wrong. Men like that put up a good front. They convince the world they're civilized. But they're still criminals, and don't you forget it. Backed into a corner, they'd do almost anything to escape. I didn't think Alvedero would send somebody after me for reporting him to the police, but that was because I figured he knew he'd only make things worse for himself if he tried to seek revenge after he'd already been arrested for possessing the stolen bracelet. But I could've been wrong. What if he'd turned out to be some kind of psycho? What if he *had* hired a thug to burst into my—*your* hotel

192

room, to teach me a lesson? My God, Mandy, you might have gotten badly hurt—or worse!"

His genuine concern touched the very center of her soul. She knew he did care for her to some extent. Yet she couldn't let that weaken her resolve. She owed allegiance to her parents, who were going through pure hell at the moment, and if she could make this disastrous time any easier for them she had an obligation to, if for no reason other than her own piece of mind. Looking steadily at Clay, she swallowed with some difficulty, loving him so much she ached to do anything to please him, yet knowing that in this instance she must follow the dictates of her own conscience.

"I know what you're trying to tell me," she said, her lilting voice lowering. "We might run into danger. But I'm willing to take the risk."

"You may be," he thundered, "but I'm not willing to let you."

She breathed heavily. "Can't you just accept the fact that I'm going wherever you go to look for Becky? It's something I have to do. I've told you that over and over, and it's true."

Uttering an explicit curse, Clay tossed back the last of his brandy, swallowed, and glared at her. But glaring was as useless as he'd suspected it would be. Under his harsh gaze, she remained as determined as ever, her answering gaze never wavering, her deep-rooted resolve written all over her face. Still, for the next half hour or so, he remained tight-lipped while she made conversation. But she was an intelligent woman, her thinking independent, and finally he succumbed, allowing himself to be drawn into a discussion of politics.

"If I hear one more Sunday-go-to-Meeting, Salute-the-Flag, or Don't-Think; Let-Me-Do-Your-Thinking-For-You speech, I may just scream," she adamantly proclaimed. "So many politicians insult our intelligence. We don't have to think exactly the way they do to be patriotic and moral. Especially when some of them don't act all that moral themselves."

"Some of them do get tiresome," he had to agree. "There's one particular senator who makes me grit my teeth whenever he opens his mouth."

They talked on and on for a couple of hours, politics soon losing out to a discussion of their favorite movies, past and present, then favorite books, and at last a heated conversation (they completely disagreed) about which professional basketball team was best all-around and deserved to win the next NBA championship.

Their lighthearted argument ended in a draw, and as a low chuckle rose up from deep in Clay's throat Mandy tried unsuccessfully to stifle a yawn. A quirky smile moved his lips. "If that's a hint that I'm boring you . . ."

"You know you're not. I'm just a little tired, that's all."

"Hard day?"

"Don't ask," she quipped. "I had to wait on triplets this afternoon—a first for me. Twelve-year-old girls, and all three wanted different dresses for their aunt and uncle's silver anniversary party. But their mother wanted them to dress alike. She lost out in the end, but it took forever for the girls to convince her they like to look different sometimes. And besides that, Saturday's always busy at the shop."

"Plus the fact you're worn out from worrying about your sister."

"Yeah, I guess that has something to do with it," she conceded, hiding another yawn behind one hand. "But I am trying to keep everything in perspective."

"Easier said than done. Come on, I'll show you your room," Clay insisted, rising effortlessly to his feet. "I think you should go straight to bed."

Bossy, making herself right at home, preceded them down a

long hallway illuminated by electric lanterns ensconced on the walls. Glancing back at them frequently, she waddled forward.

"You're getting broad in the beam, girl," Amanda said to the dog. "You're going to have to spend less time at your food bowl and more running around."

Carrying Amanda's suitcase in one hand, Clay opened a door on the left with the other, reached in to switch on a light, and bade her enter the room with an exaggerated flourishing gesture.

Amanda stepped across the threshold, eyes alight with appreciation. The decor was country comfortable. All the furniture was early American pine, finely carved, and a hand stitched, patchwork quilt in wedding ring design covered the high brass bed. The rose window curtains matched some of the quilt pieces.

"Oh, this is nice," she said earnestly as he put her canvas bag down on the antique chest at the foot of the bed. And when she saw Bossy sniffing around the room, searching for whatever it is dogs invariably search for in new surroundings, she turned to him. "Mind if I keep her here with me? If she needs to go out she can let me know."

"By all means let her stay. If she has to go, she has to go. We don't want to stop her."

Light laughter bubbled forth from Amanda.

Desire flamed up in Clay.

Her breath caught as his hands spanned her waist and he drew her to him, his lips caressing hers as lightly as the tips of butterfly wings. Her senses swam. She wanted to hold him closer and closer to her, but irrepressible uncertainty about his feelings for her overcame the clamoring, traitorous needs of her body. For a delightful instant, she kissed him back, then made herself pull away, although he released her reluctantly.

She shook her head. "Maybe we should try to be just friends, Clay."

"You're something else," he growled. "You turn up on my doorstep, invite yourself in to spend a few nights, then reject me."

"I'm not rejecting you."

"Aren't you? Sure feels that way to me."

"It's all so damn complicated. If we could just find Becky. I think we will soon. We'll hear from her and—"

"That may just be wishful thinking."

"Yes, but—"

"Good night," he said, and left her without another word.

Standing in the middle of the room, trembling, she watched him disappear. Did he really believe it had been easy for her to say no to him? If he did, he was dead wrong.

CHAPTER ELEVEN

Using the key Clay had given her, Amanda unlocked his front door Tuesday afternoon. Bossy, who had met her on the driveway, nearly knocked the grocery bags out of her arms as she tried to bulldoze her way into the foyer.

"No, girl, you stay out a while longer. You're free here. No fences. Go out in the woods and chase rabbits."

Sighing heavily, the dog gave her a look that seemed to say she was raised in the city and didn't intend to go country— ever.

"Well, you still can't come in yet. Go lie in the grass if you're too lazy to do anything else."

Instead, Bossy flopped down on the veranda and was still gazing longingly inside as Amanda pushed the door shut with her foot. Smiling indulgently at her pet's bid for sympathy, Amanda went into the kitchen, where she put the lopsided bags upon the chopping block in the center of the room. As she unpacked the perishable items, she discovered the bananas were buried under a pile of cans, and wincing, she dug them out. Fortunately they weren't bruised. She put them in the nearly empty fruit bowl on the counter, adding the half-dozen apples and oranges she had bought.

Humming softly, she took peppercorns, cloves, and bay leaves from one paper sack, then removed the corned beef from the bottom of the bag with a smile. She had left the shop in Betsy Ann's capable hands so she could get here early and start the feast she had planned as a surprise for Clay, who'd said he'd be home around six.

Bustling around the spacious kitchen, she found the saucepan she needed and then set to work, softly singing an old love ballad. When she had the meal well on the way, she decided to have a leisurely bath and freshen up before Clay got back. It was a hot, muggy day and she felt rather wilted.

Two hours later, Clay parked his Jaguar roadster in the garage, got out, and was greeted by Bossy, who loped over to him. Bending down, he scratched behind her ears. The dog trotted beside him to the front door. Taking pity on her, he let her into the house, where he was greeted by a delicious aroma. He loosened his tie as he followed his nose to the kitchen. There Mandy was efficiently moving around, lovely and enticing in a sundress with a navy background splashed with red and white flowers. Her golden hair was pinned in a loose chignon on her nape. A wavy tendril had escaped to tickle the back of her neck. She brushed at it with one hand and tried to confine it again but it soon fell back down. Her back to Clay, she didn't realize he had stepped into the room and was watching her, and so he allowed his slow gaze to travel over her from shining oh-so-touchable hair to the narrow-strapped leather sandals on her slender feet. He thought he could go on looking at her forever, but Bossy had other plans and went to her mistress.

Startled when a soft nose prodded her left knee, Amanda glanced down. "How did you get in?" Then she turned around to face Clay, her heart doing a crazy little somersault. Why is the heart so foolish and its actions so uncontrollable? she thought. The question popped into her head but was unanswerable and quickly forgotten as his magnetic black eyes captured hers.

"Something smells great," he said from the doorway. "And familiar."

She nodded. "New England boiled dinner. You mentioned you like it."

"It's one of my favorites."

"I hope you're going to love mine. It's a specialty of my Aunt Audrey. She taught me all the secrets to make it mouth-wateringly good."

Yanking off his tie and shrugging out of his jacket, Clay strode across the threshold. "Water main on your street still not fixed?"

"No. And my neighbors are fit to be tied, believe me."

"Should I believe you? Maybe you do have water at your house again but you're just not telling me."

A shadow crossed over her features as she tensed. "You don't sound very friendly."

"I guess not," he replied brusquely, divisive emotions pulling him in opposite directions. He enjoyed her company; he liked having her live in his house. But he also had a sense of responsibility. He shouldn't do anything to encourage her to stay, because when he got another lead on Becky and Brad, as he eventually would, Amanda shouldn't go with him to find them. If he led her into danger and she got hurt, he'd probably never be able to forgive himself. Meeting her level gaze directly, he shrugged. "But I know you'd do almost anything to help your sister. Even lie."

"Well, I'm not lying now," she uttered, her voice strained. His attitude was both painful and insulting and she couldn't take any more of it. "I'd better go pack my things, take Bossy, and leave. Dinner should be ready in about half an hour. Enjoy it."

He should have let her go. That would have made everything simpler. Yet he couldn't. When she started to march

199

past him, he caught her by the hand. "All right, I believe you."

"Aren't you kind."

"Don't be sarcastic. I'm asking you to stay. Why go home to a house without water?"

"I can do without it for a day or two."

"Mandy, you're just being stubborn."

"Well, you've always said I had a stubborn streak in me." She thrust her jaw out, trying to ignore the sensations building beneath his fingertips feathering the pulse in her wrist. "So you can't be too surprised."

"Not really," he admitted, giving her a slow smile. "But just remember: In this heat, you're going to want to be able to take a shower."

Both his warming smile and his logic had an effect. She opened her mouth to insist she was leaving, but closed it again. The very idea of not being able to bathe in this turgid weather, even for a day or two, made her feel clammy all over. Although a faint frown still etched her brow, she relaxed a little as she tried to make a sensible decision.

"Stay," Clay repeated. "You have to. How can I chase you away after you've made a special dinner?"

She wavered. "Well . . ."

"Besides, now that Bossy's gotten a whiff of that corned beef, she's going to feel very deprived if she doesn't get any."

"Mmm, she'd probably sulk two or three days," Amanda wryly agreed. "All right, you talked me into it. We'll stay."

Only then did he release her hand. As she walked back to the electric range, he rubbed his jaw and shook his head. He knew he should have encouraged her to leave, yet somehow he'd wound up practically begging her to stay. The woman was uncanny in her ability to twist him around her little finger.

When they sat down to dinner a half hour later Clay ate heartily, saying little at first, but showing true appreciation of her culinary talents. Soon he requested second servings of corned beef, carrots, and potatoes.

"More cabbage too?" she suggested. "There's plenty."

"I wouldn't mind a little more, then," he said, taking a sip of red wine. "This really is terrific, Mandy. My compliments to the chef."

"Thanks, but the compliment should really go to Aunt Audrey."

"My compliments to her, too, then."

Nodding, Amanda smoothed the linen napkin in her lap. "What have you been up to today?"

"Is that your way of asking if I've heard anything about Brad's and Becky's whereabouts?"

"No. It's my way of making conversation. You mentioned another case, the client in New Orleans. What's that about?"

"Privileged information."

"Don't be a spoilsport," she admonished, grinning. "I'm not asking you to give me your client's name and address. But surely you can tell me what he lost that he hopes you can find?"

"A wife, for one thing," Clay said, relenting. "*Plus* the three Picassos and two Monets she took with her when she skedaddled out of town. They've been married for over twenty years but it seems she developed a romantic interest in the golf pro at their club. She ran off with him and took the paintings to bankroll their escapade."

"How awful for your client. He must be very hurt."

"Enraged is a better word for it. I get the impression their marriage wasn't what you'd call made in heaven and he's determined to recover the paintings. He doesn't care what happens to her. To quote, 'It'll be a cold day in hell before I want to see that brainless little twit.' "

Sighing, Amanda prodded a tender slice of carrot with the tines of her fork. "Sad, isn't it? Does it bother you sometimes to deal with people who care more about material possessions than they do other human beings?"

"Sure, those are the ones I pity. But not all my clients are like that. Some of them ask me to find family heirlooms that have great sentimental value. And others come to me out of a sense of obligation. For example, the directors of the museum. They were responsible for the Shalimar rubies, and when the collection was stolen, they—"

"No. Please." Amanda hastily raised a silencing hand. "Let's not talk about the rubies. We're having a nice relaxing meal and I don't want to spoil it."

His eyes lifted; locked with hers. He nodded. "Good idea. Anyway, the lady and her golf pro are real amateurs and it's been easy to follow their tracks. I got a reliable tip, flew to New York this morning, and went to the gallery where they had left the paintings to be sold. They'd even given the manager the name of the hotel they were staying in. So I called the police. They picked the couple up and confiscated the paintings as stolen property. My client will eventually get them back."

"And his wife? What happens to her now?"

"It probably depends on whether or not he presses charges."

"Do you think he will?"

"Yes. He seems like a very vindictive man."

"But wait a minute. They're married, so the paintings are as much hers as his. How can she be arrested for taking them, even for trying to sell them?"

"They aren't legally hers. He bought them under his name, as an investment, so she did steal his property."

"How do people make such messes of their lives?" Amanda pensively questioned, then thought of Becky and quickly added, "Forget I asked that."

Clay understood, and steered the conversation in a different direction. "Okay, I told you about my day. What about yours?"

"Not quite as adventurous as yours was, I'm afraid. I didn't track a pair of art thieves to New York or anything like that," she said, smiling softly. "But my triplets did come back."

"The ones who all wanted different dresses the other day?"

"The very same. Seems they decided the selection of preteen fashions in our shop is 'bad as all.' "

Clay laughed. "Whoa. Better decipher 'bad as all' for me. Doesn't sound good."

"Oh, but it is. It's the best. Where have you been, Mr. Kendall? Aren't you up on the latest slang? 'Bad as all' is the same thing as 'super' or 'groovy' or 'the cat's pajamas,' whichever one strikes a bell in your memory."

He pretended to be hurt. "How old do you think I am? 'The cat's pajamas' was way before my time. I do remember super and groovy, though. So the triplets do like the clothes you sell?"

"Enough for each of them to try on everything. But they're nice, polite girls, thank goodness. If they'd acted like brats, I might have gone crazy while they darted in and out of the dressing rooms and made something of a shambles of the whole shop."

"Triplets," he mused, shaking his head. "On a shopping spree. I'm not so sure your day wasn't more exciting than mine. I only had to deal with two amateur thieves."

After they'd finished dinner, they shared chores in the

kitchen, cleaning up and putting pans, dishes, and utensils in the dishwasher. As Amanda adjusted the dial and started the machine, the front doorbell chimed. Excusing himself, Clay went along the hallway to answer the brief sharp rings, with Bossy trotting a step ahead of him, ears pricked up, brown eyes alert, obviously considering herself protectress of his home. A gruff bark erupted from her throat, then subsided into a low purposely menacing growl as Clay opened the door. Patting the dog's head, calming her, Clay greeted the friend standing outside on the veranda.

Following at a more sedate pace, Amanda saw a tall, loose-limbed, curly-haired man enter the foyer.

"Didn't know you'd got yourself a guard dog, Clay," he said, gingerly stepping past the suspicious animal tracking his every move with her eyes. "What's his name?"

"Her name's Bossy. But she isn't mine," Clay explained, glancing back at Amanda. He beckoned her forward. "She belongs to Miss Mills. Mandy, meet Captain Bob Mears. Bob, this is Amanda Mills."

The captain's expression didn't alter a great deal but his hazel eyes did cool a bit as he examined her face. "Amanda Mills? You're Rebecca Mills's sister, right?"

"Yes. I am."

Scratching behind his left ear, Bob Mears turned his attention from Amanda to Clay. "We have to talk. Privately."

Clay inclined his head, looking at her. "Excuse us, Mandy."

She was dismissed. And as the two men stepped into Clay's study, she actually started to walk away, but her mind overruled her feet and she tiptoed back to the door instead and pressed her ear against the panel. She felt like the lowest kind of sneak, but it was necessary for her to hear what was being said inside that room. Becky was her sister, for God's sake! She had every right to know what was happening!

The police captain accepted Clay's offer of a drink. "I'm off duty, so why not? A rye highball'll sure hit the spot. Light on the rye though."

A couple of minutes passed. Outside the door, Amanda almost didn't dare to breathe. She waited, heart thumping.

"Here you go, Bob," Clay finally said, handing his old friend the weak highball. "So? Whatcha got for me?"

"Not a lot, I'm sorry to say. The information we sent out over our computers did find a mark, so to speak. A gendarme in Paris recognized and positively identified Charles and Mills, but by the time he got the go-ahead to bust 'em, they'd already checked out of their hotel."

"Any idea where they might have been heading?"

"I—"

As Mears started to answer, Clay hushed him with a sharp gesture, went quietly across the room, and jerked the door open. Mandy practically fell into his arms, and his hands curled around her slim wrists to balance her. Her wide surprised blue eyes darted up to meet his.

"You might as well come in," he drawled. "Since you're hearing every word anyway."

"Clay, she's personally involved in this case," Mears protested, ruffling his wavy hair. "What the hell do you think you're doing? I'm giving you privileged information and she . . ."

"She's determined to keep on top of this situation," Clay finished emphatically and with an aura of resignation. "How can we stop her?"

The captain's hazel eyes swept over Amanda and he recognized her strength of will. Clay was right. She was no quitter, and he had to admire that quality. And besides, he had no information that would enable her to help her sister outrun the law. He only knew where Rebecca Mills and Brad Charles *had* been, not where they were now.

Squaring her shoulders, Amanda looked at both men, hoping to exhibit a supreme confidence she didn't quite feel. But sometimes appearances are all that count, and this was one of those times, she decided. Her bold gaze challenged the police captain.

He glared back at her a few seconds, and flopped back in his chair with a shrug.

"Sit down, Mandy," Clay suggested. "I'll get you a drink. What would you like?"

"Oh, you don't have to get up. I can get it myself." After pouring a glass of sherry, she rejoined the men, taking a seat on the sofa next to Clay. She swallowed a tiny sip and looked expectantly at the captain. "Before I, uh, came in here, I heard Clay ask if you have any idea where Brad Charles and my sister headed after they left Paris. Do you?"

"You are a spunky one, aren't you?" Mears responded wryly, pulling at his long chin. "The answer's no. The French police didn't pick up a single lead on them. But I thought Clay'd want to know where they had been. He has sources in Paris who won't talk to the authorities, and maybe they'll tell him more."

"There are a couple of people I can call," Clay agreed. "I'll let you know what they say, Bob."

Rubbing the tip of one finger around the rim of her glass, Amanda asked, "How did the gendarme recognize them?"

"Luck, mostly. Our department sent flyers out on your sister and her boyfriend to cities all over the world. Trouble is, police everywhere have the same problems—too many cases to solve and not enough manpower."

"So now Becky's an international outlaw," murmured Amanda. "Incredible."

"Not at all," the captain countered. "Stealing the famous Shalimar rubies isn't quite the same as ripping off a few hubcaps. Many people all over the world want to see Brad Charles and Rebecca Mills caught."

"So I've noticed," Amanda retorted, resentment flaring in her eyes. "But there's something we all should remember: in this country, people are innocent until proven guilty."

"Look, Miss Mills, I can understand your being upset, but don't make it sound like I've decided to be judge and jury in this case. I haven't." Glowering at her, the policeman rumpled his hair with one hand, leaving a couple of tufts standing straight up. "My job is to collect the evidence and see where it leads. This time it led straight to your sister and her boyfriend. The D.A. agreed. A warrant was issued for their arrest, and I just wish my detectives had more time to work on this case. One of the biggest jewel heists of the decade happened on my turf and I don't like that one bit. I'm not going to apologize for wanting to put the prime suspects behind bars. They'll get a fair trial. Nobody's trying to railroad them. If they are innocent, which is very unlikely, they have nothing to worry about."

"How can you be so sure of that, Captain? Sometimes the system doesn't work. Can my sister get a fair trial? All the publicity and—"

"You're right. The system isn't perfect, but it's the best damn one we—"

"Whoa. End of round one," Clay interceded. "Mandy, you know he's only doing his job, and Bob, you just said you can understand her being upset. So let's call a truce. How about it?"

As a cooler head prevailed, Amanda began to calm down. She nodded. "Okay, a truce."

"Right," Mears agreed. He said nothing else for a minute or

two as he nursed his drink, but the expression on his craggy face declared that something was on his mind. At last he came out with it. "Asking questions is part of my work, and I've got one for you now, Miss Mills. Why are you here tonight? Did you come to talk to Clay about your sister?"

"No, actually I'm here as a house guest for a couple of days. You see, the water main along my street is broken and since I didn't have any water, I asked Clay to take me in and he kindly did."

" 'House guest,' " Bob Mears somberly repeated, staring at his old friend. "Forgive me for saying so but the situation is odd. You're trying to catch her sister and she's trying to protect her but here you two are together." He shook his head. "Doesn't add up. Why aren't you staying with your parents, Miss Mills? They live right here in town."

"True, but I decided not to go to them because—well, it's hard to explain, but things have been a little tense between us lately."

"Might as well tell him the whole truth, Mandy," Clay drawled. "The main reason she's here, Bob, is to keep tabs on me in case I get another lead on Becky and Brad Charles."

"Surely you understand how important it is for me to know exactly what's going on, Captain Mears," Amanda added. "Believe it or not, I want to find my sister as much as you do. More."

"But not for the same reason."

"Don't be so sure of that. I want to learn the truth. I hope that's what you want too."

"Yes, ma'am, that's precisely what I want. But the truth might not be easy for you to face."

She gave him a dignified smile. "If the truth turns out to be unpleasant, I'll just have to handle it somehow. Help my parents handle it. And Becky."

Mears put his empty glass aside. Getting to his feet, he softly cleared his throat and smoothed his untidy hair. He stood before Amanda, hesitated a second or two, then cleared his throat again to say quite simply, "Miss Mills, I want you to know I'm very sorry your sister's in trouble."

His sincerity gained her instantaneous respect. "Thank you," she murmured, extending her right hand, smiling faintly as it was lost in the huge mitt of his. "I wish she was home and out of trouble too."

"I know it must be hard on you and your folks. My detectives and Clay have all told me she's never been a problem before."

"Not at all. If you knew her . . . Well, never mind. Maybe this will all work out better than we think."

Mears said nothing, obviously unwilling to offer what he believed would be false encouragement. He turned and flapped out of the study, loose-limbed and gangling as a modern day Ichabod Crane, although conveying far more perceptiveness and common sense. Clay followed him into the foyer, showed him to the front door.

"She's some woman," Bob commented, jerking his head back toward the study. "If I didn't know you better, old buddy, I'd be a little worried. But I guess you won't let her get in the way of trying to find her sister, will you?"

"No."

"She's a very attractive lady."

"I've noticed."

"Great legs. I've got to get out of the office more often, instead of leaving all the excitement to my detectives. Why should they get to question all the pretty women?"

Clay chuckled. "Big talk. Just remember, you're a happily married man."

"Yeah, but that doesn't mean I've been struck blind. I like looking at lovely ladies as much as the next man."

With a departing wink, Bob Mears left and Clay walked back into the study. Staring at her hands in her lap, fingers linked, Amanda clicked the ends of her thumbnails against each other, looking up when he came across the room.

"Your friend seems like a very decent person."

"Bob's the salt of the earth," Clay agreed. "Outside he seems hard as nails but inside . . ."

"There's a heart of gold?"

"Yep. That's a tired old cliché, I know, but it fits him. You made quite an impression on him too, by the way." Clay stopped in front of her. "Freshen your drink?"

"Mmm, maybe a drop or two more," she said, handing him her glass and watching as he poured her a small sherry and added ice to his own gin and tonic. In his shirt sleeves, he had rolled his cuffs up to his elbows, and the white fabric accentuated the mahogany darkness of his sinewy forearms and his strong, lean, long-fingered hands. She watched them move, fascinated by their light touch and fluid surety. Was it acceptable to consider a man graceful? She thought so. Clay certainly was. Every bit as tall as Bob Mears and nearly as slim, perhaps he should have been gangling too, even awkward, but he wasn't. He carried himself with powerful, flowing ease, and when he came back to sit beside her, his muscular thigh brushed against hers. Sexual awareness arrowed through her, causing her heart to flutter.

Fortunately good old Bossy provided a diversion. Waking from a short nap on a wonderfully plush area rug, she sat up and stretched her neck until her black nose was pointing at the ceiling. After a long yawn, she padded over to her mistress and Clay, assuming her well-practiced give-me-a-handout expression.

Clay smiled. "Sorry, old girl, but we aren't eating anything."

"Too bad one of us isn't having a martini," Amanda said, patting the dog's head. "She loves olives."

Laughing softly, he shook his head. "You mean to tell me you've actually given her olives?"

"Well, I was putting some in a salad and she was begging as usual, so I had to give her a couple. I mean, who could resist big brown eyes like that?"

"No wonder she's spoiled. I'm surprised you don't sing her lullabies to get her to sleep at night."

"Oh, don't be silly. I'd never go that far," Amanda insisted, but then had to qualify, "I *did* pat her until she went to sleep when she was a puppy. But she was such a little thing."

"And such a great con artist."

"Yes," Amanda agreed, laughing.

As the dog gave up hope of a tidbit of food and dropped down onto her side at their feet, Clay sat back on the couch. His upper arm pressed against Amanda's and within seconds she was aware of the fact that he was looking at her differently than he had before. Catching her breath, she turned her head and met his gaze. His black eyes were smoldering coals. A wild tremor rushed over the surface of her skin, knifed through her flesh, and opened a clamoring emptiness deep within her. Loving him completely, she wanted him, his touch, his kisses. She wanted to be possessed and to possess. But how crazy that was. He didn't even trust her. He had made that perfectly clear. And she wasn't at all sure she could trust him either. Bad news for any relationship. Her breathing shallow, she resisted temptation and moved forward, perching herself on the edge of her cushion.

A strained coughing sound escaped her lips. She announced as calmly as possible, "Well, I think it's time for bed."

211

"A great idea. Bad as all, as your triplets say," he said, his deep voice rough-edged. "Let's go to bed together, Mandy."

When his persuasive hands encircled her waist she longed to throw herself into his arms, but fought the pulsating need, forcing her mind to rule her heart for her own protection. Pulling away from him, she stood. " 'Night, Clay," she said. Her pace slow, steady, seemingly self-assured, she left the study, then dashed down the hall to her room as if the hounds of hell were in swift pursuit. Bossy trotted along behind her.

Several minutes passed, but the desire throbbing hotly in Clay didn't cool. Passion burned through him. Their one night in Granada, his one night making love with Mandy hadn't been nearly enough to satisfy him. He wanted her again tonight and for many nights to come. And mornings, and afternoons. She was something special. With her, he felt supremely alive, and at this moment he wanted nothing more than to feel that way again. He strode purposefully out of the study. At the end of the hall, he thrust her door open without first knocking. She stood in the center of the room, half un-dressed, her sheer ivory slip clinging to every rounded curve of her svelte body. As she instinctively folded her arms across her chest, his lips lifted in an indulgent smile and he called Bossy out into the hallway.

"Sleep out here tonight, girl," he instructed, then stepped across the threshold and closed the door behind him.

"Clay! I—you—" Amanda gasped, taking a jerky backward step as he moved toward her. "Y-you can't just barge in on me like this."

"Why not? I want you, Mandy, and you want me," he said softly, getting closer. "We need each other."

"No."

"Yes. Oh, *yes*. We do. And you know it." He reached for her.

CHAPTER TWELVE

Amanda darted behind the rocking chair, her heart triphammering against her breasts. Fiery sensations suffused her body with weakening warmth, and abiding love threatened her tenuous hold on self-control as Clay's mesmerizing eyes searched the depths of hers. And when he touched her, his pleasantly rough fingertips skimming over her arms to her shoulders, she trembled, knowing the battle was almost surely lost.

Spotting her purse on top of the chest of drawers, she grabbed it, opened it, and withdrew a check. "I've been meaning to give you this for days but I kept forgetting," she babbled. "It covers my expenses in Bermuda and Granada."

He relentlessly stepped closer. "Later, Mandy."

"No, now! I want you to take it. I don't like to be in debt."

"Okay," he softly said, plucking the check from her fingers and folding it away in his hip pocket. "Now your debt's paid. I have other things on my mind."

Scooting sideways, she put the chair between them again. "Clay, this is a mistake. We should just go on the way we have been."

"I don't want to. I need more than that, and so do you."

"But everything's so mixed-up."

"Not everything. We're attracted to each other. What could be simpler?"

He advanced. She retreated, backing across the room. "Nothing seems very simple to me anymore."

"You're just trying to fight the inevitable, but you might as well give up," he warned, his tone provocative, his smile wicked. "You can't escape me now. I'm not letting you go until I've had my way with you."

A shiver of sheer excitement ran over her and she nearly giggled, as susceptible as usual to his teasing. "You nut," she said. "What turned your motor on?"

"No 'what.' Who. You. Now come here, woman."

With lightning swiftness he reached for her but she jumped back, laughter bubbling up in her as she started to open the bedroom door, calling, "Bossy, help. I'm being attacked by a sex fiend."

Before she could open the door more than an inch, he slammed it shut with the flat of his hand, pure mischief glinting in his eyes as he towered over her. "Bossy isn't going to help you. She knows you're safe with me."

"Huh! She's just a traitor," Amanda retorted, ducking by him once more to dash back across the room.

Then the chase began in earnest, becoming more exhilarating with every passing moment. Caught up in the game, she moved from place to place, always just out of his reach. She was quick, light on her feet, but so was he, and she was almost captured more than once. When she escaped those close calls she suspected he let her get away simply to keep the game going. Laughing together, they played cat and mouse.

"Oh, no!" she squealed, pulse pounding when he managed to grasp the back of her slip. Maneuvering swiftly, she regained her freedom only to trap herself between a wall and one side of the bed. And as Clay stalked around the foot, she had to scurry across the quilted coverlet. Giggling helplessly, she sprinted over to the dresser and paused to catch her breath.

Her cheeks were flushed. Her lovely hair cascaded in golden disarray around her creamy shoulders. He strode purposefully toward her. He wasn't fooled when she tried to fake him out with a small step to the right, and at last she was cornered.

Opening her eyes wide, she pretended to feel faint. "Won't you have mercy?"

"None," he growled.

He was close enough to touch her easily, yet didn't. Instead, he twirled the imaginary ends of an imaginary mustache, his expression theatrically rakish. And when he stripped off his shirt with a wicked flourish, baring his bronzed chest, she had to laugh again. "You are a nut."

"You're a very sexy woman. And you're mine, all mine." Without further ado, he lifted her off her feet, tossed her over his left shoulder, and carried her to bed, dropping her down gently onto the mattress. As he bent over her, her small slender hands drifted up his straightened arms. He smiled, his gaze warm.

"There's only one thing wrong," he murmured. "You have too many clothes on."

"Mmm. It *is* a pretty hot night."

"And it's going to get a lot hotter, lady."

"Sounds wonderful. But there's something else wrong," she whispered, repeating his words. "I'm not prepared. We took a chance in Granada, but I just can't afford to be careless again."

"We won't be. Honey, I made sure I was prepared for this the day after you moved in with me," he told her. "I knew I wouldn't be able to leave you alone."

"Sounds like you believe I could never say no to you."

"Could you?"

"Yes."

"Are you saying no now?"

"No."

"That mean you're saying yes?"

"Maybe."

"Vixen," he groaned as she chuckled. "You enjoy teasing me, don't you?"

"Well, you do your share of teasing, too, and I have to retaliate somehow."

"Speaking of retaliation, this is what you get for leading me a merry chase round and round this room," he threatened, then proceeded to play his fingertips over her rib cage, lightly probing, prodding, tickling.

Twisting and turning, Amanda laughed so much her sides ached and her eyes teared. "Devil!" she gasped. She fought back in self defense, tickling him too, and they tumbled around on the bed until they both collapsed breathlessly.

"Now you've done it," she said, puffing. "I really am hot now."

"You know the best remedy," he challenged, propping himself up on one elbow. "Like I said, you have too many clothes on. Take them off."

Her eyes darkened as they imprisoned his. "I'd like for you to undress me."

"My pleasure."

And hers. As he slowly eased bra and slip straps off her shoulders, his feathering touch was magic. His hard knuckles grazed her skin, sending nerve endings into a frenzy of receptivity. Unhurried, with a most tender regard, he lowered her slip to her waist, unhooked the front closure of her bra, and peeled the sheer lace cups from her firm, full breasts. In the soft light, he visually explored her. His eyes wandering over

216

her were as burning as an actual caress. His strong jaw set, and she cradled his face in her hands.

"You're exquisite," he said roughly. "Such a beautiful body."

"Aw, I bet you say that to all the girls."

"Wrong. You're different, Mandy."

"Special?"

"Very, very special, honey."

Joy sang in her heart, and its precious refrain vibrated throughout her bloodstream. Overwhelmed by emotion, she shot upward into his arms, wrapping her own tightly around him, allowing herself to be truly aggressive with a man for the first time in her life.

And it was a sweet aggression he could hardly resist. Her lushly curved bow-shaped lips found his and he parted them with a tenderly possessive thrust of his tongue to taste the ambrosia deep within her mouth. He kissed her hungrily, and she kissed him back with a longing that equalled his. Her warm, cushiony breasts yielded to the firmer expanse of his chest, throbbing against him.

"I'm hot, so hot, Clay," she breathed, biting the lobe of his left ear. "Take all my clothes off."

"God, I *want* you," he growled, the hardening demand of his plundering lips echoed throughout the length of his body. Explosive passion surged up with aching pressure inside him and he removed her slip, bra, and panties with oddly shaking hands, then tossed each dainty garment away, not caring where it landed.

But when Mandy's slim fingers sought his belt buckle, he gathered together what was left of self-restraint and stilled her hands. "Wait, baby," he said, his deep voice appealingly husky. "You want to be careful. There's a point of no return and we're just about there. If we're going to take precautions we'd better do something about it right now. I'll get what we need. Stay right here."

She released him reluctantly. By the time he returned to the room, she had thrown back the quilt and slipped into bed between the cool percale sheets, clutching the edge of the top one primly up to her chin. When he walked over to her, his eyes alight with desire, she said teasingly, "I've changed my mind. I think you'd better sleep in your own bed tonight."

"Too late for second thoughts. I'm spending all night with you," he countered, kneeling beside her on the edge of the bed, prying her fingers loose from the sheet and lifting her hands to his belt again. "Now it's your turn to undress me."

"My pleasure," she whispered, giving his own words back to him as her adoring eyes surveyed his chiseled face. She unfastened his belt, undid the button on the waistband of his trousers, then lowered his zipper before she stopped, her breath catching.

"Mandy," he said, his tone endearingly coaxing, "you can't feel shy with me."

"I don't . . . but I do feel a little wanton."

"Good. That's what I want you to be—a wanton woman unable to resist me. So take my clothes off now."

She did, then turned back a corner of the sheet to invite him into her bed. And when he slipped in beside her, the heat of his solid male flesh seared through the surface of her skin, warming her to the bone. His firm marauding lips covered hers. He kissed her many times and she kissed him back, vibrantly alive with the keen thrills that arrowed through her. Straining against him, in love to the very depths of her soul, she caressed him everywhere, endlessly, and sighed dizzily as his large hands coursed knowingly over her. He cupped the rounded swells of her breasts in his palms; his fingers toyed with the aroused nipples, tantalizing the topmost tips with brushing strokes and gentle squeezes. Fire radiated from his touch to the center of her being, and as tremors fluttered over her, he took one roseate peak into his mouth, then the other, the pleasant roughness of his tongue drawing on her flesh.

Curving her hands over his slim buttocks, she tangled her legs with his.

"You taste so good," he murmured. "I could devour you."

She wanted him to. Arching up, she raised one hand to cup the nape of his neck and guide his warm lips over the slopes of her breasts again and again. The moistness of his mouth did nothing to cool her skin. She was on fire for him and she was glad, so glad, when his right knee slipped between hers, parting her legs. A wondrous sexual lethargy weakened her and she whispered, *"Clay!"*

"My Mandy," he whispered back, shifting slightly to bend over her. He kissed the tops of her slender feet, her shins, her smooth knees.

She curved her fingers around his aroused manhood, stroking up and down as he traced his lips upward along her inner thighs, back and forth, back and forth between them, tasting her smooth flesh. The balls of his thumbs brushed upward, exploring the very center of hot femininity.

"There," she softly moaned. "Yes."

"Yes," he agreed, fanning his warm breath over her.

With his lips, his teeth, his tongue, he drove her wild. Under his tongue's tender lashing, she writhed in sharply intensifying ecstasy, enslaved by his touch, trying to draw away when it became too exquisite but always arching back upward, needing more. When the shattering flutters deep inside quickened and penetrated more deeply, she moved sinuously beneath him.

"Not . . . like this," she implored, her hands between them guiding him to her. "I need all of you, Clay, now."

"Sweet Mandy," he said huskily, entering her sleek warmth, stroking gently upward as she opened to receive him and their bodies joined.

Clasping the back of his head in her hands, she held him close, feeling blissfully alive, filled with his potent strength. She scattered kisses over the taut tendons in his neck, nibbled on his earlobes, smiling faintly when he trembled in response.

Supporting himself on his elbows, he smoothed her hair back from her face and cradled her face in his hands, brushing one thumb slowly back and forth across her lips. When she lightly caught the tip of his thumb between her teeth, he slipped his other hand under her hips, arching her tighter against him, settling deeper within her, smiling at her soft sigh of pleasure.

"Oh, honey," he whispered. "You feel so good."

"You do too. So very, very good," she murmured, pulling him nearer. "Kiss me again. Kiss me forever. Never stop."

Her parted lips met the caressing pressure of his, and as her tongue boldly toyed with his, teasing and tormenting, he made a gruff tortured sound and possessed her sweet, hot mouth with unrestrained insistence.

His kisses took her breath away, made her dizzy, and she couldn't resist them. Returning them eagerly, she skittered her hands over his broad powerful back, her fingertips etching erotic designs on his skin. He remained still inside her, but for those moments it was enough to be one with him. He caressed her with rousing finesse. She ran her fingers through his thick hair as he bestowed wild, searching kisses on her shoulders, then feathered his tongue over the racing pulse in her throat.

"Your skin's soft as satin," he said softly in her ear. "And you taste like . . . mmm, how can I describe it? Like whipped cream and honey."

She smiled up at him, irrevocably lost in the warm light glowing in his eyes. "You make me sound like a dessert."

"You're as sweet as one but far more substantial."

"If you call me a meat and potatoes kind of woman, I may never forgive you."

He laughed with her but then their laughter faded abruptly. "Mandy," he muttered passionately, his mouth covering hers once more.

And as he began to move within her, she throbbed all over and wound her legs and arms around him.

They did the most sensual things to each other. Alone together in the private world of mutual desire, they delighted each other and shared the heavenly wonder of most exquisite intimacy. Unhurried, bathed in the mellow golden glow of the lamp, they made a night neither of them could ever possibly forget. Every experience was beautiful. There were no limits, and individual minutes melted into one another as time became a continuous superheated flow.

Amanda whispered messages to Clay that she knew she could never have said to any other man. Love made it easy to be free and uninhibited with him. And he was tender, so incredibly tender and caring. He was a demanding lover, determined to evoke her most ardent responses, yet he never sought to take his own pleasure selfishly without regard for hers. She adored him. Intent on heightening her desire to match the level of his, he succeeded, and she gloried in all the ways he went about gaining that success. His every kiss, every caress, every slow thrust of his long hard body made her burn hotter and hotter for him. If he meant to control her completely, he was close to reaching that goal.

Yet controlling her wasn't Clay's objective. He simply couldn't get enough of her. And, in fact, her control over him was as great as his over her, if not greater. Her shapely body, the texture of her skin, the glimmering blue light in her eyes when they met his all fascinated him. Being this close to her, holding her, being held, was an incredible emotional experience made all the better by physical pleasure. With her, quick gratification would never be all he sought. Something much deeper and long-lasting bound them together, and he wanted never to let her go.

Winding her arms upward around his neck, she slowly rotated her hips in small circles, and with a low groan, he plunged deeper, capturing her soft cry of delight in his mouth. Then he lifted his head, his eyes burning into hers. "God, woman, do you know what you do to me?"

"Tell me."

"You . . ." he began, then halted, suddenly at a loss for words. "You make me feel like keeping you in this bed for the rest of our lives."

"Then keep me," she murmured, tugging the ends of hair grazing his nape. "I'm willing."

"Be careful what you say," he warned. "I might take you at your word."

"I certainly hope so." She kissed him, nibbling his lower lip, tasting the corners of his mouth.

Sheathed in her, feeling her responsive flutter to his every possessive thrust, he moved harder and faster. Sensation mounted to near intolerable intensity.

She clung to him, giving with her whole heart and wantonly taking all he gave in return. The flutters he created became an endless acute rippling that pierced her flesh, made her tingle, and caused her senses to swim. She curved her hands over his tight buttocks, pulling him higher and closer as she soared upward toward paradise. Feeling the onrushing inevitability in him, she reveled in his need of her, and then suddenly she was borne up to the sheerest spire of physical bliss.

"Clay!" she cried out, lingering on that keen sharp edge for several seconds before the pulsations rioting in her slowed their throbbing and she began drifting down from the highest plateau of completion.

His own hot release surged explosively from him. "Mandy," he roughly groaned, driving deeper again, then once more, as warm satisfaction spread throughout him, eradicating all sexual tension and filling him with a happiness more intense than he'd ever known.

Amanda couldn't stop touching him. Her lips danced across his wide shoulders. Her hands kneaded the corded muscles of his broad back. He remained above her, his evocative weight not the least bit crushing, yet pressing her down into the mattress. His ragged breathing slowed while hers, too, became more regular, though it still came in tremulous gasps. She loved him so. And when he lifted his dark head to look down at her, she was overwhelmed by the sheer power of that love.

"Clay. Oh, Clay," she whispered throatily, her eyelids fluttering shut.

"Look at me, honey," he coaxed, smiling indulgently when she obeyed and opened her eyes again. "You can't be feeling shy after everything we just shared."

"No, I don't feel shy. It's just that I . . ." Her first declaration of love trembled on her lips but she bit it back, inborn caution keeping her silent. He hadn't mentioned one word about love. If she did, would she risk scaring him away by showing how serious she was? She wasn't willing to take that chance; perhaps the timing would be better later. If she said too much too soon and lost him . . . The thought was unbearable.

"It's just that you what?" he prompted after watching mys-

223

terious expressions play over her delicate features. "Tell me, Mandy."

"I . . . feel wonderful," she answered at last, and it wasn't a lie. A lazy little smile graced her lips. "You seem to have this knack for making me feel good, Mr. Kendall."

" 'Good,' Miss Mills? You mean content?"

"Mmm. Very, very content, Mr. Kendall."

"You're quite talented yourself, Miss Mills, because you make me feel very good and very content too."

"I'm glad."

"So am I," he whispered, withdrawing gently to flip over onto his side, taking her with him. Smiling at the drowsiness softening her lovely eyes, he kissed her flushed cheeks, laying his hand over her breast, as enamored as ever by her resilient softness and heated flesh. After kissing his chin, his neck, his collarbone, she snuggled against him with a sigh. He felt her eyes begin to close. Then the feathery fringe of her lashes lay still upon her fine skin and she fell asleep. For a long time he simply looked at her before finally reaching over to switch off the lamp.

The next day, Amanda faced a new dilemma. Called by a neighbor, she learned that water service had been restored to her street, which meant she no longer had even a weak excuse to remain in Clay's house. Yet, she didn't want to leave him. She knew she would miss him terribly if she did, and she had to keep a close eye on him because he might be able to lead her to Becky. That left her only one alternative: she'd conveniently forget to mention she had running water at her house again. And if he asked her . . . well, she'd worry about how she would answer him when and if that happened.

Her decision made, she ended another day at the shop and drove to Clay's home, noticing as she pulled into the drive that his sedan wasn't in the detached garage. So he wasn't there. She was disappointed, but she smiled as she got out of her Mustang and Bossy galloped across the lush green lawn to meet her. Since Clay never seemed to mind having the dog in the house, Amanda allowed Bossy to go in with her. As they started down the hallway toward the kitchen, the phone in Clay's study rang. Amanda automatically dashed in to answer it, just before his service picked up on the second ring.

"I've got it," she told the woman at the answering service, "and I'll be here all evening." After the woman said good evening pleasantly and hung up, Amanda spoke directly to the caller. "Hello, may I help you?"

"I wish to speak with Mr. Clay Kendall," a man with a distinct Irish accent replied. "Might I talk to him?"

His voice seemed to come from a barrel and static crackled on the line. Hoping he could hear her more clearly than she was hearing him, she asked, "Are you calling long distance?"

"That I am."

"I see. Well, I'm sorry but Mr. Kendall isn't here at the moment. May I take a message?"

"Fact of the matter is, I'd rather be talking to Clay himself," the Irishman admitted. "It's information he's seeking, I hear, and I've a wee bit for him."

Information! About Becky? Amanda tensed, but forced herself to ask calmly, "What is your name, sir?"

"James. James Mulligan. Jamie, t' my friends."

"It's nice to talk to you, Jamie. I'm Amanda Mills, Clay's . . . associate," she fibbed, feeling she must. "And since he's not here right now, you can give the information to me."

"I suppose that wouldn't do any harm, now would it?" Mulligan readily agreed. "It's like this: I hear Clay's out after some very famous rubies that was lifted from a museum."

"Yes, he is," she breathed. "What about them?"

225

"I'm hearing on the streets that they've turned up here in London. Tryin' to find a buyer, the thief is."

"Do you know anything else? Who's trying to sell or who might be willing to buy?"

" 'Tis nothing more than rumors I'm hearing but I believe 'em."

And Amanda believed him. "Thanks so much for the tip, Jamie. I'm sure Clay will want to follow up on it."

"And he should. Would you tell him I'm expecting to see him if he does get to London, Miss Mills?"

"Of course I'll tell him. I'm sure he'll want to pay you for the information."

"Ah, but a couple of ales at the King George pub will do the trick," Jamie exclaimed, adding in a lower tone, "and maybe a tenner or two for the cost of telephoning. Three or four at the most, since Clay's been a pal o' mine these many years."

"Then I know he'll want to see you," she assured the Irishman, smiling to herself. "Thanks so much for calling, Jamie."

They exchanged good-byes after she took down his telephone number, and hung up, but Amanda picked up the receiver again immediately, looked up an international airline in the phone directory, and called to book two seats on the earliest flight to London. After that task was accomplished, she dialed her parents. Her mother answered, the recently developed catch in her voice now all too familiar.

"Mom, it's me," Amanda announced. "Can Daddy take care of the store for me for a while?"

"Something's happened! You've heard from Becky!"

"Indirectly, maybe. I have to check it out, so I'm off to London late tonight," she explained. "So can Daddy take care of the store? And will you come over to Clay's house to pick up Bossy?"

Shirley Mills quickly agreed and arrived at Clay's home less than an hour later. To Amanda she looked worn and weary, years older than she had a few months ago. Deepening wrinkles lined the corners of her eyes and mouth and Amanda could have cried as she handed Bossy into her keeping.

Mrs. Mills gave Amanda a quick kiss on the cheek. "We have to find Becky, but promise me you'll be very careful. I hate to think of you in England all alone."

Pulling away slightly, Amanda shook her head. "But, Mom, I won't be alone. Clay'll be with me."

"You mean he's the one who told you Becky might be there right now?"

"Well, no, he doesn't know that yet."

"Then don't tell him! You can't! You know if he finds her he'll turn her over to the police!"

"Maybe," Amanda softly conceded, dismayed by her mother's agonized tone. "But it would be absolutely useless for me to go to London by myself. I just happened to take the message from one of his contacts there, and if I tried to follow through on my own, I'd get nowhere, fast. I wouldn't even know where to begin. Even if I did, I doubt anybody would be willing to tell me anything."

"But—"

"Mom, Clay's our only chance to find Becky soon," she reiterated, gnawing her lower lip. "We're not investigators, he is. And she's not doing a thing to help us locate her. One letter to each of us in all the weeks she's been gone! She could have been more considerate."

Shirley Mills's nostrils flared. "Yes, she could have, but they don't have a right to throw her into jail because she's been a little thoughtless!"

"If she's arrested, Mom, it won't be for that reason."

"I c-can't—" The older woman's voice broke with a sob as

tears filled her eyes. "I just can't believe y-you think she's guilty. It has to be a big misunderstanding!"

"I hope so."

"Well, if she did do something wrong, you'd better believe it's Brad Charles's fault," Mrs. Mills said weakly, her fingers pressing against her temples. "He's not right for her. Ted and I never approved of him, you know."

"Yes," murmured Amanda, ushering her mother to the front door. "Listen, I'll call tomorrow and tell you what's going on. If you need to get in touch with me, we're staying at the Kensington Royal."

"How long do you think you'll be gone?"

"Until we find Becky or run into another dead end."

"I bet she'll be able to explain everything as soon as you see her." Shirley forced a hopeful smile. "It's all a mistake. I know it is."

After squeezing her mother's shoulder comfortingly, Amanda stroked Bossy's head before letting the dog trot happily out to the car.

Clay saw the station wagon pull out onto the tree-lined road as he slowed down at his driveway. He recognized the woman behind the wheel, though she didn't seem to notice him, and there was no mistaking Bossy sitting up proudly in the passenger seat, the wind fluttering her silky ears. Wearing a small puzzled frown, he parked his sedan beside the vintage Jaguar in the garage and jogged into the house through the terrace doors. Mandy was about to go into her room when he found her, and she turned to look at him when he called her name.

"Oh, good, you're home." She gave a sigh of relief. "I was afraid you'd be late."

"I saw your mother leaving when I came in. Why'd she have Bossy with her?"

"She and Dad are going to take care of her while you and I are in London."

"Oh, are we going to London?" Clay inquired, leaning one hand against the doorjamb as he regarded her solemnly. "I think you'd better explain. Have you heard from your sister?"

"No, but you got a call right after I got here this evening. From Jamie Mulligan. He's heard someone's in London trying to sell the rubies."

"And why did he tell you that?" Clay asked, mild irritation hardening his features. "I told him to contact me personally if he picked up a tip."

"Well he did, but you weren't here. And don't get mad at him for giving me the message. I, uh, told him I'm your associate," Amanda admitted unapologetically. "When he said he had some information for you I guessed it might be about Becky, so I wanted to know what it was. And besides, I thought you'd want the information as soon as possible too."

"So you convinced him to give you the message for my sake?"

"Yes. And mine. Everybody's." She glanced at her wristwatch. "We have to get packed so we can get to the airport and have dinner there before our plane to New York leaves at nine ten. We have a short layover there, then we go on to London. I reserved rooms for us in the Kensington Royal. Hope that's okay. I have a friend who stayed there once. She liked it, and it's not outrageously expensive."

Clay's eyes locked on hers. "You certainly have everything planned, don't you?"

"I knew you'd want us to get there as fast as we can."

"Us," he repeated flatly, straightening to catch her elbow as she started across the threshold. "I don't suppose I could convince you not to go with—" He stopped, shook his head. "No, I guess not."

Stepping her fingertips up his shirt sleeve to his shoulder, she smiled provocatively. "After last night, I thought you might enjoy having me with you."

"Trying to bribe me with sex, Mandy?"

She winced. He wasn't smiling, and her own smile swiftly vanished to be replaced by tight-lipped resentment. "What a rotten thing to say! If you're serious, I—"

"You what?"

"I intend to go to London with you anyway," she vowed, her tone icy. "I won't let a nasty remark keep me here."

"Guess I wasted my time making it then, didn't I, since it didn't do any good?"

Unwilling to be easily appeased, she stared up at him, her hands on her hips. "Maybe you want to think you made that remark just to try to keep me from going, but, if I'm not mistaken, Freud believed people don't say things unless they mean them."

"Freud wasn't right about everything."

"Maybe he was right about that."

"Oh, for God's sake," Clay growled, sighing impatiently as he wiped one hand over his face. "We don't have time to argue about psychoanalytic theory. We have a plane to catch."

"That's what I've been trying to tell you," she snapped, and stepped into her room, shutting the door in his face.

Stuffing his fists into his trouser pockets, he stalked down the hall and entered the master bedroom, muttering to himself under his breath. She was an impossible woman in some respects. So damn stubborn. Maybe he shouldn't have asked her if she was trying to bribe him with sex, yet he'd had to follow the impulse, in case it convinced her to stay here out of danger. Of course it had done nothing of the kind. He should have known anger would only make her all the more determined to accompany him.

"Okay, you made a mistake and opened your big mouth. Now she's mad as hell," he mumbled as he pulled a leather suitcase out of his closet. The crazy part of it was, she was right. He did want to take her with him to London, or anywhere else he might go, for that matter. Yet a trip abroad with her would have been so much better had the circumstances been different. He didn't want her walking into danger, but at the same time, he didn't want to leave her here either. Laying the suitcase on his bed, he unzipped it with a disgruntled sigh. She mixed up his head in a way no other woman ever had.

CHAPTER THIRTEEN

The following afternoon Amanda took a nap after lunch, hoping to get her biological clock in tune with London time. She awoke about two, much refreshed, stretching lanquidly as she got out of bed. London was cooler than Richmond had been, quite comfortable. After rubbing her eyes, taking care not to smear her mascara, she once again admired the room she'd been given. No motel-chain plastic decor here. The furniture was ornately carved, a small settee and matching chairs cushioned in blue and gold brocade. And the walls were actually covered with silk. Old-world charm—she loved it. She got up to go look at herself in the oval mahogany framed cheval mirror. Her hair was something of a mess. As she combed her fingers through it and smoothed it down, she noticed for the first time the cream-colored piece of paper reflected in the glass as it lay just inside the door that separated her room from Clay's.

Her appearance forgotten, she hurried to pick the paper up. As her eyes scanned over it quickly her jaw set. The message on it was short but not too sweet, in her opinion. It read simply, *Jamie still hasn't returned my call. I know a few of his haunts so I'm going to check them out and try to find him. You stay in your room and out of trouble. Back soon. Clay.*

"Damn it," she swore, wadding up the slip of fine vellum hotel stationery in her fist. She should've known better than to trust him. He'd deliberately deceived her by acting as tired out by jet lag as she was after lunch. And she had bought his act.

"Ninny," she berated herself. "Should've known he'd give you the slip if he could!"

Although she realized one of his motives for wanting to go it alone was to keep her out of danger, he had no right to make that decision himself. If she was willing to take a few risks for her sister and her parents, he should respect her feelings.

Where was he now? Had he located Jamie Mulligan? If so, what new clues had the Irishman been able to give him? Could Clay and Scotland Yard be closing in on Becky and Brad right now? Maddening unanswerable questions tied her stomach in knots. Had she come all this way, tried so hard, only to be denied the chance to be there for her little sister when she needed her most? An awful thought. Angry as she sometimes was at Becky for getting herself into such a tangled mess, love and family loyalty still held sway in her heart. No matter if Becky was guilty, no matter how foolish—even stupid—she had been to get involved with a cad like Brad Charles (or whatever his real name was), Amanda couldn't simply divorce herself from the problem. Family is family, and sisters remain sisters forever, no matter what.

Hot stinging pressure built up behind Amanda's eyes, making her head ache a little and her nose burn. She needed to cry but refused to succumb to tears out of sheer obstinacy. What good would crying do? She was disappointed in Clay. He knew exactly how she felt, yet showed so little regard for her feelings. And she had begun to hope he truly cared about her.

"Ha!" she muttered aloud as that silly hope dwindled.

Lost in thought, she was startled when the phone in Clay's room started to ring. She reacted quickly, dashed over to unlock and open her adjoining door, and breathed a sigh of relief

233

when she found his open a crack. She picked up the ornate gold-trimmed receiver on the third ring and answered breathlessly.

"Would that be you, Miss Mills?" an Irish voice came back.

"Oh, yes, Jamie. It is."

"Might I speak to Clay?"

"He isn't here. He's out looking for you, as a matter of fact."

"At the King George pub for one place, I'll wager. Haven't had a moment to stop in there today. Would you be expecting Clay back soon, Miss Mills?"

"I don't know when he'll be back."

"It's something important I have to tell him. And it can't wait long."

"Then tell me," she quietly encouraged. "What is it?"

"It's a man I contacted this very morning. He knows more about the rubies than I do, and he said he'd meet Clay in Kensington Gardens at three o'clock because it's close to your hotel. But with Clay not being there . . ."

"I can meet him," she said firmly. "Just tell me where."

Jamie hesitated for several moments before saying, "I don't know about this, miss."

"Where?"

A long sigh came over the line. "Near the statue of Peter Pan, close to the lake."

"How will I recognize him?"

"Let me see now. I was speaking to him not more'n an hour ago and he was wearing navy blue pants, a tan jacket, and a white shirt, I'm thinking. Blond hair."

"Fairly young, then?"

"Thirties. Oh, and Miss Mills, he'll be wanting to be paid for the information."

"Of course. How much do you think?"

234

"Twenty, twenty-five pounds."

"Fine. Thanks so much for calling, Jamie," Amanda said sincerely. "As soon as I see Clay I'll tell him, and I know he'll be seeing you. You've been so much help."

After saying good-bye, she hung up and rushed back into her own room to pull on the first dress she could grab from her closet, a sleeveless, V-neck, cotton knit sheath. It was already twenty past two, so she only gave her hair a lick and a promise with the comb as she moved in front of the mirror. Since she didn't know her way around Kensington Gardens, she knew she had to be on her way. She couldn't afford to miss this rendezvous with an informant who might eventually lead her to Becky.

Ten minutes later, she passed the Albert Memorial and entered the famous grounds. The carefully manicured lawns were a lush green, and the magnificent formal gardens offered a dazzling display of flowers of every imaginable color. Scarlets and pinks, violets and blues, yellows and whites and ivories colored the varied blossoms, and sweet perfume filled the air. But Amanda had more than scenic beauty on her mind. As she walked along a pathway, she stopped a young woman pushing a pram and asked the way to the statue of Peter Pan. She found the statue flanked by thick shrubbery just as her watch read five to three.

Time seemed to drag past, although no more than ten minutes actually went by before she saw a blond man in navy pants and a white shirt approach. He didn't fit Jamie's description precisely—no tan jacket, but he might have shed that in the warmth of middle afternoon. He examined the sculptor's representation of Peter Pan for several moments, then glanced in Amanda's direction as if he knew she was watching him. His eyes held hers.

It had to be him. The informant. Gathering in a deep calming breath, she walked over to him. "Hello," she murmured, her voice husky despite her attempt to sound completely at ease. "Jamie sent you?"

"Perhaps."

The man was cautious. She couldn't blame him, and managed an understanding smile. "Jamie said you'd be here. I'm glad you came. How about twenty-five pounds?"

"Sounds reasonable enough."

"Wonderful. Why don't we go to my hotel?" she suggested, suddenly harboring a hope Clay would be there when she returned with the man. She needed his help. Questioning informants was his line, not hers. She motioned toward the path. "Ready to go?"

"Yes. But not to your hotel room, miss," the blond man replied, his words cool and precise. "The name's Ashford, Inspector Ashford, and I'm placing you under arrest."

Amanda gasped. Her eyes flew open wide and she tried to pull free when the man abruptly gripped her forearm. She spluttered.

"Come along quietly, miss."

"What is this?" she exclaimed, dragging her heels. "Under arrest for what?"

"Soliciting, miss, what did you think?"

"Soliciting!" She felt dizzy as realization struck her and she shook her head emphatically. "Oh, but you can't think I'm a—"

"You named a price," Ashford said. "We've been getting complaints that some of you, er, ladies were beginning to work the gardens. Can't have that now, can we, miss?"

"Oh, but I—but—This is a misunderstanding," she babbled. "If you'll just let me explain—"

"Explain to the sergeant at the station house, miss."

"But this is ridiculous! You can't do this. I'm an American!"

That weak argument cut no ice. The inspector herded her along the path.

Strollers were staring. Amanda ducked her head, mortified. She had never been so embarrassed in her whole life, but enough of her intrinsic pride remained to make her stiffen as they left Kensington Gardens and started down Bayswater Road. She said coldly, "You don't have to hang on to me as if I were a dangerous criminal. Let me go. I'm coming peacefully. I just want to make a phone call when we get to the station. Then you'll find out what a big mistake you've made."

The inspector smiled disbelievingly, but he did release her arm. In less than five minutes, she was standing before a weary-looking sergeant, trying once again to explain her predicament. He wasn't impressed by her story either, and before she knew it, she was being relieved of all personal items. Demanding to make one call, she phoned the hotel, nearly weeping when she heard Clay still hadn't returned. She had no choice except to leave him a desperate message, but even then she had to ask the sergeant, "Exactly where am I?"

He was clearly taken aback. A frown creased his broad florid brow. "Kensington police station, miss. Haven't you ever been arrested in London before."

"Of course not! I just got here yesterday."

"Bloody bad beginner's luck in a new city, wouldn't you say?"

Disgusted, mad, frightened, Amanda refused to attempt to explain again. Instead she relayed her location to the desk clerk at the Kensington Royal, his tone of voice clearly conveying distaste.

The holding cell they put her in was clean and comfortable enough, though Spartan, and painted a dull gray. There were

237

only two other occupants, one teenage girl sound asleep and a stringy middle-aged woman who flashed a smile with one front tooth missing when Amanda sank down on the bunk across from hers.

"I'm Amber. Me mother named me after that'un in that book," she announced friendlily. "What's your name, luv?"

"Amanda."

"What'd they pinch you for?"

"I—uh, it's all a mistake. It'll be straightened out soon, I'm sure," Amanda said, trying to convince herself more than anyone else. But at least Amber was somebody to talk to. "Why are you in here?"

"Got nabbed tryin' to lift a gent's wallet. Not as quick as I used to be," the woman admitted, grimacing. "But I've only been pinched once before so I'll get off light."

Smiling weakly, Amanda nodded.

"You don't look so good, luv," Amber added. "Have a fever? Your face is red enough."

"Not surprising. I sure am embarrassed."

"Your first time in jail, is it?"

"Thank God, yes, and I hope my last."

"Oh, it ain't so bad if you don't have to stay too long."

"Right, and if I'm lucky they'll be letting me out in an hour or so."

"You're American. My daughter, she married a G.I. two years ago. They live in Phoenix, Arizona. What's it like there?"

"I'm sorry, I don't really know. I've never been to Phoenix. I've heard it's a very nice place though."

"I'd bloody well like to go for a holiday. Meg—that's my daughter—she writes me letters that make me think she's lonely sometimes, living in a strange country. And I guess she misses her old mum."

238

"I'm sure she does," Amanda said, smiling kindly at Amber as the woman lay back down on her bunk and closed her eyes, apparently ending the chat for the time being. The sudden silence in the holding cell seemed to gather in a pall around Amanda, and with an exasperated sigh she sat back against the wall, her fingers nervously plucking at the nap of the rough blanket beneath her.

How had she landed herself in such an outrageous situation? It really was preposterous. She'd like to kick Inspector Ashford for jumping to conclusions about her. Okay, what she'd said to him had sounded incriminating, but if he'd just given her half a chance to explain she could have cleared everything up. Of course, her appearance had probably worked against her. She hadn't taken much time on her hair before going to the gardens and maybe it looked provocatively tousled. And excitement had warmed and colored her cheeks, so perhaps she looked as if she had trowelled makeup on as a come-on to men. Even so, he should have been willing to listen to her explanation. She didn't give a hoot about the complaints the police were getting about "ladies" working the gardens. None of that had a thing to do with her, and she couldn't wait to tell someone, *everyone,* in no uncertain terms that she was mad as hell.

As it turned out, she had to wait quite a while to say anything to anybody. Amber and the teenager slept, and the seconds crept by like hours as Amanda stared at the barren walls and locked door. Finally after an hour and a half the door opened. When Inspector Ashford motioned for her, she wasted no time getting to her feet and following him down a narrow corridor.

"Someone to see you," he barked, leading her into a small frosted-glass cubicle.

The instant she saw Clay, she uttered a cry of welcome and

started toward him, then stopped short, noticing his stony expression. After the inspector withdrew, Clay pointed silently to a straight-backed chair, and she perched herself on the very edge. He remained standing.

"Do you mind telling me what in blue blazes is going on?" he snapped, his eyes chips of black ice. "How the hell did you manage to get arrested for hustling?"

She jerked her head up proudly. "If you'll quit snarling at me I'll tell you."

"Start now, and it better be good."

Words tumbling out in a rush, she told him about Jamie's call and the man Clay was supposed to meet at three in Kensington Gardens. And how, since he wasn't around, she'd decided she'd better fill in for him rather than risk their missing possibly valuable information. "Jamie told me what the man looked like, and Inspector Ashford fit the description, so naturally when I saw him, I walked over."

"To the wrong man!"

"He fit the description almost perfectly! And he was in the right place at the right time!"

"That's debatable, don't you think?" Clay drawled sarcastically. "It's safer to say you were in the wrong place at the wrong time. And what, exactly, did you say to the inspector?"

"I asked if Jamie had sent him."

"And?"

"Well he didn't say yes or no, but I thought he was just trying to be careful."

"That's what you get for thinking. I understand you mentioned money?"

"Well, yes, twenty-five pounds, because that's how much Jamie said the informant expected. I wasn't asking the inspector for money. I was offering to pay it."

Clay raised his eyebrows. "That's worse."

"Not funny," she heatedly retorted, her own eyes flashing. "Are you going to try to be a comedian or are you going to try to get me out of this silly mess?"

Jaw clenched, he stared down at her. "I'll do what I can."

"Think you could convince them to let me stay in this room while you straighten things out?" she asked hopefully, her voice wavering a little. "I don't want to go back to the cell."

"I'll try. All this may take a while though," he said tonelessly. "And if I can't persuade them to release you, I'll find someone to represent you in court."

"Clay!" she exclaimed, his words causing her stomach to take a sharp dip. And when he didn't bother to answer and walked out the door, he wasn't doing a thing to help assuage her fears. Through the frosted glass, she saw two silhouettes. She heard men's muffled voices—one was Clay's, that much she could tell. But she couldn't understand what was being said. Then the locked clicked and she heaved a sigh of relief, knowing he had at least been able to convince them not to put her back in the cell.

Another long hour passed. Amanda paced back and forth across the tiny cubicle, biting her lip, unable to sit down and be still. At last, when the door opened once more, she was given her freedom and found Clay waiting for her at the sergeant's desk. Neither said a word while she retrieved her personal belongings. Then a sheepishly smiling Inspector Ashford approached and lightly touched her arm.

"Sorry for the inconvenience, Miss Mills," he apologized contritely. "My mistake."

"Yes. And I'm not in a very forgiving mood at the moment. One more thing: if you'd been right about me, my price would've been much more than twenty-five pounds," she replied, and marched with dignity out of the station house.

Outside, Clay hailed a cab. During the ride back to the

Kensington Royal he maintained a silence that kept her on edge. Several times she opened her mouth meaning to speak, only to close it again. Her nerves were stretched close to breaking point when she unlocked the door to her room a few minutes later and Clay strode inside after her, his features rock hard.

She felt his eyes boring into her back. Rubbing her own eyes, she tossed her purse onto the bed and turned around to look at him, clasping her hands together in front of her. "Thanks for rescuing me. How did you talk them in to letting me go?"

"It wasn't easy. I had to call Bob Mears in Richmond. He wasn't in, so we had to wait for him to return the call. He verified our purpose here and told Inspector Ashford he was sure your story about expecting to contact an informant in the gardens was true. You're damn lucky he backed you up, Mandy."

"I know and I'm grateful."

"You should be." With one long ominous stride Clay advanced toward her. "What the devil's the matter with you? Why didn't you stay here and out of trouble like I told you to?"

"Because Jamie called! And you weren't here. But the informant expected to meet *somebody*. So I went!"

"And approached the wrong man."

"But he fit Jamie's description!"

"Amateur," Clay said, caustically. "The first thing you learn in this business is, if you're meeting a snitch, you let him come to you. You don't go to him."

Her chin jutted out. "All right, all right, I *am* an amateur. I admit I don't know much about how an investigation should be conducted. But I did what I thought I should. I'm trying to find my sister, for heaven's sake! What else do you expect me to do?"

"I expect you to have sense enough to know when you're in over your head. What if you'd approached some man who wasn't a policeman and mentioned money, and he'd gotten the same idea? Would you have let him come back here with you to the hotel? What if he hadn't taken no for an answer when you realized what he expected from you?"

"That didn't happen."

"It could have."

"Then I would've handled him somehow. If nothing else, I know how to scream."

Clay muttered a series of curses, and his jet eyes impaled her. "Don't be naive, Mandy. Some men aren't deterred even when a woman tries to scream. They get violent, stop her screaming, and . . ."

She gulped, knowing what he said was true. But the way he said it caused her hackles to rise, and she said, squaring her shoulders, "Okay, you've made your point, but do you have to be so nasty about it?"

"Yeah, if that's what it takes to get through to you."

"Oh, go away," she said, hating to argue with him, a tight ache squeezing her chest. She'd had just about all she could stand for one day, and fighting with him was more than she could bear. She loved him, so his harshness hurt. With a flick of her wrist, she motioned him toward the door. "Just leave. I want to rest awhile. I'm tired."

"I guess so. It's not every day a woman like you gets arrested for hustling."

"Still not funny," she muttered, a knot of tears that needed to be shed gathering hotly in her throat. "You can take your cruel sense of humor and leave me alone."

"Gladly. You just be sure to stay in this room and keep out

243

of any more trouble," he commanded, stepping across the threshold of their adjoining doors then slamming his door behind him. He went to the center of his room, stopped, and stared at the floor, shaking his head. Before Becky Mills had decided to please her boyfriend and become a jewel thief, before he had met Mandy, his life had been relatively simple. It no longer was.

CHAPTER FOURTEEN

They had to wait all the next day to hear from Jamie again. Clay couldn't locate him anywhere, and each time he hung up the phone after trying yet another place, he felt more frustrated. He was close to recovering the rubies, he was sure of it. It was such a strong hunch he wanted to act on it, but until Jamie contacted him again, there was nothing to do. All his other sources in London said they'd heard only that the Shalimar collection was in the country. Only Jamie—and his informant—knew more.

In her room, Amanda tried to read, but the book she'd started didn't hold her attention. Unable to concentrate, she could scarcely figure out the plot or remember the names of the main characters, and after reading one page over three times before realizing it, she slammed the book shut with a sigh of disgust. Rising from her chair, she wandered around the room, aimlessly inspecting a brass statuette here and a picture there, stopping in front of the cheval mirror to examine her reflection. A wispy curl of hair curved over her left temple. She touched light fingertips to it, then smoothed the skirt of her lemon-yellow dress. Although she had never been particularly claustrophobic, she felt as if the walls of the room were closing in. She hated being trapped in this hotel but was determined not to leave unless Clay did, and he seemed equally determined to stay put until Jamie got in touch again.

According to Clay, the smartest thing to do was to patiently sit and wait for further contact.

But Amanda's patience was wearing as thin as her nerves. Something deep inside her told her she would soon be seeing Becky again, for better or worse. Turning away from the mirror, she looked back at the book she had left on the chair and heaved another disgusted sigh. Exciting as the novel probably was, it was wasted on her at the present time. Yet she had to do something with the time other than twiddling her thumbs. It didn't help that she and Clay had said no more than a few words to each other since morning. They had even had lunch separately, courtesy of room service.

"Okay, Mr. Kendall, enough is enough. I don't care if you're still mad at me. I have to talk to somebody or I'll go stir-crazy," she said aloud, opening her adjoining door. She knocked once on his door and when she heard his muffled response, she turned the gleaming brass handle and stepped into his room.

Propped up against pillows in the middle of his bed, he looked up from *The Times* of London crossword puzzle. With a wry twist of his lips he tapped his pencil against the paper and laconically inquired, "Know a five letter word for 'boredom'?"

"Yeah. 'Hotel.' "

He almost smiled. "I think it must be 'ennui.' It fits."

"I'm sure it does. But that must be the easiest answer in the whole puzzle."

"It is."

"Even so, I still think 'hotel' is a better answer at the moment."

"Bored, huh?"

She lifted her eyes heavenward. "That's putting it mildly."

He crooked one finger, beckoning her to him, then patted

the edge of his bed. "Come here. After I get past the easy words in the puzzle, I can use all the help I can get. *Times* crosswords are notoriously tricky."

Eager to do anything to help pass the time, she walked over to sit down beside him on the bed. During the following hour or so, they consolidated their knowledge, disagreed on some definitions, agreed on other clues, and finally, after several messy erasures, finished with only four spaces of one word unfilled.

It was after three o'clock when Clay consulted his wristwatch.

Seeing the shallow frown that nicked his sun-bronzed brow, she sensed his mood, experiencing the same impatience she knew he felt. Tense once more, she balled up her right hand, her nails digging into her palm as she asked, "What now?"

Clay shrugged. "Guess we might as well play a few hands of poker. If you're willing?"

"Sounds fine to me."

"Just remember, I won't be such an easy mark this time. I know you're a card shark," he warned her, nearly smiling again. "Now that I know I'm up against a semipro, I won't let myself be flimflammed."

"I don't try to flimflam people," she drawled, grinning. "It's just that I'm an exceptionally good poker player. So beware."

Facing each other across a round, ornately carved table, they took turns dealing, and winning, hands. True to his word, Clay strove to match her expertise now he knew she was no novice at this particular card game.

"Three of a kind," he showed her once.

"A flush," she told him, showing her hand. "Sorry."

"Two pairs," she said later.

"A straight," he countered, displaying a six-high straight.

As time passed and they exchanged wins on a fairly equal basis, she dealt the cards once more. "This is it, okay?" she suggested. "Whoever wins this hand is the champion?"

Nodding agreement, Clay discarded two cards and was dealt two new ones. His expression inscrutable, he surveyed his hand, and looked at Mandy. "What do you have?"

She grimaced comically. "One lousy pair. Threes."

"Then I win, but not by much," he conceded, showing a lowly pair of fives. Then he shrugged. "But that still makes me champion. Right?"

"Yes, O Master of Poker," she drawled, bowing from the waist. "I salute you."

Clay's answering smile slowly faded.

Her smile did, too, as they looked at each other and reality struck them both again. She took a deep shuddering breath. "Why doesn't Jamie call?"

"He will eventually. But I'm not sure the informant he found will be willing to meet me, after yesterday's fiasco."

"Well, you weren't here when Jamie called, so you wouldn't have been able to meet him anyway," she replied defensively, her delicate features set. "So don't try to blame me for what happened."

"If you'd stay'd in your room like I told you to, you—"

"You're not my boss! I'm not a slave, subject to your every order. You'd better remember that, Mr. Kendall."

"How could I forget, Miss Mills?" he retorted, his sensuously shaped lips thinning. "You've been a thorn in my side since the day I met you."

"Is that a fact? Well, you— You're a—" Her words halted abruptly. She didn't know exactly what sort of names she wanted to call him, and as they sat glowering at each other, she realized she didn't want to call him anything nasty at all. Bickering served no purpose whatsoever. Each time they argued she ended up feeling miserable, and since she already felt like inner tension was close to tearing her to pieces she didn't want to make things worse. Rubbing away the shallow furrows that marred her smooth brow, she softly suggested, "Truce?"

"Truce," he accepted huskily, looking at her. Needing her.

Staring down at the table, she began to shuffle and reshuffle the deck of cards, lifting her shoulders in a quick shrug. "You know," she began solemnly before taking another deep breath, "I've been thinking. I mean, I got arrested yesterday simply because I said the wrong things to Inspector Ashford and he assumed I was trying to hustle him. But I wasn't, which seems to me to prove that things aren't always what they seem."

Clay nodded. "That's true."

"Then you agree? All the clues that point toward Becky's being a jewel thief might not amount to a hill of beans. I was innocent yesterday, so maybe she's been innocent all this time too."

"Mandy, don't try to con yourself," he murmured, sensing her hope, emotionally wanting to encourage it while mentally knowing he couldn't countenance the idea of raising any hopes that exceeded the boundaries of his own professional common sense. Sadly, he shook his head. "What happened to you yesterday isn't anything like the trouble Becky's in. As you said, Ashford jumped to a conclusion about you, without any concrete evidence. But the evidence against Becky is much more damning."

Weary as she was, that was the last thing Amanda wanted to hear. She stood and took a step away from the table and Clay, brushing a hand over her hair. "If that's all you have to say, if you can't be more open-minded, I think I'd better go back to my room."

"No. I'm not going to let you go," he whispered roughly,

catching both her hands in one of his as he leapt to his feet. His other hand cupped her delicate jaw, tilting up her small chin and forcing her to meet his darkening eyes. "Mandy, I want you. *Need* you."

"No!" she gasped before her breath was taken away as his warm plundering lips descended upon her own, claiming their sweetness with dizzying demand. She resisted. "Clay, making love isn't the answer to everything."

"Quiet. Don't talk," he insisted, kissing her again and unzipping the back of her dress.

He was so boldly demanding she never really had a chance —and didn't really want one. As his hands roamed over her bare back, unhooking her bra in their leisurely travels, the touch of his flesh upon her own ignited raging fires she couldn't hope to extinguish.

"Oh Clay," she murmured against his deep-plundering lips, swaying against him, her knees suddenly weak. Giving him back kiss for kiss, she cooperated as he took off her dress removed bra, leaving her clad in only her sheer half-slip. She stepped out of her shoes while unbuttoning his pale blue shirt, and when he gathered her close in his arms, his hair-roughened chest tickled her naked breasts.

"I have to have you," he whispered, and took her to bed.

Lying atop the coverlet, she watched as he stripped off all his clothes and dropped down beside her to remove her slip. His fingers slipped beneath the waistband of her panties and drew them slowly down.

"Help me," he commanded hoarsely.

Amanda raised her hips, encouraging him to eliminate that last remaining barrier of clothing between them. She felt surrounded by warmth as he surveyed her nakedness.

In the late afternoon light, her satinesque skin shimmered, and looking at her was a pleasure beyond belief. Yet, he wanted to touch every fine pore, too, and to taste every sweet inch of her. Cupping the arousing weight of her ivory rose-tipped breasts in his palms, he bent over her, blowing softly in her ears, nibbling the tender lobes until he made her tremble.

"I could devour you," he proclaimed, unmanageable passion singing through his bloodstream, as his thumbs toyed with her lovely nipples, arousing them.

"Oh, yes, Clay, I . . ."

He captured her words in his seeking mouth as he once more took possession of hers, parting her succulent lips wider, groaning softly as her honeyed tongue parried the proprietary thrusts of his.

It was as if it had been weeks, even months, instead of only two days since they had last made love. A mutual hunger consumed them. They moved sinuously together upon the bed, neither of them able to get close enough. He always delighted her, but this time the ecstasy was even more intense, her womanly response more primitive, her love for him without beginning or end.

Her fresh fragrance made him crazy, as did the creamy smooth surface of her skin and the silky texture and slight bounce of her golden hair.

"I may never let you go. And I have to taste you here." His mouth closed hungrily over the swollen crest of her left breast. "And here." He drew upon the sweetness of its twin. "And here." Lowering his head, he traced the end of his tongue around and into the shallow bowl of her navel, a pleased smile curving her lips as her fingers tangled feverishly in his hair.

Enslaved by each other, they exchanged long urgent kisses that thrilled them both. Amanda felt the rapid beating of his heart against her yielding breasts even as her own heart thudded wildly. Adrift together in a special private realm of electrifying sensations, they held each other, knew each other, gloried in the bliss they shared. She plied him with intimate caresses, loving the power of virile manhood stirring against her curving palms. Breathless, she saw his sun-browned hands play between her thighs, creating deep plunging ripples that originated in her very center and radiated everywhere. He touched her with such reverence and tenderness that her love for him doubled and redoubled. With a surer knowledge of her, understanding exactly what she liked and how to arouse her desire to a fever pitch, he unhurriedly caressed her as she caressed him.

His breathing ragged, he moved between her shapely legs as she parted them for him. Opening them wider, he lowered himself. Her heels pressed tightly against his hips and as she gazed up at him, her honest blue eyes soft, he smiled gently and made her body one with his.

He was inside her, where she had ached for him to be, and she welcomed him joyously, raining lingering kisses along his neck and across his wide shoulders.

Controlling his driving need, he loved her slowly, giving back in full measure as much as he received. Her body was a temple in which to worship—and worship he did, with his hands, his lips, all of him.

Soon, so soon, she was caught up in a dizzying swirl of keen sensation, holding her breath as she waited . . . waited. Clay withdrew, shushing her soft protest. She relaxed against him as he smoothed her hair back from her face, kissed her, then kissed her again, entering her once more.

She clung to him as they moved in perfect synchronization, heightening mutual rapture until . . . until . . .

"Clay, *yes,*" she cried out, stiletto sharp fulfillment finding its ultimate peak, crashing through her in cresting waves. And as his body trembled, she knew he joined her in keenest completion. For a long moment, his breathing ceased and he stroked deep, deeper, within her. Then together, they relaxed in the magnificent aftermath, arms and legs intertwined, the coverlet beneath them atangle.

Basking in a warm glow, they cuddled. He ran one hand over her back, massaging, kneading supple muscle. She drew her fingertips around over his chest, nails catching occasionally in the fine covering of dark hair. She smiled secretly to herself. She'd never known being in love could be this sweet.

"Sexy lady," he whispered after their breathing returned to a more normal rate. "I just can't seem to keep my hands off you, Mandy."

"I don't mind."

"I got that impression."

"Oh really?" She tilted her head back upon his shoulder to look up at him. "Does that mean you think I'm easy, Mr. Kendall?"

"Easy? You! Never in a million years," he retorted, a teasing light in his dark eyes. "I could never assume that. I remember how long it took me to get you in bed with me the first time."

"I'm glad to hear that," she retorted, her gaze as teasing as his. "I'd hate for you to think I'm a pushover."

He shook his head. "Never."

For a long time they held each other, exchanging contented kisses and light caresses that were enough in themselves. Clay's lips brushed over her tousled hair; she explored his chiseled features with her fingertips. He caught the mound of flesh at the base of her right thumb between his teeth, gently nibbling. She nuzzled his taut pectoral muscles with the tip of her chin.

"I have a great idea," he announced at last, kissing her breasts. "Since we have to stay and wait to hear from Jamie, we'll order a delicious, expensive dinner from room service.

253

Then we can play cards again. Strip poker this time—I insist. And after a few hands, I'm sure I'll be in the mood to come back to bed with you again."

Amanda laughed. "You're insatiable, Mr. Kendall. Don't you ever get enough?"

"Not where you're concerned, no. So what do you think of my plan?"

"I think I kinda like it," she confessed, madly in love and accepting that as fact. She lifted herself up on one elbow, bent down, and kissed him lightly before adding, "Only you could persuade me to gamble my virtue."

"I'd better be the only one," he gruffly replied, his narrowing eyes imprisoning hers. "I don't even want you to be tempted by any other man, because you're mine, Mandy, all mine."

Emotion caught in her heart. His words, his impassioned tone, made her wonder if she dared hope what she'd been afraid to hope before—that she was really and truly special to him. Still, he had never spoken that most important word— love. Until he did, *if* he ever did, she couldn't be sure how serious he was about her.

Jamie Mulligan didn't contact Clay again until the next morning. When the phone rang beside Clay's bed, Amanda, the lighter sleeper, awoke first. Stifling a yawn, she fumbled for the receiver, sleepily turned it upside-down, and spoke into the earpiece. Blinking her eyes, she realized her mistake and corrected it, answering briefly, "Yes?"

"Ah, it's Clay Kendall I'm trying to reach," a male voice answered hesitantly. "Have I been connected to the right room?"

"Yes."

"Well, then, might I talk with him?"

"Of course," Amanda said, becoming more alert as she recognized Jamie's voice. Beside her, Clay stirred. His arm flung across her waist flexed, though he didn't open his eyes. She gently tapped her elbow against his ribs to rouse him. "Wake up. Jamie wants to talk to you."

He became alert instantly, almost miraculously. Sitting up, the sheet dropping down around his narrow hips, he took the phone from Mandy's hand and said hello brusquely. For nearly a minute, he merely listened. Then he replied, "The King George pub at ten. I'll be there."

After the call ended and he reached over Amanda to hang up the receiver, she heaved a long sigh. "I guess you're going to make me stay here again, under orders not to budge?"

"Not a chance. After the trouble you got yourself into last time, I don't dare leave you alone today," he answered flatly. "You're going wherever I go, so I can keep an eye on you."

After breakfast they took a double-decker bus to Beeson Street, since they had plenty of time. Entering the King George pub at ten to ten, they sat down at a scarred wooden table toward the back of the establishment and ordered coffee, although two of the three patrons were already quaffing down mugs of ale. Luckily, Jamie arrived less than five minutes later, but Amanda would never have identified him in a million years. For some reason she had expected him to be a short stocky man, with a stereotypical twinkle of merriment in his eyes, but the real Jamie turned out to be far different.

Tall and lank, his bony shoulders hunched, he made his way to their table staring at the floor, and when his gaze lifted, his eyes didn't so much twinkle as gleam with streetwise savvy. He was as loose-jointed as Captain Bob Mears, but there the resemblance ended. The happy-go-lucky look on his face gave the impression that he didn't take anything very seriously. Greeting Clay with a hearty clap on the shoulder

255

and Amanda with a respectful nod, he sat down at the table across from them.

"Seems we had a wee bit of a mix-up in the gardens yesterday," he said lightly. "My friend showed up but there wasn't a soul to meet him."

"That's my fault," Amanda volunteered, smiling sheepishly. She gave a brief account of what had happened. "Well, that's all water under the bridge now. I just want you to know I really tried to contact your friend."

"I'm guessing you still want to see him and hear what he has to say." Jamie eyed Clay. "Would I be right?"

"Exactly right. We want to meet him, the sooner the better."

"Well, then you'll be pleased to know he's here in the pub," Jamie replied brightly, beckoning to a mousy little man from the bar who had obviously been watching them out of the corner of his eye. Carrying his mug of ale, his gaze darting here and there, he wound his way between tables to join them and quickly sat down. "Miss Mills, Clay, this is Ian. Cautious he is because the bobbies like to keep a close eye on him. It's sticky fingers you have, isn't that right, Ian?"

"I ain't tried to filch nothing for weeks," the little man protested. "My Mary, she said she'd toss me out if I was nabbed one more time."

"I understand you have some information for us?" Clay spoke up, getting straight to business. "About the Shalimar rubies?"

"I'll be needing some money for . . ."

"Of course. How about fifty pounds?"

Ian's face lit up and he bobbed his head up an down. "Well, I hear things. First it was that them jewels was here. Then three nights ago, I happened to run into an old pal o' mine and he said the people what's got the rubies are staying at the Royal Knight Hotel. A swanky place, that is."

Amanda and Clay glanced at each other, neither of them breathing for a second or two. Clay asked the informant, "Is this pal of yours usually reliable?"

"Well, he's been known to tell a tall tale or two when he's been having a drop too much to drink. But it was just one whiskey he had when I saw him this last time."

"So you believed him?"

After taking a swallow of ale and wiping his mouth with the back of his hand, Ian nodded.

Clay paid him, taking several bills from his wallet, which the man swiftly accepted. Glancing furtively around the pub as if it was a longtime habit, he pocketed the money and wasted no time leaving.

Jamie grinned. "Ian's a good sort. A wee bit henpecked."

"But you think he's trustworthy?" Clay asked. "He wouldn't have made up a story just to pick up some easy cash?"

"Not on your life. Too skittish, he is. Wouldn't want to have to fret about somebody coming after him for telling a lie. If he says his pal told him those blokes are at the Royal Knight, it's telling the truth, he is. I can't be vouching for his pal though —he might not be above weaving a yarn."

"Even so, it's the only real lead we've had for a while. Thanks for getting in touch," Clay told Jamie, taking more money from his wallet. "Worth at least a hundred, I think."

Jamie's eyes widened with appreciation. "Saints be blessed, this is dandy. Never hurts to have a few extra quid. To save for a rainy day, mind you."

"There'll be more where that came from if this lead falls through and we need your help again. I'll be in touch to see if you've heard anything else," Clay said, standing and looking down at Mandy. "Let's go check out the Royal Knight Hotel. If Becky and Brad are there, we'd better hurry. They have a knack of slipping away just as we're getting close to them."

As they traveled across London in a cab several minutes later, Amanda sat staring out her window, unconsciously unzipping and rezipping her leather clutch purse. Finally Clay reached over to still her hand.

"You're very uptight," he quietly commented. "Care to tell me exactly why?"

"I feel kind of sick," she admitted, her cheeks slightly pale. "I . . . I just have a feeling we're going to find them this time. Call it woman's intuition, but—"

"I can't call it that because I have a hunch you're right—we are going to find them."

Amanda sighed. "After all these weeks of searching for Becky, I should've figured out how to handle the whole mess and what to say to her, but right now my mind's a perfect blank. What *can* I say when I see her? I have no idea how she might react. Maybe being with Brad has changed her completely and she'll be tough to deal with. I mean really tough."

Soothingly stroking her fingertips, Clay shook his head. "She may have changed some, but from what you've told me about her, I doubt very much she's become a gun moll."

Amanda smiled humorlessly. "No, I can't see her in that role either, but she's obviously not my dependent little sister anymore. She might not be willing to listen to a word I have to say."

"We'll just have to take it as it comes. I'm not really worried about Becky's reaction. Brad's the real problem. He may panic when we confront him, and panicky people can be very dangerous. But I'm prepared." Opening his jacket, Clay allowed her to see the shoulder holster he was wearing. "I hope a gun won't be necessary, but there's no use taking chances."

258

"But you've never carried one before!"

"Oh, yes I have. I just didn't tell you I had it with me when we contacted Bernie Cooper and Juan Alvedero."

Suddenly she felt even sicker, knowing she was in over her head. Dealing with thieves and fences, riding around with an investigator who toted a deadly weapon—it was insane all the way around. She should be in her store, where she belonged. Instead she was speeding through London, headed toward a confrontation she had no idea how to handle.

The Royal Knight Hotel was indeed "a swanky place" as Ian had said. A red-and-gold striped canopy covered the sidewalk from curb to entrance, and after Clay paid their taxi driver and they got out, a doorman in gold and scarlet livery opened the brass and glass doors for them with a stiff bow. Thick red carpet covered the floor of the grand lobby from wall to wall, and the furniture was upholstered in plush gold velvet, while gilded moldings, realistically ivylike, climbed Ionic columns. All the opulence might have been gaudy but was saved from that fate by the sedate, nearly regal atmosphere that graced the area.

"If they're here, they're really living high," Amanda said, looking around at all the expensively and tastefully dressed people either chatting in low voices or perusing *The Times* of London. "It must cost a lot to stay here."

"After selling that bracelet to Alvedero, they don't have to worry about the price of a hotel for a while," Clay reminded her, his fingers lightly touching the small of her back as they approached the richly gleaming teakwood desk. When one of the clerks turned to them with a polite smile, Clay smiled back and said, "I believe you have a Mr. and Mrs. Brian Walters here as your guests." He was taking a chance on giving the name Brad had used in Granada.

"Walters, sir?" The clerk quickly scanned the register, then shook his head. "You must be mistaken. We have no one by that name staying with us."

Laughing, Clay tapped the heel of his hand against his forehead. "So they're up to their old tricks again. Brian and Bernice are a little eccentric. They enjoy checking into hotels under false names." He looked at Amanda. "Isn't this just like them, dear?"

"Uh, why yes, just like them." She forced herself to laugh too. "They get quite a kick out of being offbeat sometimes."

"Indeed?" The clerk pursed his thin lips. "Well, I'm sorry I can't tell you if they're actually staying here if you don't know what name they may have registered under."

For a second, Clay pretended to look crestfallen. Then he brightened, tapping one hand against his chest before removing two photos from the inside pocket of his jacket. "What luck. I brought along the pictures we took of the two of them the last time they visited us. Thought they'd enjoy seeing them. And if they are staying here, you'll be able to recognize them."

The clerk glanced quickly at the pictures of Becky and Brad. "Ah yes, the Campbells. Or so they call themselves. Yes, they've been our guests since Saturday, I believe."

Amanda's heart stopped. She looked up at Clay and tried to return the pleased grin he manufactured for the clerk's benefit.

"Of course, Campbell," he said. "They've used that name before, haven't they, dear?"

Unable to speak, she simply nodded.

He asked the clerk, "Are they in at the moment?"

Glancing back over his shoulder, the clerk nodded. "I assume so, sir. At any rate, if they went out they didn't leave their key."

"Which room are they in?"

"I—er, perhaps I should call up and tell them you wish to see them."

"We'd rather you didn't. We'd like to surprise them. Matter of fact, I was hoping you could tell me where I could buy a bottle of champagne so the four of us could celebrate seeing each other again."

The clerk relaxed. "I could have a bellman deliver a bottle to the Campbell's room, sir, if you wish."

"Terrific. Just make sure it's the best you have. And wait about a half hour to send it up, please. Now, what room are they in?"

"Room four twenty-three, sir."

"Thank you," Clay graciously said, and headed with Amanda toward a bank of elevators.

"You're such a convincing liar," she told him for the second time since they had met. "You almost had me believing we were just visiting a couple of old friends."

Clay had no response to her comment. A troubled frown furrowed his brow as they waited for an elevator, and jaw setting, he at last shook his head. "This may be crazy, Mandy. I think I'd better call Scotland Yard in on this before we go upstairs. Normally, I'd handle a situation like this alone, but I don't want to drag you into something dangerous."

"Not the police," she pleaded, laying one hand upon his right forearm. "Please, Clay, not yet. L-let me talk to Becky first, or at least try to. I want to make this easier for her if I possibly can."

Gazing down into her lambent blue eyes, he realized he'd reached a point where he could deny her almost nothing. He gave a curt nod of his head, ushering her into the first elevator that opened.

As they were borne slowly upward to the fourth floor, she nervously plucked at his sleeve. "I have an idea. Let me go to

261

the door first, alone. Becky will let me in right away when I tell her it's me, I know she will. And I'll be sure to leave the door open just a crack so you can come in after a minute or two and catch Brad off guard."

His frown deepened. "But he's not going to be overjoyed at seeing you. And he's going to want to know how you found them. What can you tell him?"

"I—I'll think of something. I guess I can be a convincing liar too, if I have to be. I'll say Becky called me and told me where she was. She won't understand but I think she'll back me up."

"I thought you were afraid Brad had changed her completely."

"She's still my sister! Surely she won't turn against her own flesh and blood. I'm sure she won't. So let me get into the room first. I really believe that's the best way to handle this."

Despite some reservations, all of them concerning her safety, he had to agree. Perhaps her plan would be the safest approach. She'd go in. Brad would be preoccupied with her unexpected appearance and Clay could burst into the room, gaining the advantage by the element of surprise. Still, he couldn't help feeling uneasy when they stepped off the elevator on the fourth floor, then stopped a few feet away from the door to room 423. When Mandy gave him a quick nod and started to walk away from him, he caught hold of her hand, his fingers squeezing hers tightly.

"You be damn careful," he instructed, his deep voice strained. "If anything—and I mean *anything*—starts to go wrong, you scream as loud as you can and I'll come running. Got that?"

"Got it," she whispered, raising her other hand to tap her fingertips upon his cheek, adoring him. "But I just know it's going to be all right."

He wasn't so sure.

And to tell the truth, neither was she as she lifted one hand to rap her knuckles lightly on the door marked 423. She waited. No response. Shaking all over, she tried again, knocking harder, louder.

"Y-yes?" a squeaky woman's voice finally answered. "Wh-who is it?"

Despite the squeakiness, Amanda knew it was her sister speaking. Swallowing hard, still feeling rather nauseous, half afraid of Brad's possible reaction when he saw her, she mustered up all her courage to call out, "Becky, it's me, Amanda. Open the door. Let me in." Then she heard a soft sobbing cry and in less than two seconds, Becky flung the door open and hurled herself into her arms, sobbing wildly.

"Oh, thank God you're here!" Becky babbled, pulling Amanda into her room. "I—I was j-just trying to d-decide whether or not to call you. Oh, Amanda, it's so awful, *so* awful. I—I don't know what to do!"

Surreptitiously making sure to leave the door to the corridor unlatched, Amanda stepped into the room and looked around quickly, her gaze fixing on a closed door, which she assumed opened to the adjoining bath. Even as she hugged her sister close, she forced herself to ask, "Where's Brad, honey?"

Rebecca Mills burst into tears, ran her hands through her hair, which was already unusually untidy, and yanked at strands of it as she mumbled, "He's gone!"

"Gone where?"

Before Becky could answer, Clay lunged through the doorway in a crouch, gun drawn, his left hand supporting his right wrist as he took aim.

Becky gave a startled cry.

Waving a hand at Clay, urging him to put the gun away, Amanda explained, "Brad's not here."

After surveying the room carefully, he replaced the revolver in his shoulder holster and asked, "Where is he, then?"

"Where is Brad, Becky?" Amanda repeated, patting her younger sister's heaving back. "Becky?"

Becky stared at her older sister wide-eyed, then glanced at Clay. "Wh-who is he? How d-did you find me?"

"Clay's a private investigator, hired to find the Shalimar rubies," Amanda bleakly explained. Then she gave in to raw tearing emotion. "Becky, how could you let Brad convince you to steal them?"

Becky's horrified look told its own story, and the torrent of tears she wept verified it. When Clay stepped closer to hand her a neatly folded handkerchief, she wiped her eyes, but nothing could stanch the flood that washed down her cheeks for several minutes. Finally she began to compose herself. Ducking her head, she stared at the floor.

"You can't believe I h-helped Brad steal the Shalimar collection," she said, her tone hopeful, her voice full of grief. "I didn't. I swear. Oh, he stole them, but I didn't know that until the day before yesterday." Words tumbled out of her in a torrent. "I—I . . . he was gone and I decided to get a book from his suitcase. I was bored, you see, and I thought if I had something to read. . . . Oh, God! Instead of the book, I—I found the rubies! I couldn't believe what I was seeing but there they were. Wh-when we were in New York, I saw the newspaper headlines about the theft, but . . . but Brad always kept me from buying a paper, saying we had to catch a cab, or that we'd lose our reservation at a restaurant or something. He told me the rubies were stolen *after* we left Richmond but now I know he replaced them with fakes to give himself time to get away. He even admitted that when I told him I'd found the real rubies in his luggage! I begged him to give them back but he . . . he laughed at me, and then he

264

left. I didn't know what to do. I wanted to call you or Mom and Dad but . . ."

Tears gathered in Amanda's eyes. "Are you saying you didn't help Brad steal the rubies?"

"I . . . Of course I didn't! I mean, not on purpose. Now I know he was just using me when he pretended to be so interested in my work, wh-when he asked me to take him to the museum at night to show him new exhibits. I guess that's how he figured out the security system and made a schedule of the guards' patrols. And then he—he went in one night and took the rubies. And I ran away with him because he said he loved me. And he told me not to let you or Mom and Dad know where we were, since you didn't like him and he was afraid you'd try to take me away from him. I believed him! I've been so stupid!"

"Becky, Becky," Amanda comforted, hugging her younger sister close. "You've just been naive. But . . . I have to tell you."

"Wh-what?" Becky asked, sobbing.

"The police in Richmond think you were a willing accomplice to the robbery," Amanda forced herself to say. "Becky, you're in trouble, but I want you to know Mom and Dad and I will do anything in the world to help you."

"Help me? How can you help me if they think I'm a thief?" Becky shrilly exclaimed, wringing the handkerchief. "Oh, God, I'm going to be arrested and sent to prison!" She raised frightened eyes to Clay's face. "Is that why you're here? To take me back so they can toss me in jail and throw away the key?"

"Try to calm down," Amanda said soothingly, squeezing her sister's shoulder. "You're getting hysterical."

"You'd be hysterical too if you were on your way to prison!" Becky practically shouted. "But you're not. *I* am."

"Listen to me," Clay intervened, avoiding the question Becky had asked him. "You say you didn't know Brad planned to steal the rubies, that you didn't even realize he had done it until weeks after the robbery. That's your defense. With a good lawyer, you'll be able to convice a jury that you didn't know how he meant to use the information you gave him about the museum. They'll go light on you—probably put you on probation for a couple of years, at the most."

"But I don't want to be on probation! I don't even want to be tried!"

"If the D.A. doesn't believe your story, he'll have to request a trial. That's his duty."

"I don't care about his duty. I didn't do anything wrong!"

"But Becky, in a way you did," Amanda was forced to say. "You willingly gave Brad information about how the security system worked."

"But he said he loved me and wanted to know everything about my work!"

"You should've told him that details about security were confidental."

"I did, but he said that if I loved him, I wouldn't want to keep any secrets from him."

"And you bought that line?" Amanda asked impatiently. "For heaven's sake, Sis, you should've known something was fishy the minute he said that."

"Oh, you think you're so smart!" Becky retorted thickly, a new torrent of tears pouring down her cheeks. "So wise. You just don't understand how much I love Brad."

"You didn't have to be a simpleton about it." The moment those harsh words were out of her mouth, Amanda tried to brush them aside. "Forget I said that. We're both just upset. But you said something that really bothers me. You said I don't understand how much you *love* Brad. Does that mean you still think you're in love with him even though you know what he did?"

Becky sniffled miserably, pushing back her tangled hair with a limp hand as she shrugged. "I don't know how I feel right now. I'm so confused. But . . . but it's hard just to stop l-loving somebody. I mean, he treated me like a princess."

"Yeah, I'm sure he's a real con man. In fact, he's proved that."

"Becky, I have to ask you some questions," Clay gently announced, motioning both young women toward a damask-covered love seat and taking the chair opposite it. He leaned forward, elbows resting on his thighs, his fingers steepled, as he offered the younger sister a compassionate smile. "You may be able to provide me with some valuable information. Now, we know that you met a man in Granada, Juan Alvedero."

"Y-yes, Brad said they were old friends."

"Señor Alvedero is a fence. He didn't want the entire collection, but he did buy the bracelet."

"When I found the rubies yesterday, I—I noticed it was missing, but Br-Brad wouldn't tell me what he'd done with it."

"It's been recovered. So you're saying the rest of the collection is intact?" Clay continued, and when Becky nodded, he gave her an encouraging smile. "It helps me to know that. Now, has he introduced you to any people here in London?"

Becky nodded again, still twisting the damp handkerchief. "I was really impressed when he took me to see such wealthy friends."

"Can you remember their names?"

"Of course. First there were Peter and Margaret Stafford, who own a huge estate in Essex and live in a beautiful Tudor mansion. Margaret was very nice. She showed me all over the house and grounds while Br-Brad and Peter talked. And then

we went to see Arthur—no, *Alfred* Cromney, some rich indus-
trialist, not really very friendly. Then last week we visited
Jane Edwards in her town house here in London. She's a
widow, very dignified."

"And you didn't meet anyone else?"

"They're the only ones. Why?"

"Looks like Brad's decided to cut out the middle man,"
Clay said to Amanda. "He's not going to the fences this time.
He's trying to sell the collection on his own."

Becky gasped. "You mean you think all those people . . ."

"Were potential buyers," Clay finished for her, his finely
hewn features arranged in solemn lines. "Yes, that's exactly
what I think. So tell me, was Brad planning to see any of them
again, do you know?"

"I . . . Yes. We were invited to dinner at Alfred Cromney's tomorrow night."

Clay slapped his hands against his thighs. "Bingo. Now we
have something to go on. We know who's interested in buying."

Amanda swallowed with some difficulty. "And . . . what
now?"

Clay's black eyes captured hers and seemed to plumb their
depths before he turned his attention back to Becky. "Do you
have any idea where Brad is now?"

"He . . . he said he's was going to get a suite at the King
John Hotel and that if I wanted to stop acting like a crybaby, I
could find him there."

Clay's gaze locked with Amanda's once more as he rose
lithely to his feet. "Lucky for us he didn't think you'd turn
him in, so he even gave you the name of his hotel. I can't let
him get away this time. Since I wouldn't be able to go to the
States and get back here fast enough to trap him with the

rubies in his possession, I'm not going to be able to make Becky return to Richmond."

"I guess not," Amanda breathed, her blue eyes fixed on his. "But . . . you could turn her over to Scotland Yard."

"I could."

He could but he wasn't going to. Suddenly that fact was clear to her. Despite all the things he'd previously said about not being able to let Becky go if they found her, he was now giving her a chance to flee. But *why?* Amanda's heart fluttered. Could it be he had changed his mind because of their intimacy during the past weeks? She could only hope so. When she jumped up and headed toward him he held up one hand stopping her in her tracks.

"But I have something to say to you both," he murmured. "Especially to you, Becky. You should go back home even though you're scared to. The alternative is to run away, and if you do that, you'll never be able to stop, never be able to go home again. I don't think you want that."

Biting her lip, Amanda gave her younger sister a nod. "He's right, Beck. We have to go home. You can't run away forever."

Becky sobbed. "But I *am* scared! So scared. I don't want to go to prison."

"I have a feeling you won't have to," he said. "I know a great lawyer. Name's Jake Brewster. As soon as you get home, call him and tell him I sent you. He's a whiz in a courtroom."

Amanda nodded. "I'll call him as soon as we land."

Clay nodded back, then looked at Becky again. "Does Brad have a gun?"

"A . . . gun? I—I don't know. I never saw one."

Since she hadn't seen the rubies until yesterday, her answer wasn't particularly reassuring. Amanda went to Clay, worry written all over her face as she cupped his rigid jaw in her

269

hands. "Don't let him hurt you," she whispered, an abrupt pressure stinging her eyes. "Please be careful. Oh, I wish you weren't going after him alone. I should go with you."

"But you can't. You and Becky should take the first flight home," he whispered back, tapping the end of her nose with one fingertip and adding teasingly, "Besides, I wouldn't want to take the chance of you getting in my way, Nancy Drew. I have a jewel thief to catch and a fortune in rubies to recover."

"Be that way, then, Mr. Independent," she tried to retort lightly, a tremulous smile briefly curving her lips. "Just be sure you call me the moment you complete your mission. Okay?"

"Yes," he said, then turned and opened the door just as a room service waiter started to knock.

"Your champagne, sir."

"Oh, yes, I ordered it, but we're not in the mood for a celebration right now," Clay said, paying for the champagne anyhow, and telling the waiter to keep it himself.

After the man voiced a surprised thank-you and left, Clay looked at Amanda one more time and started to speak again, but changed his mind. He stepped out the door and disappeared down the hall.

CHAPTER FIFTEEN

The flight home to the States seemed to last forever. Finally, during the last leg from New York to Richmond, Amanda helped Becky settle down by asking a friendly steward for a brandy for each of them, which they followed with another round. Exhausted by shock and disillusionment, Becky at last fell into a fitful sleep. But unfortunately, even two drinks didn't provide Amanda with the same blessed release. Thoughts churned in her head, nagging at her, making her heart beat double time with a very real fear. If Brad was armed . . . If Clay got hurt, or—or worse . . . Such horrifying possibilities weren't easily dismissed, and so she gnawed upon her lips until they felt raw.

It was something of a relief when the pilot set the big jet smoothly down on the tarmac at the airport and taxied to the terminal. Amanda gently nudged her sister awake, and when they disembarked and passed through the airline's aseptic lounge, they found their parents awaiting them, both in tears. After much hugging and kissing all around, she left her mother and father reassuring Becky while she went to find a pay phone and call Jake Brewster. After explaining to his protective secretary that Clay Kendall had told her to call, she was allowed to speak to the lawyer. As briefly as possible, she explained the predicament her sister was in and was impressed when he said authoritatively, "Have Becky meet me at police headquarters, central division, in an hour. As an unwitting accomplice to a crime, she'll make a much better impression if she surrenders willingly."

Pleased he remembered Becky's name, Amanda readily agreed, hung up, then rejoined her family to tell them what they must do.

"But I don't want to go to jail," Becky said, sniffling. "Isn't there something else I can do besides give myself up?"

"There must be!"

"I can't let my baby be put behind bars! Can't we just take her home with us?"

Voiced simultaneously by Amanda's mother and father, these unrealistic comments struck a raw nerve. She looked at both of them, then at her sister, her jaw grimly set. "All right, I guess Becky could go home with you tonight, but sooner or later the police are going to know she's back in Richmond, by tomorrow for sure. And they'll come for her. So what would you rather have? A mob of policemen dragging her out of your house in handcuffs? Or do want to make it easier on everybody, especially Becky? If she gives herself up, which will give the whole affair a bit more dignity, Jake Brewster assures me he can have her out on bail in a couple of hours. It's your choice."

Shirley and Ted Mills seemed to age years in a single second, but their common sense at last sustained them. And even Becky acted as if she understood the logic of Amanda's appeal. So, as a family united, they left the airport and drove to the police station, where Jake Brewster soon met them and escorted them inside.

Clay had been sitting in the lobby of the King John Hotel twenty-two hours straight, except for brief visits to the men's room and time out twice for coffee and a quick bite to eat in the adjoining restaurant. His eyes felt gritty from lack of sleep; he needed a shave and wanted a shower. But such are the inconveniences of surveillance. After learning that Brad wasn't in his room but hadn't checked out, Clay had found himself a chair from which he could survey the entire lobby, and there he settled down to wait. Yet he hadn't expected to wait this long. Midnight came and went. The hours dragged into dawn and still Brad didn't make an appearance.

Cup after cup of strong black coffee kept Clay awake. By nine in the morning, as he pretended to read a newspaper, the print was beginning to blur before his eyes and his thoughts were occupied by Mandy. He knew she was back in Richmond now. Unless Becky had refused to go. He doubted that. Mandy could be very persuasive, and Becky had seemed extremely susceptible, especially to someone she knew loved her. As Mandy did.

Despite the inordinate amount of caffeine running through his system Clay started to nod off, and had to fight sleep with a vengeance. Jerking his head up, forcing his eyelids open, he suddenly sat up straight as Brad Charles, alias whatever, strolled cockily across the lobby to the front desk.

His weariness fleeing in a burst of adrenaline, Clay watched as his prey walked over to step into an elevator. Never foolhardy, always cautious, Clay hastily found a phone, called Inspector Ashford, explained he had cornered the man who'd stolen the Shalimar rubies, and requested backup.

Less than fifteen minutes later, Ashford arrived at the hotel with a cordon of men, all plainclothes, mercifully inconspicuous.

"I'll go up first," Clay said, "to make sure he has the rubies in the room. That way, if he's stashed them someplace else you won't burst in on him and he won't have grounds to sue you for false arrest. All right with you?"

Reluctantly, the inspector nodded. "But my men and I will be right outside in the corridor."

"Glad to hear it," Clay said with a grin as they made their way up to Brad's floor.

Once again Brad had set himself up in luxurious accommodations. Gilt-framed oil paintings accented the oyster-shell walls of the hallways, where the carpets were inches thick. Getting off on the sixth floor and leaving Ashford and his men to follow at a distance, Clay strode nearly to the end of the corridor and stopped at the carved double doors of Brad's suite. He knocked twice, sharply, then had to wait several seconds before the man inside cautiously called out, "Yes, what is it?"

Clay had his line prepared. "Mr. Cromney sent me," he answered matter-of-factly. "I have a message for you."

Without hesitating another instant, Brad Charles opened the doors, put on one of his most charming smiles, and eagerly motioned Clay inside. "Well, well, I'm sure anything Alfred asked you to tell me must be important."

Clay agreeably inclined his head. "Mr. Cromney asked me to express his regrets. He won't be able to entertain you at dinner this evening after all."

All Brad's charm vanished. His face went red and he started sputtering. "But he said . . . does this mean he's no longer interested in buying the . . . uh, merchandise I offered to him?"

"The rubies? Ah, yes, he is still most interested," replied Clay, adroitly getting past one hurdle, certain now that Brad and Cromney had been negotiating a deal for the collection. "He simply has to postpone the dinner tonight, but he should be able to see you tomorrow evening. If, of course, that would be convenient for you?"

"Oh, sure, fine. The sooner the better," Brad responded,

becoming his slick smarmy self again. "Tell Alfred I'm look-ing forward to finalizing our little deal."

"I will. One other thing though," Clay added, glancing around the elegantly furnished sitting room. "Mr. Cromney wants me to look at the rubies. I assume you have them here in the suite?"

"Well, yes, I could hardly ask the desk clerk to put them in the hotel safe. Can't take a chance on anyone recognizing them, especially since photos of them were all over the news-papers a few weeks ago."

Clay nodded. "I understand. Now, may I see them?"

"Why does Alfred want you to look at them? He's already examined them himself."

"Yes, and he does have some knowledge of gems, but I'm a gemologist, so he wants me to examine them too," Clay calmly said, using the same ploy he and Mandy had used on Alvedero in Granada. He smiled. "You know the old saying: 'Let the buyer beware.' It's Mr. Cromney's motto, which is one of the main reasons he's as wealthy as he is."

Buying every word of the explanation, Brad shrugged as he started out of the room. "If he wants you to look at them, it suits me. I'll get them."

A couple of minutes later when Brad returned carrying a medium-size velvet box and handed it to Clay, Clay cocked one eyebrow. "I'm sure you didn't get the collection through customs in this."

"Certainly not. I never even tried to get through customs with the rubies. When they started X-raying luggage, suitcases became obsolete for taking stolen property from one country to another. I use plaster statuettes these days, hide the goods inside, then mail them general delivery to the main post office wherever I'm heading."

"Mmm. I've heard of smugglers doing that," Clay said,

sitting down at a Queen Anne desk and placing the case atop it. "Of course, there's always the chance the merchandise could be lost in the mail."

"A very slim one. I've never lost anything yet," was Brad's smug answer as he walked across the room to the small bar. "Get you a drink . . . er, I didn't get your name."

"James," Clay lied. "Edward James. And thanks but no thanks. I don't drink while I'm working."

"I bet old Alfred is a bitch to work for, right?"

"He pays me well. I'm sure you know he often adds to his private collection, and that's why he wanted a gemologist on his staff." As Brad turned his attention to dropping ice cubes into a glass and pouring a generous measure of expensive Scotch, Clay unhooked the brass clasp on the case and opened the velvet-covered lid. Suppressing a satisfied smile, he looked down at the Shalimar collection resting in a black plush bed, the individual pieces arranged to show off their magnificence to best advantage. It was a great feeling to have them right in his hands after all the searching, and he decided to put an end to the charade now in progress. After closing and latching the case, he tucked it under one arm and rose just as Brad Charles turned away from the bar.

As the debonair jewel thief raised his glass toward his lips, he suddenly stopped, the glass halfway to his mouth, a puzzled frown creasing his forehead. "Thought you were supposed to examine the rubies. You haven't even had time to get started."

"I've seen enough. I know the gems are authentic," Clay replied, adding, "The game's up, Charles, or whatever your real name is. I'm not Edward James. I'm Clay Kendall, and Alfred Cromney didn't send me here. I was hired by the museum to recover the rubies, and now I have. By the way what *is* your real name?"

For a moment Brad was stunned by this turn of events, but he recovered quickly and gave a short cocky laugh as he put his untouched drink down. "I'm not going to tell you my name. And if you think I'm going to let you walk out of here with that collection, you underestimated me."

"Make it easy for yourself," Clay counseled somberly. "You've been caught with the loot. There's no way out."

Throwing back his head, Brad laughed again. "Just tell me one thing. How did you track me down?"

"It wasn't easy—your false passport, the false names. We came close to catching up with you in Bermuda and Spain. Then a couple of days ago, we were tipped off you were in London. Yesterday someone directed us to the Royal Knight Hotel."

Brad's laughter ceased, even the too confident grin was wiped off his face as his handsome cleft chin set. "So you went to the Royal Knight and Becky sent you here?"

"In a way. She admitted you said you'd be here."

"Damn her! That little twit!"

"That 'twit' was in love with you," Clay said tersely, his own strong jaw rigid. "And you used her."

"And I offered her everything! She could've shared the money from the sale of the rubies. I told her that. The money would have set us up for life. But no, she had to be Miss Goody-Two-Shoes and get hysterical at the very idea. I should've just walked out on her without telling her where I'd be if she changed her mind. The little snitch. If I could get my hands on her now . . . Where is she?"

"Back in Richmond. Telling the police how you tricked her into giving you information about the security system in the museum and the guards' routines. In case you don't know it, the authorities think she was a willing accomplice. You got

277

her into a hell of a lot of trouble that she doesn't deserve to be in."

"I know. I read the newspapers even though I didn't let her see them. But she'll get off."

"Maybe. But you won't."

"Wanna bet?" Brad snapped, sneering as he flicked open the blazer he wore, reached behind him, and withdrew the revolver tucked into the waistband of his trousers. He pointed it straight at Clay's chest. "You must think I'm some kind of fool. I don't let anybody touch those rubies unless I have a gun handy. Now, hand them over or I'll—"

"Or you'll what?" Clay challenged, his voice steady despite the fact that he was mighty uneasy looking into the barrel of the gun. "You won't shoot me. You don't dare. The sound of a shot would bring people running. And besides, you don't think I was stupid enough to come here alone, do you? The police are outside in the hall, just waiting for you to try to make a move."

"You expect me to fall for that old trick?" Brad hooted, gesturing with the revolver. "Just put the case down. I'll have to tie you up and gag you so I can get out of here."

Turning around, shaking his head, Clay started toward the double doors. "Not a chance."

But he had misjudged Brad Charles's propensity for violence. Before he had half a chance to reach for his own gun, the thief fired. Tearing pain ripped through Clay's left upper arm and as he staggered slightly, all hell broke loose. Inspector Ashford and his men slammed through the doors, and seeing he was vastly outnumbered, Brad dropped his revolver and surrendered, cursing.

Clay groaned, his arm throbbing. He allowed an officer to take the velvet case from his right hand as Ashford hurried over to examine the wound.

"You're bleeding badly," he pronounced morosely, making Clay feel even lousier. "Can you walk?"

"Sure. At least, as far as the elevator. I can't guarantee how I'll feel by the time we get to the lobby," said Clay, gritting his teeth with the pain. "I've never been shot before. I could have done without the experience."

"Better you than me, chum," Ashford quipped, but his expression was anxious. "Never could bear the sight of blood, especially my own."

In answer, Clay managed to muster a weak grin.

Amanda had chewed one fingernail close to the quick waiting in vain for Clay to phone. Oh, the telephone had rung several times. Two wrong numbers. And her mother had called once, her father twice, and each time they had insisted she speak to Becky, who was still in a severely troubled emotional state and barely capable of listening to anyone's comforting words. Amanda had done her best to reassure her sister, although every second she talked she wondered if Clay was trying to get through to her. Her father was preoccupied with Becky's trouble and didn't want to go to the store, and since she was afraid to take a chance on missing Clay's call, Amanda decided not to go either. She called Betsy Ann, who readily agreed to take care of business.

But Clay's call didn't come. Over twenty-four hours had passed since she'd left him in London. She had spent a sleepless night, worrying herself nearly sick about him. The very thought of food now made her ill, and as she curled herself into a tense ball on the sofa that afternoon, even Bossy was subdued and lay on the cold hearth, resting her nose on her paws, her ears down.

"Why don't you call?" Amanda exclaimed aloud at last, her voice catching. What was happening in London? Had he found Brad? If so, why hadn't he let her know? Or what if he couldn't? What if he'd been hurt or he was . . . No! She couldn't even think such things. Biting back a tortured moan, she gnawed on her knuckle, then jumped nervously as the phone on the table next to her jangled shrilly in her ear. She tried to compose herself. It was probably just her mother or father calling again—or another damn wrong number. Yet her voice quavered as she answered, putting a stop to the insistent nerve-wracking pealing.

"Miss Mills?" a distinctly British voice inquired. "Inspector Ashford here."

She stopped breathing. Her heart leapt up into her throat as she stammered, "Wh-what's wrong? Why d-didn't Clay call me? Where is he. Is . . . is he okay?"

"He'll be fine, Miss Mills, I promise you," Ashford hastily told her. "But he's been shot and is in hospital."

"Shot?" she cried, practically choking on the terrifying word, forcing her fingers through her hair. "How bad is he? Please, please tell me the truth."

"I am telling you the truth. Brad Charles put up a fight and shot him, but it was a clean wound through the arm. He really will be all right. He lost a great deal of blood but he's much better now since he's been given transfusions."

"You mean that? You're not lying to me, are you, trying to make it easier?"

"Miss Mills, Clay is conscious, resting comfortably in bed, and he himself asked me to call you."

Believing the inspector, she nearly wept with relief. "I want to see him."

"And that's why he asked me to call. He'd like to see you too, if you can possibly get here."

"Get there! Of course I'll get there! If I can't get a flight soon, I'll sprout wings and fly," she vowed, laughing and crying all at once, thanking God he was going to be all right and wanted her to come to him. After a few seconds she composed herself. "Should I get in touch with his family? Maybe he'd like some of them to come too?"

"I've already contacted his parents and told them he's in no danger and should be home soon. And he only asked that you come, if you will."

"Oh, I'll be there as soon as I can," she said huskily. "And thank you so much for calling and for your kindness, Inspector Ashford. I even forgive you for thinking I was a . . ."

He chuckled. "You're the one who's kind, then. It was a stupid mistake. I'll ring off now and tell Clay you'll be here soon."

The instant they said good-bye, Amanda dropped the receiver into the cradle and jumped to her feet, startling Bossy considerably. Her ears pricking up curiously, the dog trotted after her mistress into her bedroom, where Amanda carelessly tossed clothes and shoes into a suitcase and threw a few cosmetics into a matching tote bag.

Less than ten minutes later, Bossy was in the front seat of Amanda's Mustang as they sped across town and came to a screeching halt in front of Shirley and Ted Mills's house. Bossy, loving Amanda's parents dearly, bounded up the sidewalk, her tail wagging furiously. Before Amanda could knock on the door, the dog was scratching at it, and she leapt inside to nuzzle her nose against Shirley's knee the moment she came to open it.

"I have to leave Bossy with you again," Amanda blurted out, her cheeks rosy, her eyes alight. "I'm going back to London. Clay's been hurt. He needs me."

"Clay—Clay Kendall?" her mother stuttered, as her husband appeared and Becky stepped out of the shadows in the hall.

"He . . . *He* needs you and you're going to him!" her younger sister cried. "But you can't go. *I* need you here. And —and besides, he's the man who hunted me down. How can you go running off to him?"

"Oh, grow up, Becky," Amanda snapped without meaning to. "He's also the man who would have let you go in London, and you'd better remember he could have turned you over to Scotland Yard. But he gave you a chance to get away, although he knew you'd spend the rest of your life running if you went. He didn't have to advise you that you'd be better off coming back home to get the whole ordeal over with. And damn it, I *am* going to him. He needs me now more than you do. Mom and Dad and Jake Brewster will take good care of you. Besides, Becky, you can't use me as a crutch forever, you know."

"But—"

"But nothing! Brad, that great love of your life, shot Clay. He *shot* him! The *bastard*. Now Clay wants to see me, and I'm going to him because I love him."

"But—"

"Brad Charles isn't even his real name! Did you know that?"

Becky burst into tears. "Oh, how can you be so cruel to me?"

"I—I don't want to be cruel," Amanda murmured, relenting enough to embrace her younger sister. "But I can't go on babying you. We've all babied you too long. If we hadn't been so protective, maybe you would've been wise enough to see right through Brad from the start. Maybe it's as much our fault as yours that you didn't. Regardless, it's time for me to help you break that dependency, and I'm going to the man I love because I want to."

"You should go," their mother said softly, coming forth to

hug both her daughters and nodding at Amanda. "If you love him, you have to go to him."

"Yes," their father agreed, kissing Amanda on the cheek and draping his arms around his wife's and younger daughter's shoulders. His smile half glad, half sad, he inclined his head toward the front door. "Go on. Catch your plane and call us tomorrow. We'll take good care of Bossy."

Tears of affection filled Amanda's eyes. Then she turned quickly and walked back out of her childhood home to her car.

Delivered by taxi to London's St. Thomas' hospital several hours later, Amanda paid the fare, adding an outrageously generous tip for the driver, and ran lightly up the stone steps into the building. Lack of rest should have exhausted her, but she was sustained by nervous energy and hope as she asked the woman at the reception desk for Clay's room number. When she entered his room, adoration and some fear ballooned in her chest as she saw him lying upon the stark metal hospital bed, equally stark white sheets covering him. On tiptoe, she approached him, her heart thundering until she saw that even though his eyes were closed, he seemed to be breathing deeply and steadily. And no tubes or needles were attached to his lean body. His color was good, healthy even, and for many long minutes, she stood by his bedside, simply looking down at his face, loving him.

He was asleep. She hated to disturb him, yet she was soon overcome by the need to hear his voice again. Leaning toward him, she touched his cheeks, whispering throatily, *"Clay.* Clay, I'm here."

His eyes opened slowly, black as coal and mysterious as they met hers. Then he smiled softly, reached up, and captured her hand between his. "Hi," he murmured. "I wasn't sure you'd come."

"Then you're crazy," she retorted, bending down to brush her lips over his. "How could I stay away, you big dummy, when I love you so much I'd go to the ends of the earth for you?"

He tilted his head to one side on his pillow. "Would you? I hoped you would, but I had to be sure. That's why I told my doctor I'm in too much pain to leave the hospital. I wanted you to come see me like this and feel sorry for me."

"Sorry for you! I was, but now I feel sorry for *me*. How could you manipulate me like this?"

"Why do you think I did?"

"How should I know?"

"You have to know by now. You must know that I love you too."

"How can I know that? You've never said so!"

"Then I'm saying so now. I love you, Mandy. You've turned my life upside down and made me happier than I've ever been."

"You really mean that?"

"Let me show you, honey," he whispered, pulling her down to sit on the side of the bed and raising up to claim her parted lips in a hot, possessive kiss that deepened and lengthened. And when he finally released her, a warm lazy smile shaped his firm mouth as he ran his fingers through her hair. "In fact, I love you so much, I'm willing to make you a partner in my business."

"A . . . a partner?" she echoed, sea blue eyes searching his. "That's all?"

"And my wife, of course," he added, stroking the slender column of her neck. "It's in the Bible, isn't it? 'A good wife, her value is far beyond rubies.' Or something to that effect."

"More valuable than the Shalimar rubies?"

"What do you think, love?"

"I think yes," she murmured, kissing him ardently again. "You would've let Becky get away the other day. I've been wondering why, and I've started to think you would've let her go for . . . for me?"

"Ah, now you're beginning to understand," he said gruffly, throwing back one corner of his sheet. "So get into bed, woman. I want to be close to you again."

As he drew her down onto the mattress she tried to protest. "But your arm, Clay. It must hurt."

"Some. But it feels much better now that you're here to comfort me. Come here. I need to kiss you, to make love to you."

"But Clay, we can't, not here! Somebody might come in."

"Don't worry, Mandy. I bribed all the nurses on the floor and told them that when you got here, we didn't want to be disturbed. They understood. We'll be left alone, I promise."

Unable to resist any longer, she took off her shoes and slipped into his bed, cuddling close as he pulled the sheet back over them. A soft laugh bubbled up from her throat as he kissed her forehead, her temples, the bridge of her nose. "Bribing the nurses! You never miss a trick, do you?"

"Not if I can help it."

"Oh, Clay, I do love you."

"Love you too, so much," he growled, quickly undressing her, pulling her atop him, making her his once again. "Oh, Mandy, you are more priceless than all the rubies in the world."

"So are you," she breathed, her body cleaving to his as they joined as one, more precious to each other than anyone else could ever be.

In each other, they both found ultimate completion.

Two souls intertwined, bound in mutual love, they had found heaven on earth, setting out on their own private journey to that destiny they both knew would sustain them all the days of their lives.

Lovers.

Best friends.